THE LATE-SUMMER PASSION OF A WOMAN OF MIND

THE LATE-SUMMER PASSION OF A WOMAN OF MIND

Rebecca Goldstein

Farrar, Straus and Giroux
NEW YORK

The author gratefully acknowledges permission to quote from the following published works: *The Republic of Plato*, translated by Francis M. Cornford, copyright © 1941 by Oxford University Press, published by Oxford University Press, all rights reserved; Plato's *Phaedrus*, translated by R. Hackforth, copyright © 1972 by Cambridge University Press, published by Cambridge University Press, all rights reserved.

The author would also like to acknowledge excerpts used from the following published work: *To the Bitter End*, by Hans Bernd Gisevius, translated by Richard & Clara Winston, published by Houghton Mifflin, 1947.

Library of Congress Cataloging-in-Publication Data
Goldstein, Rebecca.
 The late-summer passion of a woman of mind.
 I. Title.
PS3557.0398L38   1989   813'.54   88-24404

FIRST EDITION, 1989

For my mother
Loretta Newberger

We said, did we not, that love is a sort of madness. And that there are two kinds of madness, one resulting from human ailments, the other from a divine disturbance of our conventions of conduct.

PLATO
Phaedrus

I

We are all masters of self-deception.

Eva Mueller was staring in mild wonder at the line she had just typed. Why had it been written? Had she even been aware of these words before they materialized under her fingers and onto the waiting page? So unanticipated were they, so untouched by the prod of conscious intention, that someone (not Eva) might have suspected some kind of mystical agency, an unbidden eruption of literary ambitions from beyond the shady veil. And even Eva, who detested mysteries, who felt them as unclosed and uncleansed wounds in need of the poultice of solution, even Eva Mueller was mystified.

She switched off her electric typewriter, leaned back in her chair, and considered, her features poised in their characteristic frown, her hands against her chin in the praying position. Could these possibly be the words for which she had been waiting, the words that were to introduce the long-delayed summation of her book, *Reason's Due?* She had been actively working on this book for the past ten years, thinking about it even longer. One might have thought that by now, so near the end, she would be striding over the mountaintop in a nimbus-glow of glory, instead of crawling soft-belly to the ground, as uncertain of each move —no, worse—as when she had begun.

The problem was, and she knew this, that she expected a great deal of this final chapter. Final chapter—there was something vaguely chilling in the phrase. Up until now the book consisted of a meticulously laid-out trail of logical deduction. It was in the closing words that Eva hoped to reveal the heavy blooms and ripened fruit, the beauty and the salvation that lay enfolded within the logic. But so far her repeated attempts had not pleased her. Strange that she could not bring her most deeply held beliefs to a form of expression that did not disgust her.

So near the end, and now to have to sit and wait. It will come, her wiser self assured her weaker. One cannot push, or press, or tug. But both selves chafed at the passivity implied by the injunction. Passivity is pain. And it was ironic—was it not?—that the creative process itself, the most perfect, almost godlike expression of human freedom, must be fettered to the ball and chain. The waiting-for-it-to-come. And even when it did: the disquiet in the midst of rejoicing, the small quiver within the sigh of relief, for the plain brute contingency of the fact. It came, and the rest was determined. It came . . . but had it not?

And now this. Words arriving that made no sense, that did not speak to the point at all.

Eva impatiently pushed her chair away from her desk and strode over to the large window of her office. The venetian blinds were firmly drawn, effectively effacing the outside view. This was because it was spring, and Professor Mueller hated spring.

Her office, upon request, was on the northern and less scenic side of the building. She might even have considered asking for one of the windowless basement rooms, occupied by graduate students and lowest level lecturers, were it not for the impropriety of depositing a person of her rank in such a space.

Eva lifted a bottom corner of the blind, sending a rattling shiver up through the narrow slats. She squinted her eyes against the invading brightness. Down below was a slice of the well-kept lawn of the quad. And strewn about it, like limp-limbed dolls discarded by a spoiled child, were the sunning bodies of students. "Bodies," she repeated to herself; she would not vouch for the presence there of any minds. For the hour of the hedonists is upon us, she intoned silently to herself, the corners of her mouth lifting mirthlessly, and the weak-minded shall inherit the earth.

It was only late April. The snows had been melted a mere month. This was, in fact, the first truly warm day of the season. And yet none of the bared skin displaying itself beneath Professor Mueller's window retained its natural pigmentation. Enviable diligence, she thought grimly. They not only squander the hours but court skin cancer in the process. How long before the simple sensibility begins to associate tanning with destruction and disease instead of health and the leisure of affluence, to feel the appropriate revulsion at the sight of seared membrane and again reserve its praise for pallor? It would come eventually; for such contingent associations are the essence of the untutored taste in beauty.

There were a few random spots of activity on the lawn. A few students sauntered, singly or in groups, on the walks crisscrossing the quad. And almost below Eva's window were two boys, in cut-off jeans and no shirts, tossing about a Frisbee. One was thin and ran awkwardly, hurtling himself forward in a manner forcefully suggestive of the possibility of skinned knees. The bared chest would be better covered, looking visibly susceptible to infection. Eva could almost see a mother hovering, her soul's focus the fearsome rumblings of that slight cavity. A terrible thing, to be the mother of such a chest.

But the other boy, with long yellow hair that rose and fell as he ran, had a fine-looking body, lean and well developed. A swimmer's body. The faded jeans were sliced at the middle of his firm browned thighs. She watched as he raced backward and then, in a beautifully liquid movement, leaped high into the air, triumphantly clutching the absurd orange disk in his hand. Was it a deception induced by the sun's glare: that he seemed to hover in suspension for a moment, sucking in the air and light, his pectorals swelling above his narrow waist and hips? It seemed to Eva so. Ard in the expanded dimensions of that moment her eager eyes collected details: the play of light and shadow on his profile, the darker golden hair curling beneath his upward-reaching arm, the jeans slipping down over his sucked-in belly as he hung there inhaling. He landed lightly on bare feet. Eva found she was smiling, her tongue behind her slightly parted lips. She quickly looked away.

Her eyes passed haphazardly over the rest of the lawn. She couldn't make out any faces from this height, but it was yet possible for recognition to impose itself upon her. It would be irksome to discover some of her own students down there among the sunning supine, especially now, with the semester all but over, after she had given them all she was going to give them. One more lecture to deliver tomorrow, and then the class, the cohesive whole to which she had administered weekly, would decompose into scattering individuals, some to return next semester, or in future semesters, others gone forever. So hard, so hard, to let go.

But it was, after all, nonsense, this dull ache at the end of each term. There would be more students, flowing in and flowing out, like the river of Heraclitus. And really did it matter in the end, their individual identities? Philosophy does not concern itself with stories, with the accidental details of particulars with histories. History has no place in the philosophical perspective. They were students: that was all that should concern her, there to learn what she had to teach. She let the blind drop with a clatter and turned back to her desk.

There in her typewriter was that piece of unassimilable absurdity. Her long slim fingers tentatively touched her forehead, which was high and very intelligent, too high it had seemed in her youth, when her face did not yet carry the depth of character to support it. She still possessed her beauty, though it had undergone, over the years (she would be turning forty-seven at midsummer), a purification which now left it perceptible only to those who were themselves of a certain spiritual development. Grosser souls, against whose intrusion not even her carefully crafted life was proof, would perhaps dismiss her as . . . brittle.

She was painted in a pale and delicate palette, her hair ash blond, her skin marmoreally smooth and white. Her bone structure was elegant, and her figure, if anything, slimmer and more girlish than it had been in her softer, fuller youth. There was little softness now lingering about her. The simple straight skirts and blouses or sweaters she wore did not interfere with her natural style. Her one extravagance was shoes: always expensive, always European. Her younger, and almost invariably more fashion-eager, students usually suffered in comparison.

It was true that Eva's male colleagues had by now ceased to joke among themselves that a hopeless crush on Professor Mueller ought to be included among the requirements for the major in philosophy, but this was not because the students no longer fell in love with her. They did, at a rate which had of course slackened over the years but was still not inconsiderable. It was an irony —of course quite lost on Eva, who was steadfastly oblivious to the dramas in which she figured—that many who sat raptly listening to their professor's lectures on the "futility of the passions," on the need to transform the passive emotions directed toward objects and people outside ourselves into the active emotions of the intellect, were swollen with an advanced case of that same passive desire whose elimination was being eloquently, even passionately, urged upon them. She would hardly have approved, had she gained an intimation, of the sort of thick and heady excitement often found pulsing on the other side of the lectern. She would have been profoundly bewildered, and just as profoundly appalled. She had no wish to be entangled in others' inner lives;

had, in fact, a very active desire to the contrary. Knowledge of the yearning would have added no warmth to her life but, rather, would have diminished her sense of vocation, besides inducing a painful pity, which it would then be her duty to overcome. For pity, like all the painful passions, is not only irrational but harmful and *wrong*.

There were times: when Professor Mueller was standing before her class, quoting from memory from Plato's *Phaedrus* or Spinoza's *Ethics,* her eyes focused on some distant plane where the words she was effortlessly reading were inscribed; there were times when her features underwent yet a further purification and she seemed, to those already under her spell, to radiate an unearthly beauty. At such times, when she herself was under the trance of her philosophy, the utter remoteness of their professor was revealed to her students, and a certain percentage were then suffused with a throbbing knowledge of the futility of the passions.

An inspiring teacher. Eva Mueller was appreciated as such by her department, which had grown tolerant of her eccentricities, her tendency to approach various departmental matters, from tenure to budgets to student requirements, with dense ethical arguments, unleavened by any touch of brio or humor. It is true that their tolerance had increased in proportion to their ceasing to think of her as really female. Her appeal, at least to the impressionable young, was called to mind only when someone or other tried to explain away to himself the woman's uncanny ability to attract huge numbers of students, a success unshared within the department, especially in this time of appalling pragmatism among undergraduates, clinging to their majors of pre-law and pre-med and pre-business as to a life preserver which would float them gently to the safe and shining shores of material comfort. There were those among her colleagues, particularly those who had initially felt Eva's charms, who now regarded her as something of a perversion, the ultimate proof of the basic incompatibility between the life of the mind and the female state. For was it not obvious that the triumph of her reason had brought with it the desiccation of her womanhood? Still, one and all in the department were grateful for the "Mueller numbers," which they could tote triumphantly before a college administration grown increasingly vigilant on such matters.

We are all masters of self-deception.

Eva leaned down over her desk and ripped the paper out of the typewriter with a show of unnecessary violence. For a moment she considered copying the sentence onto one of her index cards, now numbering in the tens of thousands, which would then be filed away in accordance with her elaborate system, a frozen fugue of logical relations. No, she decided with force. Either it is a floating bit of nonsense or it is a genuine insight. If it is the first, better to forget it. If, by some utterly remote possibility, it is the second, it will not be forgotten.

We shall have to see, Eva told herself, what follows.

Eva Mueller left her office earlier than usual that day, unable to throw off the restlessness that had settled over her like the itch of an allergic reaction. It was often like this on the first spring-like day of the year. A certain agitation, a certain . . . sadness. Odd, the sense of loss that mingled with the scent of the newborn season. Almost like the loss of death, it seemed; the sun's long rays probing through to the skull beneath with its emptied eyes.

Eva was uncomfortable; she was inappropriately dressed. The wool of her skirt and sweater were clinging to her unpleasantly. She had found herself reading the same passages again and again, and still the words would drift off unpossessed, wisps of smoke spiraling away into thin air. Several times she exchanged her book for another, or went to peer yet again through the slats of the blind into the bright outside, sprinkled with the golden boys and girls, more gilded still by the sun. But she had forced herself to remain until a respectable hour before closing up shop. It could not be—impossible thought!—that she was fleeing her office. Her place at the university was her refuge and her sanctuary, the blessed domicile of her truest self. This was especially so now that the warm weather had arrived, rendering the outside world inhospitably alien.

Spring always comes late to this town in upstate New York. The campus lies cradled in its low valley, which it shares with Lake Seyuc, tucked into the shadows of the sheltering mountains and their low-hung and leaking clouds. As a rule not much sun gets through from October to April. It is the formation of the surrounding mountain masses, people say, which traps the wafting waters of Lake Seyuc and accounts for the invariance and density of the overcast.

The fact that the university is enclosed within its own weather system deepens the already profound—and, for many of the inhabitants, pleasurable—sense of isolation. But not all find themselves in their element here, in this meteorological pocket of sun deprivation. And perhaps the unusually high suicide rate among the students (a tragic seven in one semester is the record to date) is not unrelated to the prevailing atmospheric conditions. It is also more than possible that nature has further contributed to the sad statistics, not only in the sunlight withheld, but in the means proffered: two deep gorges lying at the extreme ends of the campus, traversed by high bridges—one, on the southern side, over which cars can pass on their way into the campus; the other, more favored by the unfavored, an even higher footbridge at the darker northern end. From here one can look down several hundred feet to the cold, heedless rush of the water, on its way to Lake Seyuc. And so it is that an indifferent nature conspires, together with the tensed fragility of youth, to push so many, quite literally, over the edge.

This gloominess of climate had always suited Eva, ever since she had come here twenty years before. The winters were not unlike those she had experienced as a child in her native Germany. And, in any case, cold is so much more conducive to the life of the mind. The spring could never arrive too late for her taste. During the long ice-encased winter, when recklessly high-spirited undergraduates drove their cars onto the solid lake, making bets as to how far out the ice would hold, the air was pure and odorless, and the snow, which never entirely melted, simplified and unified the rugged landscape. Eva would tirelessly hike the surrounding mountains and feel her powers of understanding soar. She had her favorite paths through the forested silence, the only sound the crunch of the snow beneath her boots and the muffled murmurings of the fir trees. Eva knew then that she had achieved freedom. She was, as far as it is possible, without a history. The facts, of course, remained; they would always remain. What she had shed was the awful sense of them. Even that story from long ago, told in the hushed and distant nighttime voice of her father, seemed hardly real. She had struggled free; and she was happy.

But then in late March the ice of the lake would break, in a great unearthly noise, the booms exploding into the midnight quiet like the sounds of the gods at war; and Eva retreated into the shade of her blinds-drawn office. The oozing thaw brought with it earthy, unclean smells distasteful to her sensibility. And when the sun finally did break through, and Eva glimpsed the students, who in class had seemed so earnestly receptive, now stretched out semi-nude on the rough boulders rising out of the wild waters coursing through the campus, their radios blaring their odious music, which Eva could tell, even without being able to make out the grunted lyrics, was a celebration of all that is low and anti-philosophical in life, she would feel profoundly betrayed. (Nonsense, nonsense, she chided herself. So unreasonable to take it personally.) But the truth was, she had deceived herself once again. She was not in the business of lifting them out of their soul muddles and up into the empyrean circle of light. She had not produced in them the horror of that mediocrity, intellectual and moral, which they breathed in daily. Despite her teaching they remained prisoners of *eikasia*, the lowest form of consciousness; confused and irrational, beguiled by illusions, dissolving images on water.

As Eva was leaving her office she caught sight of a coppery bobby pin lying under one of the chairs provided for students visiting her office. It had to belong to the girl who had come to consult Eva earlier that day, the weepy one. Eva rarely learned the names of her students, since there were so many; and in any case, she had a poor memory for such things. But she did have, associated with many of the faces, a short descriptive phrase she used privately to designate an individual, based on his or her philosophical performance; so that this one she remembered as "muddled" *(ein Wirrkopf)*, that one as a *"tabula rasa,"* and the next as "promising, perhaps."

The girl who had occupied that seat earlier in the day had been one of the many that Eva lumped under the heading "sleeping, do not disturb." But henceforth, should Eva have reason to recall her, she would be "the weepy one." She was one of the many who had been lured into the course by Eva's campus-wide reputation but who had absolutely no business being there. Not all are meant to study philosophy; not all, therefore, are marked for redemption. This is the hard insoluble truth encased in Plato's "one noble lie," to be told the inhabitants of his utopia: that some souls are composed of gold, others silver, and yet others, the vast indistinguishable majority, iron and brass. Or perhaps copper, Eva thought, thinking of the weepy one of the afternoon visitation. She scooped the hairpin up with a tissue, depositing it into the trash.

Eva had been surprised to see this student at her door, but the very first sentence out of her mouth accounted for the unexpected event. Of course, Eva thought, with a resignation brushed with amusement: the girl had come to make excuses for the lateness of her paper, still hovering in the realm of non-being. She pleaded "personal problems." Indeed, Eva thought, taking in the girl's heavily applied makeup—the eyeliner so thick she looked like a raccoon—and short denim skirt; I can well imagine. However, it was not to be left for Eva's powers of imagination but was poured out all over her, the tumid, murky mess that was this creature's life.

Strange, the things the students told one. It was because they were American, she had decided. Discretion was as alien to them as lederhosen. But still, that they should choose her as mother confessor! Over the years she had learned to take it all in stride and to think of such sessions as part of her duties as teacher. It was fine, very fine, she had decided, that they came to her. Disengaged but attentive, she would listen, trying to grasp the sensibilities—so very different from her own!—that animated their situations. And quite often the students went away inspired to take not only Professor Mueller's advice but her person as their model. For they were in a state of frenzied flux, these students, in transition from the gaseous formlessness of childhood to the final solidity of adult life. And they flowed; my God, how they flowed, first this way, then that, in that hormone-thickened syrup of their prolonged adolescence; when the options between different modes of life are quiveringly alive, and each encounter with a personality who seems a "type" brings with it the thought: Perhaps that is how *I* should be. Professor Mueller represented one of the possibilities. For her part, Eva tried to sound the voice of reason. But quite often she suspected that what they really wanted from her was not counsel but expiation.

And so it had seemed, at least at first, with the weepy one this afternoon. She was a very soft and yielding kind of girl, no hard surfaces or sharp angles to thwart another's will. A pretty girl, Eva supposed she would be called, if one did not scruple to label so true a picture of banality. In any case, her prettiness would not stand the test of time. Already vulgarity was seeping in, dulling and slackening. There was a charm in the questioning wonder of her wide-open eyes; but with time they would look simply stupid. Her voice was whispery and her mascara-gooed lashes clung shyly to her cheeks.

The next half hour brought Eva a reluctant acquaintance with the nature of the girl's personal problems: a married man who was "trying to decide" between the lachrymose narrator and his knowing, but forgiving, wife. Eva doubted the girl's grasp of the situation. The silly child was being duped. This was not, Eva was quite certain, the kind of female to win out over a spouse. The very word "wife" suggested a substantiality that could only be seen as desirable when placed beside this puddle of a person, awash in her blackened tears.

A few more sobs and shudders and it trickled out that the married man was her English professor. Aha, Eva thought, then your unhappy fate is immitigably sealed. Austere as Eva's own life was, the revelation left her unshocked. Her years in academe had inured her to the indiscretions, and worse, of her esteemed colleagues. There was something in the professor-student relationship, a certain power dynamic, that proved very tempting to the morally sluggish. And then, in dealing with a professor, one is dealing with someone whose personal identity is largely constituted by the ideas he holds. To effect an infusion of those ideas into the consciousness of another was to achieve a kind of intimacy after which the sexual might seem almost anticlimactic. But anticlimactic or not, the erotic suggestion does often hover in the vicinity of the classroom.

It was, of course, the girl's own stupidity that had landed her in such a pathetic position of passivity. And yet Eva felt a momentary anger toward the man who would avail himself of this opportunity, who would submerge himself in this open wound of a female. (Oh yes, she could well imagine.) This was not only a lapse of propriety; it showed an unpardonable lack of taste.

"I don't blame anyone. Nobody's at fault," the girl was blubbering. "I keep thinking of that song, 'There Is No Blame, There Is No Shame,' by the Cheaps Thrills, you know?"

"I don't." They take their ethics from the popular junk in which they marinate their brains. Really, what was the use? Let the Cheap Thrills go and teach them philosophy.

"It's just that he wants both of us."

"He wants," Professor Mueller repeated. But her tone, and its import, were quite lost on the child.

"I'm just really falling apart. I can't concentrate on anything.

]15[

I haven't finished the work for any of my courses, not even Art Appreciation, and all we had to do there was go to the museum."

Eva stifled her desire to smile. The girl was seriously stupid. Eva had done a three-year stint on the Admissions Committee and knew the devious paths often traversed by final decisions. She quickly calculated. No, she had not been on the committee when this girl, a junior, had dripped through the sadly porous system. Eva, by her own standards the only sensible person on the committee during her tenure there, had often been dismayed by candidates others had championed in the name of student diversity, an altogether dubious aim from Eva's perspective. Her own standard had been simple: Would I want to teach this person?

Now she said to this girl, whom she did *not* want to teach: "You must see that happiness is impossible for you in such a situation. You've put yourself into a position of passivity. All the power over your future has been handed over to another."

"You mean Fr . . . I mean, you mean my English professor."

It would have been a simple procedure at this point for Eva to deduce who this girl's lover was. But she would not allow herself even to consider the possibilities. Such gutter-knowledge did not stir her interest. But oddly, some recalcitrant element of her psyche, with a mind of its own, had apparently immediately gone to work on the problem and now produced the answer: Frederick Simmons, the chairman of the department in question. She remembered that years ago, when they had done a stint on the Honors Committee together and he had displayed a certain flirtatious gallantry toward her, which she had answered, as was her unwavering policy, with an exaggerated stiffness. Frederick Simmons. Eva pushed down the name with a feeling of distaste. Really, she didn't want to know.

"Yes," Eva said. "Your professor."

"But I love him," answered the girl in her tear-thickened voice.

"And this love: is it good for you?"

"I don't know. I mean, I'm miserable and all."

"Well," Eva said with a patience that she willed, "that sounds as if it is not very beneficial."

"But I'm in love." The child sniffed loudly.

"I don't quite understand how that is a sufficient refutation. Does your being in love conduce to your well-being despite the fact of your misery? Or is it, rather, that you believe being in love overrides your well-being?"

"I don't know. I'm not really sure what you mean. Could you run that past me again?"

Eva sighed. Really, where did her pedagogical duties end?

"Look, you've gotten yourself into a rather unfortunate place. I can't tell you what to do with your life. It's your decision, of course. That is the very point: it *must* be your decision. Not mine, not your English professor's. Waiting around for someone else to make up his mind about what will happen to your life can only be very painful. Passivity is pain."

"You mean I should leave him?" Her wondering eyes dilated.

"Well, at least that would be *your* decision, your move. And there would be pleasure in simply becoming an active agent, being the one to take the decisive step. Surely you can see that."

"But I don't *want* that change," the girl literally wailed. "I don't want him out of my life. I can't just decide to stop being in love."

Eva imperceptibly shrugged her shoulders. This was becoming tiresome and there was work to do.

"You know what it's like," the girl continued. "I mean, you're a woman and all. I mean, that's why I came to you. You're not just a professor."

Eva stared at the girl, for whom, despite her scruples, she was beginning to feel a slight disgust.

The student, dull as she was, sensed she was losing her audience. She made an effort, her voice even more whispery and halting: "You said that passivity is pain. And you say that sort of thing in class, you know, that stuff about freedom, you know, that we're free only when like our own needs are making us act?"

"Yes," Eva answered quietly. "Our *true* needs, which it takes some wisdom to discern." She was the slightest bit impressed, in spite of herself. Apparently, the girl hadn't been sleeping as soundly as Eva had judged. Something had gotten through. Of course, what the child made of the words was anybody's guess.

"Well, I mean I don't really understand that."

"Don't you?" Such a shock.

"I mean, it seems kind of selfish. And it seems to condemn a person to a life without, you know, real affection. I mean, does freedom mean never loving? Cause, you know, when you really care about someone, well then, like *their* needs kind of affect you. You just can't be a closed system. You know, like no man is an island?"

Quite a speech. It seemed there was something cooking after all, on however small a flame, beneath the copper head of hair. The girl had contrived to engage Eva on her own turf and Eva was obliged to answer. But still she hung back, staring into the girl's vacant eyes, her dissolving face. Eva believed passionately in the education of the young—it was the very foundation of her existence!—but really: there was a limit. This girl, whom she could quite easily imagine as attractive to a certain kind of man, represented what Eva herself found most distasteful in woman-hood. This heaving, viscous pool of feelings and sensations, with nothing firm and ungiving to get a grip on. It was a fact Eva had long ago faced: the members of her own sex for the most part disgusted her. How to explain to such a creature that to be mis-tress of one's own future means that others can*not* mean too much. That one's attachments should be loose and easily severed. Friendliness, not fervor. Detachment, not desire. That, or risk relinquishing one's inner peace, becoming a helpless hostage to the vicissitudes of others' attitudes. Passivity is indeed pain.

"Well," she plunged in, "according to Spinoza . . ."

"Excuse me, Professor Mueller, but I don't really want to hear another lecture on Spinoza." The girl's impatience, or perhaps fear at her own temerity, gave a certain husky substance to her voice. "I came to you to hear what *you* would say. After all, you're a woman. You have the heart and feelings of a woman, the body of a woman. Spinoza could never understand what I feel, but you could."

Eva felt a swell of outrage gathering within her. Just who was this idiotic child, this common little chit with her smeared makeup and her repulsively short skirt, to speak to a professor in this way? Eva stared at the student, her heated contempt giving a sharpness to her observations: the orange lipstick caked into a flaking mosaic, the drop of water suspended from the tip of her reddened nose. And really it seemed to Eva that there was a certain smell in her office emanating from the girl, a damp intimate feminine smell, extremely offensive to Eva. Her nostrils —the most expressive feature of her face—quivered in disgust.

"Now it is my turn not to understand you," she said quietly, her accent, usually carefully subdued, breaking through. "I am a woman, it is true. But so far as I know, philosophical understanding is not gender-specific. Spinoza's flawed sex seems to me not to undermine his fundamental validity. But since I have nothing whatsoever to say to you *as a woman*"—she emphasized the words with sarcasm—"perhaps we had better terminate our discussion now."

It had taken Eva several minutes to still the roiling of her undammed anger. Really, to be so stupid was pitiful. But to be so assertively and self-contentedly stupid bordered on the immoral.

Another student had visited Eva that day, a refreshing contrast to the weepy one. It was of him that Eva now thought as she left the building and ventured out into the waning, less relentlessly probing sunlight. His name was Michael Fields. He was one of the few undergraduates in a very long time whose name Eva knew, although at the beginning of the semester he had been christened "clever but glib." Not only did Eva know his name, but he had the (as far as it is remembered) unique distinction of having made the professor burst out laughing in class.

The class had just begun the reading of Spinoza's *Ethics*, one of the high points of the semester. For the students all knew Professor Mueller's passionate regard for the "God-intoxicated atheist." Plato and Spinoza, those were her masters, the two great apostles of redemption through philosophical understanding.

Professor Mueller had recited, her eyes focused on that remote place, the very first words of the monumental work, a definition: "By that which is self-caused, I mean that of which the essence involves existence, that of which the nature is only conceivable as existent." By proposition ɪɪ, Spinoza would have proved that this Self-caused, or God, necessarily exists.

"Who can tell me what this definition means? What is Spinoza trying to do here?" she had asked, her eyes, their blueness blazing, focusing back in on the students before her.

And Michael Fields had answered, glibly, but cleverly: "This is where Spinoza makes his first mistake."

The class at first did not react, but waited, watching Professor Mueller. And she too stared for several seconds, finally surprising both the students and herself by breaking into delighted laughter, light and musical. She leaned back against the blackboard and closed her eyes, in brief abandonment to merriment. And her class joined in with equal heartiness, loving her in this moment of unusual levity as they loved her in her more natural solemnity.

Michael Fields had continued to attract Eva's attention throughout the semester. Slowly he had lost his cavalier attitude and had become intensely interested in deciphering this most grandiose of all rationalist systems, which makes all the claims for reason that have ever been made. Eva had been moved to witness such a transformation, and such susceptibility to the power of Spinoza. For really, there were few students indeed who could begin to appreciate him. It sometimes struck her as almost laughable to be lecturing to these uncreased faces on such a thinker. What could they make of him? What could they understand? The good students would approach the system as an intellectual exercise. The others could not approach it at all. But none of these children could see it for what it was: a heroic attempt to reconcile the human spirit to the tragic possibilities of life.

Michael Fields was one of the good students; but sometimes Eva suspected that he might be something more, something very rare and wonderful: a philosopher, formed of the brilliant stuff, the gold of Plato's fable. "It is true, we shall tell our people in this tale, that all of you in this land are brothers; but the god who fashioned you mixed gold in the composition of those among you who are fit to rule, so that they are of the most precious quality." In his midterm exam he had written in such well-reasoned appreciation of Spinoza's goals that, for the rest of the semester, Eva felt as if she were lecturing to him alone. She read her cues from his face. If he looked puzzled, she continued to explain her point. When he seemed satisfied, she moved on. But, of course, as she found reason to remind herself, there had been gifted students before him; and there were others still to come.

Today Michael Fields had come to her with a proposition. He wanted to set up a private tutorial with her for over the summer, to complete the five parts of the *Ethics*. (In class they had concentrated only on the first.) She had told him to come back tomorrow for her answer.

She was seriously tempted, although she had promised herself to take on no more students. She was currently supervising the doctoral theses of five graduate students; that was more than her required share. And even though it was the more formless undergraduates whom she really enjoyed teaching, she felt a greater obligation to take on the graduate students. After all, they had so much more at stake.

But really, it would be a pleasure to go through the *Ethics* with this boy. He seemed to possess such a surprisingly intuitive understanding. So rare in a child his age. So wonderfully rare. How had he come by it?

On the other side of the question, there was her book. It was an absolute necessity that she complete her book this summer. Her former editor, who had been the one to approach her initially with the project and who had patiently awaited the final product for ten years, dear, kind Horace Fraser, had suffered a stroke this past winter. He had survived, but as a frightening facsimile, almost a physical parody, of his former self. The right side of his face was paralyzed. Eva had had to overcome a strong reluctance to visit him in New York. She had been afraid of how he would look.

(Papa's face after his stroke, the twisting snarl of a mouth, as if stitched into a caricature of evil. It had been a terror, that face, a terror to nullify all memories. I thought: In dying he gets the face he deserves.)

The editor who had taken Horace's place was a young man, maybe thirty or so, with a young man's impatience. Ira Cranshaw. Eva did not like him. For the first time Eva was working under a deadline. But even without the deadline she would have been anxious to complete the book at long last. It was time. And now, without Horace's solicitous and respectful patience . . . Ira Cranshaw did not share Horace's enthusiasm for *Reason's Due*. So far as Eva could discern he had little acquaintance with, or sympathy for, the philosophical enterprise. It was good that she had so little left to do: the very final chapter. It would be done by summer's end.

Eva had come to the high footbridge strung across the northern gorge which she crossed daily on her way to and from the campus. Today, on an impulse, she turned left onto the narrow path that led gently down into the ravine. It was a favorite walk, densely shaded. About halfway down there was a huge boulder where Eva sometimes sat, and onto which she now pulled herself with ease. (She was quite strong for someone so slender.) Through the trees one had a lovely view of the abyss. There they were, far below, the faithful heliolaters, stretched out on the sheer rock rising from the foaming waters, as devoid of movement—and reflection—as lizards.

Eva had not been there five minutes, however, before they bestirred themselves, gathering their things together and finally scampering down from their perches and wading thigh-high back to shore. Their day's work was completed. The sun's rays were now too weak to summon forth the coveted melanin. Eva leaned back in contentment. She had decided to take on the boy. Michael.

"Hi there. Mind if I join you?"

Eva slowly turned her head in the direction of the baritone voice, her face already composed in an expression of arch dismissal. It had happened often enough before. Some young man would approach her and, taken with her shoulder-length blond hair and slim build, mistake her for a student, fair game for the hunter. She had long ago—twenty years, really, when she had just become an assistant professor—devised the expression she now wore, conveying her elevated status and the insufferable effrontery of any approach. Over the years many a young male had beat a flustered retreat.

Eva's eyes fell now on the hopeful petitioner, a strutting young pagan. Short and muscular, dark curly hair, perhaps nineteen or twenty. Tight, rather bulging jeans. An undergraduate. She stared at him for a few seconds, waiting for her scorn to penetrate. And then something unexpected happened. The boy looked aghast. He actually looked frightened and . . . . disgusted. He mumbled, "Sorry, ma'am, my mistake," and lunged down the path.

Eva understood. She did not deceive herself. After all, what reason had she to elude the trivial truth? There is cause for self-deception only concerning issues that personally matter. And the dashed desire of an estrous undergraduate was surely of no consequence to Eva. Actually, it was mildly amusing. Expecting a face as callowly blank as his own, he had been confronted with a mature woman. There was no denying the look of startled . . . repugnance.

Eva could well imagine the reaction of *other* women. The throbbing vanity, the inward howl at the injustice of it all. And yet, of course, it is just; eminently just. We grow old or we die. In this world of foolish vanities, none is so foolish as the pride of the young. Did they do something special to earn the right to be young? Shall they be young forever? No, it is given, given to all . . . for a time. Eva knew her own time was ending. It did not concern her. For another woman, she knew, such a little misadventure would constitute a trauma of significant proportions. For such a woman the thought that she is losing her sexual allure is like a little death. Eva had read of the melodramatic displays of self-pity exhibited by some of her sex in the face of their "change of life," upon which she herself had recently, without regret, embarked. In fact, if anything, she had greeted the process as liberating. She had always resented the monthly mess thrust upon her by her anatomy, the days of cramps and discomfort, interfering with her thinking. Really, if there was any injustice to rail against, it was that of being born a woman, involuntarily saddled with the apparatus of procreation. Of course, such a complaint was also absurd. Still, Eva was not sorry to be deprived of this aspect of femininity.

But these other women, who placed all their worth in the hollow uterus within and the flimsy flaunted integument without. Eva could only pity such women. She never had, and never would have, anything to do with them. Wasted lives. If that is the loss one mourns, then one has led a truly wasted life. That a tight-jeaned, half-baked male in heat should disdain her company? Was such a rejection to constitute a personal tragedy? Bosh!

(How long now since the world gave up its ghost of intrigue? How long since I've looked on another as an empire of possibilities, dense with pounded promise, Anaximander's inexhaustible *apeiron*, bounded by a body?)

Eva slowly slid down off her perch—how many of her students could maneuver the movement so gracefully?—and continued on the path down which the terrified young suitor had just fled. The itchy restlessness of the afternoon was creeping back upon her. She decided to walk it off. She had no wish to return to her apartment just yet. She left the path and plunged deeper into the woods.

But the agitation of the afternoon only increased as she walked, quickening her pace. Something rank and obscene had been awakened in the forest by the thaw. The ground underneath was soft with mud. And everywhere, pushing themselves up through the mire, were the raw pale-green sprouts of new life, still wet with the slime of birth. Aristotle had posited the *threptikē psychē*, the vegetative soul. And it seemed to Eva, in a wave of squeamish sickness, that she could almost hear the silent screaming into life of this multitude of souls, mouths open and greedy for breath. She turned to find her way back out of the woods, and in her haste slipped on the slickened earth, catching her arm around a tree to prevent her fall. But she was shaken, deeply shaken.

And, as she stood there for a few seconds, composing herself, willing her heart back to its normal rate, she caught a whiff of a scent she had encountered before in the springtime woods, a bittersweet pungency piercing the heavy air. It was a distinctive smell. It smelled like . . . semen. Eva's sharp nostrils quivered. Was it some species of plant, or the remains of some undergraduate escapade? As she quickly moved on to escape the unpleasant odor, she was assaulted by a quick series of images, more than twenty-five years old, wrapped away in her mind like an old wedding dress in blue tissue paper. A dark bedroom in New York's Morningside Heights, a tousled bed, a younger Eva, naked, with a man beside her, facing away. He was slowly turning toward her. Eva closed her eyes very tightly before she could see his face, squeezing them together as hard as she could, grimacing in the effort, fracturing the image into a multitude of flashing points of brilliant color.

Eva's apartment was in a very large and elegant stucco mansion, built in the 1890s and subdivided some twenty-odd years ago. Many of the mansions of the Heights, overlooking Lake Seyuc, had suffered a similar fate. Eva's apartment was large and airy, with high ceilings trimmed with carved plaster moldings and paned French windows. The walls were painted a pale gray, the plaster trim was white. The apartment contained one of the original stairwells, graced by an elaborately carved oaken banister. She had one very large room —probably one of the sitting rooms, now her combined living and dining room—on the bottom floor, and another heroically proportioned room—her bedroom—above. Off the first-floor area was a small kitchen, added when the apartments were carved out, modest but adequate. Eva had furnished her rooms almost entirely with antiques which she had acquired over the years, in the few shops in town and at sales out in the surrounding countryside. There was, throughout, the feel of a faded past.

Eva moved quietly around her little kitchen, gathering together the components of her evening meal: some bread and cheese, a bottle of mineral water, an orange, and coffee. She very rarely cooked, at most broiling the occasional chop. Food had long ago ceased to be of any importance to her; and when she was deeply involved in her writing she would forget to eat for long stretches of time, finally reminded by a sudden attack of light-headedness or the trembling of her hands. She arranged her food on a tray and carried it out to her round oak trestle table. Found in a barn sale some twenty miles out of town, the table had come with four ladder-back chairs covered in sapphire-blue velvet; but she never had need for more than one at a time, and the other three were piled high with papers and journals.

Eva switched on the small silk-shaded lamp she kept on the table. She never used the overhead lights but, rather, the small lamps she had scattered throughout. There was always need, no matter what the time of day, for artificial lighting in the downstairs room. The apartment was at the very end of the house, shaded by a cluster of poplar trees growing a few yards from the house. They tapered off about twenty feet into the air, and so Eva's bedroom got some late-afternoon sunlight. But then she was never there in the late afternoon. Eva had also been able to purchase the heavy blue brocade drapes that had graced the tall paned downstairs windows since the days when the house was privately owned. She kept them drawn shut, opening them only at night. So her living room was always dark.

Eva had taken a few mouthfuls of food when she returned to the kitchen and switched on her little radio. The radio was tuned to the college station, which was broadcasting the day's news. Listening to the radio's newscast during dinner was a concession she sometimes allowed herself to the state of living alone. She never permitted herself to read during meals. Even if one lives alone, or perhaps especially if one does so, one must be scrupulous in the observation of the conventions of civilized living. Mealtimes in the Mueller household had been extremely formal. Eva remembered how strictly she had been trained, as a child in Germany, down to the correct posture while dining. If there was one aspect of her adopted country which still produced a shock, hardly dulled by repeated exposure, it was the manner in which its inhabitants ingested their daily sustenance. When she had first arrived on these shores she was barely able to eat in public without staring in dismay at the wild spectacle of flailing silverware, engorged mandibles open and conversing, teeth and tongues flagrantly exposed in the act. Even the relatively better bred among them ate in a way which no German parent would tolerate in a child older than four.

After the news came a program of classical music, succeeded by hours of popular music, of the sort favored by the young. There was once a time when she might have left the radio on for the classical program, a time when she had loved music. It was a love, of course, that ran in her family. (Her father on the violin, her mother on the piano: how many times had Eva fallen asleep as a child with the sounds of their playing drifting up to her bedroom high on the fourth floor, lapping gently around her bed.) But for some time now Eva had found it quite impossible to listen to music.

After Eva had washed, dried, and put away her plate and cup and glass, and swept her table with her little whisk broom for any stray crumbs, she settled herself down in her cushioned rocking chair with a book. She never read fiction. She had, in fact, great disdain for the novel, mucking about in the dark holes of others' lives. A low form of knowledge that, dressed-up gossip, the pointless wagging of women's tongues. Plato had banished the whole lot of storytellers from his ideal state, where reason reigns.

Tonight she sat with a rather obscure German work on Kant's conception of freedom, written in the late nineteenth century.

The text was thickly encrusted with neo-Kantian jargon and pedantic, curlicued prose—German scholarship gone berserk. But Eva sat there trying to chip her way through. One never knew when one might happen upon something useful, a stranded remark that could lead one to yet another tiny corner of the blacked-out vastness. Those were the very precious times. Those were the times one lived for. Her entire book had emerged from the quiet unfolding of one such gathered moment. (Will there be more?—other moments? other books?) Toward midnight she got up to open the windows to the cool night air, standing there for several moments, breathing deeply, and then returned to her chair and her reading.

Eva awoke with a start in her rocking chair. Her little lamp was still burning beside her, her wristwatch ticking: 4 A.M.

There it was: the music. He was at it again. The nocturnal flutist. Somebody on the Heights had taken to playing his instrument in the dead of night. The long thin rays of the flute's voice entered now through the window, pushing aside the heavy drapes, together with the stirred-up breeze. Seven, maybe eight times before in the last month Eva had heard the music, always between midnight and dawn.

Eva listened for several moments. It was a French Impressionist piece tonight. She thought she recognized it: Debussy's "Song for a Flaxen-Haired Child."

Tentatively, she moved her stiffened limbs, slowly rising from her chair. She walked over to her tall opened window, leaning out, trying to determine from which direction the music was coming. It was impossible; the breeze, almost a wind now, made it impossible. What manner of soul was it who poured his music out onto the nighttime wind? Somewhere on the Heights swelled the figure of Marsyas, hurling his tragic challenge to the god. Why do you pull myself from myself, he will cry out in the agony of his flaying.

But why a "he" with "*his*" agony? Why had she always taken

the maleness of the flutist for granted? Was it that she imagined all women, in love with their creature comforts, safely asleep at this inconvenient hour? She was not like other women. Here she was, awake to the night, leaning out of her window, trying to place the direction of the flute's long voice. *Mein Gott, wie schön!*

(Mama at the piano! Darling Papa at the violin! *Wie schön,* I would think, drifting slowly into sleep, *Wie schön ist die Musik!*)

So softly, so surely did the music make its way into the room . . . it seemed the very voice of the night. And the flutist: the night's own soul. He played well. He played . . . beautifully. So beautifully that it was beginning to hurt.

And yet she continued to stand there at the open window, marveling. How could such tender desire send itself out into the cold silence of the night, to venture forth like that, strain after longing strain? Oh, it was a fallacy, reckless and unsound, to expose oneself like this, to go out into the world asking. It was the fallacy from which followed, with a necessity almost mathematical, the full dimensions of the human tragedy. One must keep one's questions and questings confined to those one can answer for oneself. Otherwise it is all pain, a pain beyond bearing, to nullify all memories. And for what? This, beautiful as it was, was a mistake; but a mistake of such sublime and noble courage!

At every moment she thought: Now it must stop; surely it can no longer be borne. But still the music pushed on, trembling and unprotected—but persistent, so persistent in its claims. Each phrase fully alive for its moment, and then just as fully dead.

And Eva stood there, in wordless wonder, hearing it out until the end, in reverence and humility, for all that it cost her to let such music enter. But heroism of such proportions demands some gesture in response. And when the last notes had died, she closed her windows and climbed her heavy oaken stairs, to bed . . .

. . . and the sun-dampened boy floating free in mid-flight, landing light on bared feet. And my words, which you will not hear, which you have willed not to hear. Why have you torn out my tongue, *meine kleine Fee?*

]31[

There was always a cluster of students who remained after class, surrounding Professor Mueller at her lectern, asking questions, listening to her expound on the finer points. Finally, she would excuse herself; otherwise it could go on all day. Come see me during my office hours, she would say. You know when they are? Oh yes, they knew. The other department members were always amused to see the students lined up outside her door. The legion "Mueller numbers." What was she handing out, anyway? Sugar-coated Spinoza? Kantian kisses?

But today she did not linger after class. She said her words, her final words for the semester: always inadequate, never doing justice to her subject. She watched her sentences drifting up, thin wisps of meaning trailing off into the silence. Her last chance for the semester to make the fire leap the lectern; and this was all she could muster. If they ignited any spark out there, it was indeed a miracle. And then she fled the room quickly. Usually the students applauded the last class: whistles, bravos. This time she would not have been able to bear it. As it was, something powerful and hurting was threatening to burst open her chest.

Sometimes she received anonymous gifts: flowers, once a rare edition of *Leaves of Grass*, the occasional attempt at home-made poetry: ". . . So heady on her words/That we barely no-tice what we've done/That we have entered the labyrinths of logic/Are walking firmly on the abstract plane/And are ad-vancing, behind her, on human freedom!" Never once had she tried to guess the identity of the donor. The gifts were from "the students." They loved her class. That much was clear. It was fine, very fine, that this should be so. She was giving them something they needed, quite obviously, something they held precious. Even if they didn't yet fully grasp its significance, unhandled by life as they still largely were. (What had *she* known at that age? What had *she* been?) Still, the words would be there for them in the years to come: though submerged and unheard beneath the debris of a noisy existence, they would surface someday, when they were needed, when the pain of life came crashing down. It was her hope as a teacher. Other-wise, what was it all for?

She was sitting in her office, her heart pounding, her breathing labored. This is ridiculous, she told herself. It's only the end of semester, not a major catastrophe. There would be other classes . . . other students. Nothing was lost. Nothing was really over. It seemed that after all the years, all the effort she had expended toward the goal of perfect rationality, she was still a damnably silly woman. *Schluss damit!* Enough!

There was a knock at the door. Had they followed her en masse to her office? Had they trailed her here, sloshing their messy youth and love? She could not bear it. She could not . . . She squeezed her hands together, tight, tight, the knuckles white. Then she got up from her desk and opened her door.

"Oh—ah, hi, Professor Mueller. I hope I'm like not disturbing you or anything. You kind of rushed off. But I think I'm like supposed to talk to you."

It was the boy. Michael. Michael Fields. He looked uncomfortable, uncertain of himself. And he so self-assured in class. But young. The young found so much to embarrass them. They, who were so blithe and unashamed of the most intimately personal facts, who snapped their fingers and shook their bodies while mouthing the vulgar lyrics of their unmelodious music! But they blushed and mumbled at the sight of sorrow.

But then, what was she thinking? He would not know, could not know the state of her mind. He was uncomfortable because she was the professor. He didn't know whether he was intruding, doing the right thing. A young boy. And she was the adult. The teacher. The authority. It was enough for her to see what had to be done. She became the professor, impregnably rational, a figure impossible to imagine wringing her hands till the knuckles went white.

"Come in." She smiled. "Yes, we were supposed to talk today. About the tutorial."

"Yeah." He smiled with the relief of his embarrassment.

"Come, take a seat. Well, I think we can work something out."

He grinned. "Wow! This is really great! Now I have a bona fide excuse for staying here all summer. My parents have been hassling me to come home. You know, stay with them. They're in California. You know what it's like." He laughed.

Eva stared at him. So this is what he wanted from her, the hours that she was going to carve carefully out of her writing time. The unthinking selfishness of them! They only took, took, took, never even realizing there was someone there giving, giving, giving. Had he no idea what time meant to her? Did he think she just sat around in her office staring out the window, waiting for a student to find some purpose to put her to? And she! How foolish of her. Such a meaningless sacrifice.

"I was prepared," Eva said stiffly, "to give you some few hours —you must understand I am quite busy—because I was under the impression that you had a serious interest in the *Ethics*. However, if your end is quite other, if you mean only to frustrate your parents' holiday plans for you, then I am afraid I have not the time."

Now he stared at her: hurt, dumbfounded.

"Oh, God," he groaned. "I am such an idiot. I can't believe I said that to you. It's just that I'm, well, I guess sort of like nervous. I mean I really want so much to study with you this summer. I was just, you know, babbling. I was so scared that you would turn me down, because you're so busy, of course you're so busy, and then I was just so, so . . . well, I guess, happy. I was babbling. I guess I'm still babbling." He sat back, his face very red.

Eva considered. Was the boy telling the truth or cleverly covering his *faux pas?* It was hard for her to believe in others' deceptiveness. And yet, over the years, she had been forced to accept mendacity as a not altogether unnatural occurrence among the students. They knew what to say, some of them, said it to save their skins, with such conviction, such earnestness. Eva was not so easy to fool as she once had been.

But she wasn't all that hard either. For she believed it to be a very bad thing, a fearsomely wrong act, to disbelieve a person who is telling the truth. She would, on the whole, rather risk being duped.

She looked at the boy. His fair skin was mottled red. So mortified, dejected. Like a little boy who has wet his pants, she thought. And if it had been, after all, only nervousness, if he were in earnest . . . She liked it that he didn't try to argue with her now, only sat there waiting. Oh, the expression on his face!

"Okay," Eva said, not allowing the smile she felt to form itself. "I will believe you. And you will convince me that I am not now

]3 5[

making a grievous error by working very hard for me over the summer."

"Yes!" he fairly shouted. "That's exactly what I want. To work very hard for you over the summer."

She leaned back and permitted herself the smile. How wide open he looked. What an easy thing it was for the brand-new wrapping of sophistication to come undone. They are just feeling their way into the world, still wet and wobbly.

He *looked* like a California boy: lean and athletic, his eyes a shade of blue rather similar to her own. Like a fallen piece of the German sky. (*Blaue Augen, Himmelsstern/Küssen alle Mädchen gerne,* the little girls had sung as they jumped rope through the summer months.) His hair was a light brown flecked with gold, straight and rather long, falling into his eyes. His nose and mouth were small and well formed; and there was an almost childlike roundness to his face. Poignant, she thought unexpectedly. Yes, there *was* a poignancy to that unstable mixture of child and man, before the final precipitation into full maturity. But his voice was deep; in his voice he was a man. Although perhaps it was a bit self-consciously modulated.

"Shall we meet every week for an hour, or every other week for two hours?"

"Let's make it every week," he said quickly. "And thanks. That's really more than I had expected. That's really terrific. Do you think we can finish the whole *Ethics?*"

She found it impossible not to smile at his enthusiasm.

"Yes, I think we might. I'll want a few written pages every week. Just two or three, to help you organize your thoughts. So we can use our time together most productively."

"Okay. Sure. Sounds great. What day of the week?"

Eva pulled out her black academic calendar. She had to balance him against the graduate students, the dissertations in various stages of incompleteness. "Fridays, say between eleven and twelve?"

"Good! Great!" He stood up. He was only one or two inches taller than she, maybe five eight. She wondered if he might still grow. His face, at least, looked as if it had a lot of developing to do before it settled itself into manhood.

"Well then, I guess that's that." He took a big breath and then laughed. She laughed too.

"Yes. That is that."

Eva was sitting in her darkened living room, only the little lamp beside her on, her round trestle table stacked with columns and columns of blue exam books. Like a penance, she thought. For the sin of pride? So proud of her success as a teacher, the classes so much larger than her scornful colleagues'. Now the excessively high piles to mark.

She had made herself a large pot of coffee to get herself through the night. Here was the moment of truth, for them and for her. Had she managed to teach them anything? How much had she gotten across? She knew only too well that a certain percentage of the booklets would be a battering agony to read through, to see her words and the words of the great thinkers they had read come back smudged and hollowed, and lisping like a mockery.

She had sorted the booklets out. She would read the better students' first. Then she would have a standard by which to assess the others. On the very top of the first column was his: the boy's, Michael Fields's. She stared at where he had printed out the Honor Code, meant to discourage cheating. It was somehow charming to think of his writing it out. Why, she couldn't say. All the students had done the same.

She leafed quickly through the booklet, to see which questions he had chosen: 2, 4, 5, and 8: the most difficult, the most challenging. The last question, in particular, she had posed for only the most gifted students. Here is where they could show what stuff they had. (She hoped the others had had sense enough to leave it alone.) She poured herself a cup of black coffee and began to read through the exam, quickly, nervously. Had she made a mistake?

When she had read it once, she began again, this time more slowly, pausing now and then to look up and reflect. Finally, she closed the book and set it carefully down. He had done well, very well. In fact, he had done quite marvelously. It was among the best exams she had ever gotten from an undergraduate. He had covered all that needed covering; but more than that, he had moved with self-assurance and grace, even wit and originality. (It was a rare and wonderful thing to encounter wit and originality in the dreary landscape of the bluebook.) He had made the material his own.

A+, Eva wrote on the cover of the booklet. She looked up and smiled in triumph.

It was strange, the way it finally happened. Such a small occurrence to have made such a difference, the change so sudden and so utterly complete. Like a phase transition in matter, the ice becoming water; a degree's fluctuation and suddenly there is an entirely different kind of stuff.

He was in her office, puzzling over a difficult passage in the *Ethics*, when Eva got the telephone call. It was from her new editor, Ira Cranshaw. He had just skimmed the chapters she had sent him, he said, and he wasn't completely happy with them. He wasn't saying he was an expert or anything but he really didn't think it was going to work—as it was, that was. The arguments all seemed so long-winded. Obvious points belabored. And where was it going? A great complex mosaic, but the picture just wasn't emerging. He was sending it back to her, with more detailed criticisms and questions. She should get it in the mail within the next few days. He was sure it was nothing she couldn't fix up. Well, goodbye.

Eva hung up the phone, her ivory skin gone several shades whiter. She was stunned, her body cold and numb.

And then she looked up and saw the boy watching. She had entirely forgotten that he was there beside her, the opened *Ethics* between them. He was looking at her now with a face full of sweet sorrow. It was as if he had heard every word, every bruising syllable the man had hurled down the wires from New York. Unaccountably, tears suddenly started in her eyes, fast and scalding. And she saw that his eyes—the blueness he shared with her—were also watering. It pierced right through her: he was crying for her pain. It struck her with the force of a revelation: *he was crying for her pain!* It was beyond belief, beyond any conception she had available. She had so completely forgotten the touch upon the soul of a sympathetic apprehension. There was a warmth now, in that place where it had brushed her, a gently stirring warmth, so long ago forgotten.

They shared their look, brimmed with a mutual knowing, in silence.

And then Eva shook herself out of it, this dangerous tunnel of a moment, its unseen end lying in some unknown place. What had she been allowing? she asked herself in horror. Had she gone mad? To let somebody in like that, to let in *a student?*

She blinked her eyes quickly, quickly, feeling the wetness on her lashes, blinking it back, willing the water *back*.

And then she immediately returned to the proposition of Spinoza's that they had been discussing:

For I have shown that we in no case desire a thing because we deem it good, but contrariwise, we deem a thing good because we desire it.

But the released tears would not be reabsorbed. They filled her eyes for the remaining twenty minutes that they discussed the passage, distracting her and making her feel uncomfortably unfamiliar to herself. And when he left she let them well over and trickle down her cheeks, where they remained until they dried, leaving her face feeling streaked and grimy, like a very young child's. But she didn't wash them away.

She had difficulty falling asleep that night, and then she kept waking up. Each time she tried to remember what had occurred, what had changed. Nothing, she would remember. Nothing of significance.

She had spent the evening at her little table, her entire manuscript laid out before her. She was reading, from the beginning, the words of Ira Cranshaw playing in the background like a taunting *basso ostinato*. Was he missing the point, was he an unqualified judge, or was there really something seriously amiss in her conception? Surely when she completed the final chapter he would see how it all fell into place, how each piece was a necessary link in a tightly wrought deductive sequence. There *was* a picture, and it would emerge at the end.

What felt seriously wrong was that she didn't seem to care. Again and again she went over the man's words and was startled by the lack of effect they had on her. Her mood—oddly elated—did not fit the situation.

Her mind kept drifting back to that moment of such sweetness. That is why I cannot think on those words with pain, she thought.

But really, had anything of importance transpired to have called forth such an overheated response? The boy is kind. He has the gift of empathy. The important thing, surely, was what that man had said, throwing doubt on the work of so many years. That is what she must think of, concentrate on. But the recognition did not still the sudden spray of joy playing within her.

Early in the week Eva sent to the Dean of Students for the boy's complete file. She sat at her desk with all the facts of his academic existence laid out before her.

He was twenty and would be a senior in September, with a major in philosophy, as she had known. He had graduated from La Jolla High School, first in a class of five hundred and thirty, where he had been editor of the school newspaper and captain of the swim team. (He looked athletic, with a slim but well-developed build.) She read through the essay he had written for admission, smiling at the tone of slightly sardonic sophistication he had affected, his heavy-handed use of the qualifiers "quite," "somewhat," and "rather." She already knew him well enough to see how this was in character, could in fact hear him pronouncing his essay in his self-consciously manly voice. Then Eva looked at his college transcript, glancing approvingly down the columns of A's, and noted that he had just been granted early admission into Phi Beta Kappa. He was still involved in swimming, she saw, and also worked for the college radio station. Goodness, she smiled, reading that he was a disc jockey on a nighttime music program. The fact tickled her somehow.

Eva meant to listen to the boy's program that night. She was curious to hear the kind of music he played, how he handled himself on the air. But at nine, when his program began, she was too involved in rethinking a section of her book to leave off.

It had to do with Plato's doctrine of *anamnesis,* or recollection, according to which all learning is a kind of remembering of a world the soul saw before its birth, the vision of which it loses in the process of becoming embodied, but of which it can be reminded by carefully selected promptings. These promptings constitute the true process of education; and the prompter, the teacher, is engaged in a most sacred, and solemn, task—a fact which the great majority of Eva's colleagues conveniently forgot, resenting the students as a category of distraction, pilfering time from the first-order business of research. She had tasted the bitterness of their coiled cynicism.

All knowledge is a matter of recovering the world we lost in being born to body, which in Plato's doctrine is the world of the Forms: transcendent, abstract, and universal.

Of that place beyond the heavens none of our earthly poets has yet sung, and none shall sing worthily. But this is the manner of it, for assuredly we must be bold to speak what is true, above all when our discourse is upon truth. It is there that true being dwells, without color or shape, that cannot be touched; reason alone, the soul's pilot, can behold it, and all true knowledge is knowledge thereof.

A good part of Eva's book was an attempt to trace the connections between the ideas of freedom within this life and immortality beyond this life in the systems of Plato and Spinoza. Both ideas, for Plato and for Spinoza, are a realization of the yearning to break through to the other side of our bounded egos. This sounds, on the face of it, paradoxical, since our desires to be both free and immortal would seem to speak to an intense focusing in on our own particular identities. But not in the thinking of either Plato or Spinoza, as Eva was intent on showing. And the doctrine of *anamnesis,* which is utilized by Plato in both the *Phaedo* and the *Phaedrus* as part of an argument for immortality, was central to Eva's argument.

But *anamnesis* draws one into one of the major ambiguities scoring Plato's position. The use of the Forms in this doctrine presents a picture of entities unconnected with the sensible realm, as dwelling in "that place beyond the heavens," a picture which is challenged by other metaphors in which concrete particulars are spoken of as "participating" in the abstract Forms. For Eva this was a difficulty forever stalking.

The existence of the abstract Forms is offered by way of explanation for the given sensibles. This is, in fact, the manner in which the soul's pilot, reason, can "behold it," by seeing how the one realm, which we sense, can be explained only by positing the other realm, which we infer. Spinoza had been both Platonic and poetic when he wrote: "For the eyes of the mind, by which it encounters and sees, are none other than proofs." But if this is so, if we are to encounter the one realm in the process of explaining the other, then the two must be joined in the profound intimacy of ontological relatedness; and this relation must itself be fully accessible to reason. But how can there be the necessary connection between the one domain: transcendent and timeless; and the other: entrapped in the rigid matrix of space and time, not even fully real, according to Plato, because of the countless contradictions with which it is beriddled?

The Forms constitute a region fully penetrable to the processes of reason. But the world we encounter through our senses confounds our minds, for it is a place of the maddening co-mingling of opposites. It is this defect of the sensual realm which, more than anything else, more even than its slippery transience, reduces and darkens it, removing it, for Plato, from the irradiating grace of being fully real. Whereas the relations between the Forms are determined by the transparent weave of logic, the opaque world foisted on us by our senses is one in which the same object can be, at the very same time, both noble and base, profound and ridiculous, calling forth our love and esteem and our unforgiving and unforgetting hatred and contempt. The consistency-craving faculty of reason is inclined to decree such a world nonexistent and be done with it once and for all. And yet, of course, it cannot. It is compelled to acknowledge the reality of these hideous deformations of the rational fabric, and must even attempt to assimilate them to the perfection that dwells beyond, if it is ever to make its way into that beyond. And so the dilemma of Plato himself, equipoised in the tension pulling between the ways up and down.

In rereading this section of her book, Eva felt she had given preferential attention to the view of the Forms as "dwelling elsewhere," in the isolated splendor of their eternality and beauty-shedding coherence. She had not been true to the vigorous ambivalence of Plato's own position.

And so it was that she missed the beginning of the boy's show. When she turned it on, shortly after eleven, a woman vocalist was wailing, so far as Eva could make out, the words:

> *It don't take no book learning*
> *My body's all hot and yearning*
> *We're gonna get it on tonight*
> *One wicked night will do us right.*

So it was as bad as all that, then. This was the kind of loathsome anti-art by which she was so often assaulted in the vicinity of the campus, played out with such a deadening sameness of rhythm and melody that so far as she was concerned it could all have been

one song, repeated at varying tempos by different, barely mediocre talents. And of course she had never bothered to listen to the
lyrics. She had wearily regarded these rude disturbances of the
public atmosphere as just so many more of the all too numerous
indications pointing to the difficulties encountered by those who
would prod the young into a reluctant recollection.

Eva shared Plato's almost hostile suspicion of the arts, especially, in Eva's case, of music, whose treacherous ways she well
knew: to seep in, drop by tremulous drop, gathering itself into a
power capable of washing away the most laboriously erected
structures of reason. The universal force of the medium is *prima
facie* odd, since it is the most abstract, least narrowly human, of
the arts (although what she was hearing now successfully
obliterated this fact). Our response to music—true music—
is almost like a parody of the processes of true reason, our soul's
stretch after the impersonal and transcendent. But only parodic:
for it is of the essence of music that it be in time. And yet the
isomorphism is sufficient so that the god of Plato's *Timaeus* pre-
fers music—in an inaudible form, of course—to all the other fine
arts.

This notion of an inaudible music was one which had struck
Eva's sensibility deeply. She found in the phrase, at first pricking
as with the thorn of a contradiction, the very essence of the
matter. Music itself would wish not to be heard. It would, if
possible, bypass the ear and be taken in, pure and whole, by a
mind equally unsullied and undivided against itself. But we are
bodily creatures, imprisoned in the iron cages of our sensual
selves. And so music too must cover itself, coat the radiance of
its form in the cloudy film of passion and clotted sentimentality.
And, perhaps because her true nature is so contrary, the seduc-
tiveness of her sensuality surpasses all other artistic forms. "She
is a Kundry," writes Thomas Mann in *Dr. Faustus*, comparing
music to the ambiguous character of the temptress in Wagner's
Parsifal, "who wills not what she does and flings soft arms of lust
round the neck of the fool." And so it is that God alone can have
his inaudible music. For God, yes, music was safe; and for those

godlike in their purity, who, in being carried away, need not fear the place of final destination.

It is an irony, given the unsuitability of most minds for the philosophical quest which music shadows, that this art should sound an almost universal appeal, the vastness of its popularity a product of the means by which it would disguise itself. Very few lives are completely without its presence. For many it is the only touch with the Form of Beauty, though, too often, Beauty so dimmed and diminished as to be barely recognizable (as in these noises now being expelled from her radio). Even the culturally starved among the students (which was almost all of them), who knew and cared nothing for painting or poetry, literature or the theater, loved these crudely crafted compositions of theirs.

About six or seven songs were played, all sounding very much the same to Eva: crazed and irredeemably depraved. The atavistic thud in the bass, the revolting predictability played out in the melody and harmony above. What you hear is what you get. The concept of actively seeking out one's Beauty, of reconstructing the unifying vision so that one's apprehension itself partakes of creation: had such an idea ever visited the consumers of these brutally unsubtle sounds? This was the aesthetics of passivity, suited to the tastes of the troglodytes sitting dazed before their flickering screens.

It was hard, for the most part, to make out the lyrics, though all seemed to be about sexual passion. Such an obsession, and not only in this music of the young, with its apotheosis of cheap thrills. Were there no other human experiences that could move the soul to sing? What of adventure, risk, heroism, understanding, creativity, freedom?—all those transcendent experiences which arise from the soul's own intercourse with itself. All the important struggles are internal, waged within the self's own borders, fortified in solitude. And yet the eyes of most gaze out with hunger, their arms desperately reaching for . . . what? Only one thing, if this music was any indication. Why was it that whenever people put words to their music—which to Eva's mind was already a mistake, whether in opera (which she quite detested: all the splash and spectacle, the yearning irrationality erupting from the stage and orchestra pit) or in this kind of popular junk—they thought only of "romantic love"? Eva thought with irony of the complaint voiced in Plato's *Symposium*, that "for all the hymns and anthems that have been addressed to the other deities, not one single poet has ever sung a song in praise of so ancient and so powerful a god as Love." Plato must have started something.

But then, for most, romantic love is the most moving of all lived events, the only experience capable of seizing the center of one's concern and ripping it out of the iron cage of ego; of reversing the vectors of attention so that the reality of something outside oneself is at last, if only fleetingly, encountered. It is, for most, the only glimpse beyond. Did not Plato himself, in the incomparable *Phaedrus*, identify the erotic as a divine disturbance? It is a kind of madness, he says there, the result of either genuine illness or a perturbation sent by the gods. (And by what means does she who is possessed determine whether hers is a dementia divine or pathological?) In that urgent pull toward another, which wrenches us away from the dulling conventions, we are reminded of the Form of Beauty we encountered before our birth. And if we were to be so reminded of the Form of Wisdom, then what a frenzy of love would be awakened within us! Then how the wings of our souls would beat out the rhythms of our joy!

Plato was in a strangely softened mood toward love in that dialogue. Did some fetching Athenian youth lurk behind a corner of history in explanation? He casts an eye of toleration even on that love which does not manage to separate itself from its lustful urges, which he elsewhere, for example in the *Philebus*, excoriates as reminiscent not of Beauty but of its opposite, and best left to the "hours of darkness." But here, in the *Phaedrus*, Plato goes so far in the opposing direction (the vigor of the ambivalence!) as to claim that *anamnesis* itself is most perfectly accomplished in the desire we direct toward the beauty of the young beloved. "The soul that has seen most of Being shall enter into the human babe that shall grow into a seeker after wisdom or beauty, a follower of the muses, and a lover."

No wonder, then, that this tainted art should sing of this imper-

]49[

fect love; these are the faint and wavering images of real Beauty, but in a form accessible to even the most muddled of minds. For even they, stooped low and stunted as they are, yearn after the beyond.

No. Even Plato's disdainful pessimism over the "mortal trash" we humans are had been far too optimistic; for Plato had not been forced to listen to *this*. These sounds were the grunts and moans of spiritual grotesques. Just as romantic love is but an approximation to the philosopher's quest, so the object upon which these impoverished psyches were fixed was but the vaguest approximation to romantic love. This was not a love dragging along a soiled underside, but rather lust itself, unanchored and set adrift in an ocean of confusion. No wonder the sounds emitted seemed so little human. How could anyone detect Beauty's form within? Or had the artistic urgings of the young somehow detached themselves from so dated an object?

> *I can't wait another minute*
> *My body wants you here right in it*
> *I will have you*
> *I will have my way and I will have you, boy.*

Was this, then, what she had been up against all along? Were these the songs her children sang when out of her hearing? As they sat in her classroom dutifully taking notes on her lectures, were these the words which beat in the background and held them captive? If so, what chance had she? She ought to have listened to this music of theirs long ago.

She had stood before them and lectured on Spinoza, trying to awaken them to the wisdom of the *Ethics,* which speaks of the strength of the emotions as the state of human bondage: "Human infirmity in moderating and checking the emotions I name bondage; for when a man is a prey to his emotions, he is not his own master, but lies at the mercy of fortune: so much so that he is often compelled, while seeing that which is better for him, to follow that which is worse." How had such ideas the dimmest shadow of a possibility with minds saturated in a music such as this? In the myth of creation in Plato's *Timaeus*, the Demiurge assigns the task of incarnation, together with the devising of a functionable human psyche, to his young subordinates, who, in their youth, inject in a rather too generous portion of those "dreadful and necessary" emotions required for human survival. Dreadful and necessary, indeed. Here, in this music, one heard necessity; but where was the appropriate dread? These songs were a *celebration* of the state of human bondage.

The music was so odious that Eva wondered how it could even be effective in producing its intended reaction. But then, what was the response desired? She hadn't a clue. The oblivion of madness, perhaps. She, who was so painfully sensitive to music, could listen to this without feeling anything. Or rather, her pain now was of an entirely different sort.

Her student came on the air after this last song. Now she understood the self-conscious deliberateness displayed in his vocal precocity. His was not the soul of a future philosopher, as she had passingly thought, but of a would-be disc jockey. How very foolish he sounded, with that slick sophistication covering his trembling rawness. Cool, she supposed they would call it, if the idiom was still circulating. (She didn't know; she dealt daily with the students, but mercifully, she didn't know how they talked among themselves. They kept their uncreatively recycled slang out of her hearing.) He read the names of the songs and the groups responsible for them, making some limpingly witty remarks. He seemed to be attempting some sort of insider's joke, revolving around the phrase "This group is really cracking," whose precise explication she could not have given but which she suspected had something to do with illegal drugs. He read an ad for one of the town's discos, his false smoothness breaking at one point while he stumbled over a word. And then he introduced the next song.

"Now here's a song that goes right to my core. I mean, like this song makes me feel go-od. This song makes me feel like it's just fine to be me. You all know the one I mean."

]51[

Eva listened to the first few bars, sung by a woman to a pathetically shallow little tune.

> *The bad boys come*
> *The bad boys go*
> *They move so hasty*
> *They move so slow*
> *There ain't that much*
> *That they don't know*
> *Oooo . . . those bad boys*
> *Sure make me feel good.*

Enough. Eva switched off her radio in disgust and went back to Plato's description of the soul's forgetting and recollecting.

II

We live our lives by telling ourselves stories. There is *the* story, of course: the story of what happens, which in real life has no teller, at least none that we can hear. And what one wouldn't give for the certainty that there exists the Impersonal Narrator, putting it all into words, as in: "In the beginning was the Word." For then one might live in the hope that maybe, someday, one could hear it: the definitive unabridged version, told not in the halting voice of the first person, the half-truths of even our most honest attempts, but in the triumphantly omniscient third person, Proustian in its precision, near-Jamesian in its exhaustiveness.

But *the* story—the one we live but cannot hear—is very largely generated by the versions of it the participants tell themselves. It's these internal reconstructions that determine their actions, which is why the narrative mode is so much better suited for the explanation of human behavior than some more straightforwardly causal account, something to be read, perhaps, in the novelistic case studies of Freud, though he himself, of course, insistently reiterated that his was a science like any other.

One has to try to recapture an agent's telling in order to grasp the significance of his or her actions; that is, to provide the matrix for saying what, in fact, the action is. Some people have quite a few narrative forms at their disposal; others tell themselves the same tale repeatedly. But were a complete inventory to be undertaken I think we would find that our entire stock of story forms is quite manageably small, countable in single digits. This is a fact some might regard in the depressing light of a collective humiliation, a sobering reminder of the limits of imagination. But then, our human creativity is, for the most part, exercised not in the production of new forms but rather in the finding of ways to force our material into the finite available few. We trim off and discard into forgetfulness the incoherent bits that won't go into any kind of story we can tell ourselves—incoherent *because* they won't go in; that is, if we notice them at all.

And really, it's difficult to say which task presents the greater challenge to the imagination: the work of the novelist in fabricating material to fit a chosen story or the work of living, which requires that we come up with some story into which to shape the material we are presented with. In any case, we ought to be quite grateful for our limited supply of the sorts of stories we can tell ourselves about what it is that we and others are doing. For, were it otherwise, we would have even more difficulty in understanding one another than we already experience.

There are some general rules we employ in going about making up the stories we tell ourselves; and a few, to our credit, are principles of aesthetics; for we are, none of us, completely indifferent to the claims of Beauty in the telling of our tales. Take, for example, the profound pleasure we derive in the apprehension of a whole, which is, as Aristotle tells us in the *Poetics,* with staggering simplicity, "what has a beginning, a middle, and an end." The aesthetic preference for wholeness will often lead us to actions we would not otherwise undertake.

But the rules are by no means such as to determine that all the participants in the story will be telling themselves the same stories. In fact, quite the contrary is true: the rules forbid this, if only because in each agent's story the teller is the central figure, with all the others assigned roles whose meaning lies in the relationship with the teller. (This particular rule of construction is clearly not derived from any kind of *aesthetic* consideration.)

What this means is that there are no shared stories—one of the various ways of coming upon the bottomless enclosure of our aloneness. There is interaction only on the surface level of actions, where we splash about together; never in the underlying stories generating the actions. She says, "This is the story of how a good, loving woman saves a renegade man," and invites him to dinner. He says, "This is yet another story of how a convention-bound female attempts to entrap a free man," and declines the invitation.

It can be a soul-shattering experience to catch the drift of the tales others are telling themselves about the events we are engaged in together. There is the potential here for great pain, if also a few long moments of laughter.

Eva herself knew some of these truths, had learned them from her time with Martin Weltbaum, with whom she had lived for eleven months many years ago; with whom she had believed herself truly and deeply in love. It was almost another life; it was difficult to connect the Eva of that time with the present Eva, and so she very rarely thought back to it. But she actively believed the things she had learned from the pain of that period. Perhaps the most important lesson she had carried away with her was the necessity of keeping herself out of others' stories.

For here's a funny thing. Although we live our lives by telling ourselves stories, those who make up the best stories don't necessarily live the best lives. Too much fancy can get one into trouble. Eva had constructed a very good tale indeed about her relationship with Martin Weltbaum, fraught with moral import, as are all the best narratives—for the aesthetic sensibility has a great affinity with the moral. And then she had caught the drift of *his* version.

Eva had met Martin at Columbia University, where she was studying. He was an instructor at the Law School. They had met on the steps of Low Library, on an unusually warm day in February. Eva had been one of the many sprawled out all over the massive stone area in a mood of celebration, drinking in the sun and warmth, the just uncorked and sparkling spring air. She had stretched herself out near the top of the stairs, not far from the feet of the famous alma mater statue, her eyes closed against the sun, which was making hot, sizzling patterns on the inside of her eyelids. She turned her head lazily, looking down, and noticed a tall, slouched figure making its way up the stairs, determinedly picking its way over the bodies. He looked out of place on a day such as this, when a general dispensation of irresponsibility had been granted to all. His clothes were all wrong. He was wearing a white shirt and dark suit pants, the matching jacket hooked over a finger and carried over his sloping back. It made Eva feel warm and sticky just looking at him. And there was a clammy vapor of seriousness clinging to him, delineating him from the frivolous surroundings. About halfway up he seemed to notice her watching him, and gave a quick smile and a half bow; at least she thought it was directed at her. Perhaps there was a friend of his nearby for whom it had been intended. But she smiled in return, then felt herself foolish, thinking that the salutation had probably not been hers, and turned her face back toward the sun. A few minutes later, she was addressed, and she turned to see that he had seated himself beside her and was giving her that same quizzical smile. He was very tall, quite a bit over six feet, and slightly stooped, intellectual-looking with his horn-rimmed glasses, over which his longish black hair kept falling. He was still enfolded in his private pocket of intensity, even while relaxing against the steps, glancing again with a playful smile at Eva and then down at her long legs in a pair of red shorts.

"I'm Martin Weltbaum. I teach at the Law School. Great day, isn't it?"

She had known even without hearing the name that he was probably Jewish. Recognizing Jewish faces was one of the first things she had learned since coming to the States. (It had amazed her as a child when, sometimes, as her mother and she were walking in the city, they would pass someone and her mother would whisper "Jew." How could she always tell?)

"I'm Eva Mueller. I'm a graduate student in philosophy. And yes, it is a wonderful day. Much too wonderful to work, to even think at all."

"You have great legs, Eva Mueller. And I like your accent too. Where are you from?"

"I'm from Germany." She watched his face closely to see if there was any reaction. She was always slightly uneasy when she first mentioned her origin to Jews. One never knew.

"Is that so? Berlin?"

"Münster."

"Ah, Münster. The beautiful old capital of the flourishing province of Westphalia."

She stared at him, surprised. "You've been to Germany, then?"

"No, actually I haven't. Not in body. But I've read a lot. And heard a lot of stories. My parents were originally German."

Echt German? she thought to herself. Or Jewish German?

"So how long have you been here, Eva Mueller von Münster?" He pronounced it in perfect *Hochdeutsch,* high German.

"Two years."

"Is that so? And what made you come to America?"

"It was far from Germany." She laughed.

"I know what you mean," he answered seriously. "I was born and grew up in New York, went to school here, and now I teach here. It's probably a mistake. Even in a city like New York it's possible to become provincial."

"Oh, I don't think so. New York is so many places. You go just a few short blocks from here, from Morningside Heights up to Harlem, or down to the Upper West Side, and you go into totally different worlds."

"So you like New York?"

"Oh yes. I love it. I want to stay here for the rest of my life."

"Well, from what I hear about the doctoral programs in this university, especially in the humanities, you may just get your wish." He smiled, again glancing down at her legs.

Her heart was pounding throughout these first meager attempts at small talk. It was very strange: the force with which she immediately responded to him. She was certainly used to being the object of male attention. She knew she was beautiful. Of course she was considered very much more beautiful here in America, where blond hair and blue eyes didn't always come with the territory. She had become somewhat spoiled in her four years here.

But what was it about this serious young man that was making her blood run thick and strong, so that she could feel its dull thumping in her head? Was it just his name, and his undeniably Semitic looks? He seemed at once so exposed, dressed in those serious clothes amid the frolicking students, and yet also powerful and subtly threatening.

They ended up, a very short time after having exchanged names, back at Martin Weltbaum's cramped and sunless apartment, in a cavernous building a few long blocks from the university, in his narrow unmade bed. Even on this very first occasion there was a violence that ought to have alerted Eva, that ought to have warned her to run, and would have, had she not already begun the fall into that heaviness of being that would remain with her for months to come. Already, the pattern of inverted responses was moving into place: his cold contempt warmed her, the ferocity of his attacks lulled her more deeply into the semiconsciousness of approaching sleep. She knew, the very first time they made love, that there was something dangerous here: beneath the solemn, studious air there was a half-crazed anger. She was aware of its presence from the beginning, knew even that her body would become its focus. But she didn't run. For to know this was already to enter into a different system of logic, where the rules of what follows from what were, though radically altered, still just as inescapably determined.

Neither of them left the apartment for the next week; and when Eva did, she already moved with the deliberate slowness of a body walking in water, pushing against a resisting element. She made her way back to the apartment she shared with another graduate student and, against the background noise (coming from so far away, it seemed) of her roommate's protestations, gathered up her things, stuffing them into suitcases and boxes, hailed a cab, and dragged them all over to Martin's place. (She promised to continue to pay half the rent of the apartment until her friend found someone else. And within two days Martin had demanded that she take on half his rent if she was to live there. She would have to worry about money in the months to come.)

They had barely slept at all that first week. Martin spoke as tirelessly and obsessively as he made love. He did not need sleep or, fearing it perhaps, had trained himself out of the need. She would never know what lay at the bottom of him, whether the deepest level was constituted of fear or rage, or something altogether different. He answered no questions. More than once his unceasing wakefulness brought Eva to the edge of despair. It was one of the most terrible things about him. He could stay awake for days and days, and then sleep a few hours and be ready to begin all over again.

He spoke, that first week and in the months to come, of his family: his mother and father, for that was all that there were. His parents had been Jews living in Berlin when Hitler came to power—they were the wrong sort at the wrong place in the wrong time, he said smiling. He often spoke of these things with a calm, almost child-sweet smile on his face, at the sight of which her stomach tightened in tenderness and terror. And he had jokes, cruel jokes, about the war and its atrocities. ("The war," to both Eva and Martin, meant the same place, the same time.) He thought they were funny, even if they weren't: Which is better, a tall Jew or a short Jew? A tall Jew, because he burns longer. He laughed deep down in his throat, a mirthless, strangled laughter.

Both his parents had possessed different families, complete with perfect children, before the war. As far as Martin could see, the core of their union was derived from their having been slightly acquainted before the time of the Nazis, having attended religious classes together at the Jewish community center in Berlin. They hadn't been friends then, had probably never even exchanged a word. But within hours of stumbling upon one another on a street in a scorched and blackened Berlin, they had decided to marry and go to America together.

And yet they were rather well suited to one another. Both of them were crazy, if that was any foundation for matrimony. His mother was completely nuts. Anyone could see that after speaking to her for about five minutes. His father was the stable one: you had to spend a good half hour with him to see that he was a lunatic. During that time some topic would be sure to come up —domestic or foreign—that would make him explode, blowing his loose-fitting lid of rationality sky high.

When they came to America they moved into an apartment in the Washington Heights section of Manhattan, where they still lived, in a tight little enclave of transplanted German Jews. In their heyday (for now they were dying out) the area had been known as *kleines* Berlin.

They were Orthodox. Part of his father's insanity took the form of his becoming increasingly pious, ever on the lookout for more prohibitions to complicate Martin's and his mother's lives. He remembered the inspired madness in the man's eyes when he arrived home from the synagogue one Sabbath morning to announce that it had been discovered that the wine being used in a certain vinegar was not a kosher wine, and that this vinegar was widely added to many processed foods, from Heinz ketchup to Hellmann's mayonnaise. After the Sabbath he had attacked the refrigerator and cupboards, violently discarding the tainted items.

Even though his parents had insulated themselves and him, sending him to a school up on the Heights for boys from families exactly like his own, right down to the fillings in their dumplings and the rolls in their *r*'s, Martin had always known that this was a false world. No; worse than false: unreal, as nonexistent as the past which had ceased to be. The ghouls haunting the Heights were necrophiliac perverts, living in a filth of decomposing memories. Everything about them was unclean. He remembered how his mother used to leave a little glass of water outside the apartment door when his father went to funerals; a glass of water and a towel, so that his father could wash the uncleanliness of death from his hands before entering. And he had thought, What a farce to go through such a ritual, when it is *in* you, that uncleanliness of death, escaping from your mouths when you talk, reeking from every one of your darkened pores.

The prevailing memory of his boyhood was of just this feeling: the taint of the people he knew, the atmosphere they exuded. It happened, sometimes still, when he was walking down Broadway; he would pass one of those old people who had clawed his way out of one of the cavernous buildings lining West End Avenue, and he would get a whiff—and all that world would come back to him in full, reeling detail.

God, how it stank! He was completely baffled as a child that nobody else seemed to smell it. He knew from that smell alone that they were all crazy. It made him feel very lonely, knowing that he was the sole sane person there, profoundly and utterly lonely. But also very powerful.

He had given some thought as he was growing up to the question of whether he was unjust in hating his parents and their world. In terms of the traditional moral attributes, the kinds of things he was taught about at home and in school, like kindness and honesty, they certainly weren't bad people; they were no worse than most, probably better than a good many. Was it wrong to hate people for things that they couldn't help, hate them for being ugly, for example, or stupid or sick? Stupidity, ugliness, and sickness were certainly bad things, but did that make the people partaking of these states worthy of hatred? He had finally decided it was a moot question, like all philosophical questions unresolvable and really beside the point. For the fact was, he was biologically determined to hate those who carried death within them. His revulsion at the sight and sound and smell of them was instinctual, an indication of the essential vigor of his health. His hatred was an organic part of him, making it as silly to question whether it ought or ought not to exist as it was to ask whether he ought or ought not to be six foot four. He wasn't proud of his hatred, but he wasn't ashamed of it either.

Of course he had once loved his mother: what choice had a small child but to love that warm cow body sheltering it? The memory of this love was hard to recollect. He retained an ancient image of himself sitting on her lap, loving her moist warmth and smell, the soft cooing sound of her. But the woman could not keep from talking, endlessly, incessantly, of the life before. She would talk of the dead children. His father had had two sons and a daughter, his mother two daughters, two perfect little round dumplings. She cried whenever she saw a beautiful little girl on the street.

What right had she to tell a child these things? The terror of it was overwhelming, that these parents of his, on whom he was so utterly dependent, were born to be victims. But it was just a child's nightmare, dreamed in ignorance. He had seen that at last. He had seen that he had nothing in common with them. He was nothing at all like either of his parents, nothing nothing like the dead children who had called them Mama and Papa.

The worst place of all had been the synagogue where he was dragged every Sabbath and holiday: the packed bodies, with a steam of sour stench rising from them. He was squeezed in between his father and some other man, usually some friend of his father's. Those men were always damp, winter as well as summer. His mother sat upstairs with the other women, in a little curtained-off balcony. He wondered whether it smelled as bad in the women's section.

On the holidays when the special prayers for the dead were said, the unholy stink would intensify until it was unbearable, and he would hold his breath until he had to gasp. Those who had lost no close relative left during this prayer (but on the Heights very few did so); he was forced to stay because of his five half-brothers and -sisters.

Then, one Yom Kippur, when he was nine, the crisis came, or as he put it, the abscessed boil finally burst. He knew that the synagogue was packed with the dead, that the death in the people around him had called forth the great pressing throng of their beloved. He could hear the hiss of them, under the chanting, like their smell made audible, and kept looking around to see if the others heard it too. But of course they were oblivious. Morbidity was their natural medium. They continued to pray, to shake, and to weep.

The hissing was the most terrible sound imaginable, and it was deep within his ears, trying to bore its way into his skull. He pressed his palms against his ears, but this only made it worse. He knew that if he breathed in, they would enter his lungs, infiltrate his bloodstream, and feed off him forever. After what seemed an excruciating eternity, he passed out, waking up in Columbia Presbyterian Hospital. But the experience, as traumatic as it had been, in the end turned out to be well worth the price exacted. For the first and last time, his mother prevailed against his father, and he was not forced again to stay during the prayer for the dead.

It was autumn when this happened; for that is when the New Year is celebrated by the Jews: at summer's end. He had always liked the season: the extravagance of the botanical palette, the feeling of change, transition. There wasn't much in the way of nature to be observed around his apartment building, of course; but not far away, about a ten-minute walk, in fact, was The Cloisters, a museum built of the ruins of five monasteries, French, Italian, and Spanish, transported in the thirties by one of the Rockefellers to house his collection of medieval art.

Perhaps it was the name itself, The Cloisters, that appealed to him. He loved the idea of an enclosed separate world opening up within the lifeless heaviness of the Heights. He didn't like the monastery itself, didn't feel comfortable in it. All those pictures of the man dying on the cross. Horrible stuff. Sick. It was the park surrounding the monastery that he loved: full of grass and trees and winding paths he would try to lose himself on (but, really, he knew them too well).

Not long after his Yom Kippur experience he had another which also had consequences for his future. He was sitting on one of the little stone benches in the park, a cluster of brilliantly colored trees before him. The sky was very blue that day, a blue rarely seen on the Heights. And the vivid yellows and oranges and reds against the blue were beautiful. And, suddenly, the thought occurred to him, such an obvious thought, really, but there it was for the first time: Those colors shouldn't be called *vivid*. They weren't colors of life, but of death. He supposed it sounded pretty jejune now. But at the time, the sudden realization completely knocked the breath out of him, like the fist of truth landing him one right in the stomach. What he had been sitting there and admiring was *death*. He stared at the colors and it was as if he could almost hear the screams beneath the quiet.

What a farce, what a cruel piece of humor, this one perpetrated by nature itself. Covering up its filthy secret with pretty colors, like gift wrapping in shiny paper some foul, putrifying animal corpse. And so the sentimental and childish, in other words almost everybody, end up actually *admiring* what ought to sicken and revolt them. It was something like those creepy pictures hanging in the monastery itself, so lovingly depicting the long-drawn-out dying of that man.

It was also at about this time that he became a vegetarian. His mother was a permanent fixture in the kitchen, forever engaged in the preparation of food. He returned home from school for lunch, which was always meat, potatoes, and vegetables, with a whole other pot of chicken or meat cooked up for supper. There was always stuff boiling away on the stove. He had never known his parents' apartment to be free of that smell. But this wasn't at all a comforting or reassuring fact of the household but, rather, unbearably oppressive. There was an unwholesome desperation in his mother's attempts to feed her family. She herself hardly ever put anything into her mouth. In fact, all three of them were emaciated. Almost everything she cooked was destined for the garbage. But she persisted in her preparations, carrying out her offerings in a haze of steam and triumph to the dining room, where his father and he waited without enthusiasm. She would pile food onto their plates, giving a running commentary on it: whether the meat had been too fatty, how much she had trimmed it, the spices she had added, how she had used turnips in addition to carrots. Neither he nor his father spoke a word. They'd put a small fraction of the food she dished out into their mouths (Martin learned early how to rearrange what was on his plate so that it looked as if he had eaten more of it), all the while his mother urging them onward with her soft little pigeon noises.

But then one day, as she was apportioning her stewed chicken, she asked him whether he wanted a breast or a thigh. And these words felt like a slap across his face. Breasts and thighs were parts of bodies. It was no longer possible for him to think of the substance on his plate as food but rather as parts of the dead. He had never again eaten meat. It had been rather a struggle, given that his mother's postwar existence was fixed on those simmering pots of corpses. Desperation, even the quietly whirring sort of his mother, was a very hard obstacle to come up against. But there was no choice for him. And, in the end, it was probably to his mother's advantage, since she now had the meat and chicken for her husband, the rice and vegetables for her son, to cook and then discard.

For a while he was quite furious, thinking of the wrong his mother had done him: trying to give him life by nourishing him on death. But then he considered the fact that most people feed off the dead, and that, therefore, it wasn't just his parents' world up there on the Heights that was unwholesome and unclean. The whole world stank. This realization had deepened his loneliness, while at the same time making him feel that much more powerful.

Martin *was* powerful. His power filled Eva, saturated her completely, so that her own sense of self passed away unmourned, barely noticed. It was not only her body which, in being made his object, had been transformed so that it no longer seemed her own. Everything within her, even her own voice, had been stilled. If she thought at all now, if any words at all broke the soundless stillness within her, they were enclitically his, spoken in his tones, with his New York inflection. It was all part of the not unpleasant languor of being suspended in the moral medium she now occupied, dense and airless, with no room for questions or deliberation. She acquiesced in this state, in fact she did what she could to deepen it. She wanted to make of herself the perfect receptacle, to draw up within herself the full thrust of his talk, his anger, his sex. If only she could take it all within her, blotting it up with her blankness of being, then she might be able to drain him free. And, of course, she understood that it was not really she whom he hated.

There were moments when it would happen, if only she hung on long enough, mustered the strength to see him through to the end. When his voice would grow hoarse and he issued his commands with swelling ferocity, then she knew they were there, almost there. But it was important, very important, not to rush the moment, to leave him unspent, his energy half drained. That was more dangerous than anything else. So she had to know when to slow down, when to gently thwart him in his frenzy, until this: the great surge of him within her, and the cry of him welling up from the bottom of his poor hurting soul. Only if he cried out, in that sob ripped out of him against his will, would she know that they were there. That now he could be still, as still as she herself; the almost crazed intensity of his eyes growing dim, and finally going out. And then he would sleep. Eva would stroke his forehead, his long black locks of hair, brushing them away from his eyes like the solicitous mother she then felt herself to be, brushing the hair back from his transformed face, which was, in sleep, remarkably childlike, the long, dark lashes resting on his cheeks. This is his true face, she would think with love. If only I could free it forever.

Sometimes he would cry in his sleep. They were the most awful sounds Eva had ever heard, like a child's thin wail of hopeless terror. She sat beside him, herself soundlessly weeping.

But sometimes she was weak. There were times when she felt she could not take it; a time, even, when she had run crying out into the night, into a pouring rain.

Nothing had been able to quiet him that night. She had let him do with her as he would, as always. It didn't humiliate her. Quite the contrary, she felt herself strangely elevated in meeting his demands, no matter what they were. But that night there was no satisfaction. She had taken and taken, had opened herself up in ways she would not have thought possible. But the demon in him was out and could not be made to quit.

The evening had begun so well, with almost a hope of a normal time before them. They had gone out to see a movie, quite a change for Eva, for at this point she very rarely left the apartment, not even to buy food. Martin brought home the cookies and apples and beer that they lived on. But the movie playing on campus was *The Blue Angel* with Marlene Dietrich, Martin's favorite film, far superior, he said, to the book by Heinrich Mann, brother of the famous Thomas. That moment when the professor crows in utter abjection expressed the most fundamental truth about the relations between men and women, maybe even between all people. The second law of thermodynamics was as true in the emotional, as in the physical, realm: Everything runs toward chaos. There is a natural inclination toward degeneration in all relationships. The greater one's knowledge of the other person, which would seem on the face of it to be an increase of order, the more accelerated, in reality, becomes the process of disintegration. The trick was to know the right moment in which to pull out.

When they got back to the apartment, Martin had been in an unusually buoyant mood, almost playful. Eva had recently bought some sexy lingerie, silly things: a black camisole top and a garter belt, trimmed with lace and red ribbons, almost a parody of the look of the classic vamp. Martin ordered her to put them on now and sing the famous Dietrich song, in the famous Dietrich pose, legs straddling a chair. And then he played games with her, composing his rules, as always, with great seriousness. Tonight it was that some part of her must remain in contact with the chair at all times.

But gradually the play took on an unfriendly tone.

"Over! Turn over! Don't move, don't dare to breathe."

"Kneel!"

"Stoop!"

"Over, over!"

The demands became frenzied and, finally, unsatisfiable. Her body had grown leaden with fatigue until she could think of nothing but the peace of unconsciousness; and at last she asked to be allowed to go to sleep. Her plea had the effect of a spark to gunpowder. His rage exploded. His face, which was leaning almost into hers, was torn apart into such ugliness that for the first time she felt a ripple of alertness coursing through her body, jolting her fully awake.

He will kill me.

Slyly, so that he would not see, she glanced around for possible avenues of escape, as he rose to his knees over her, his face, red and swollen, close over her, so ugly that she had to squint. She was a cow. She had grown fat and grotesque. Why did she have to lie there like that? Why wouldn't she do what he wanted? She was half dead, even when awake. If she fell asleep now she would look like a corpse, a bloated, rotting corpse. She stank like death itself. Look at how swollen and disgusting her breasts had become, the nipples enlarged and darkened. He squeezed them hard, hard, so that tears started involuntarily into her eyes, welling over. What had happened to her? he was screaming. Had she really been beautiful when they first met?

Eva knew what had happened, why her body was swelling into strange fullness; her stomach, once taut and flat, now protruding so that she had to push the elastic of her panties down beneath it. It was because she had made herself so still. It was for this reason that her body was no longer her own, that all of its physical processes had slackened, so that even her pulse was dimmed. She understood this, knew that it was right that it should be so; and so took pleasure in it. But she couldn't explain all this to Martin. It took such an effort to explain anything at all, and, really, there was no reason to. What was happening to her was of no consequence, except as it affected her ability to meet Martin's demands.

And, of course, there was no saying anything to Martin now, with his face hidden behind that mask of ugliness. She noticed his arms tensing, the right one beginning to rise, and she knew the violence to come. Something within her took over. With silent speed she slid out from beneath him, and had shed the tattered remains of lingerie, pulled on a dress lying crumpled on the floor, and run for the door, before he came after her. Once on the street she ran and ran, overcome by her panic. She doubted that he would come after her, though. He had too much at risk. He was an instructor at the Law School. He could hardly be seen chasing a weeping barefoot woman down Broadway.

She ended up going back to her old apartment that night, the one she had been living in when she met Martin. Her former roommate let her in reluctantly. She had found someone else to take Eva's place, but she let Eva sleep on the couch. The two roommates left the apartment early the next morning, barely exchanging a word with Eva, as if afraid of contamination. Stupid girls, Eva had thought; running to their lectures, caught in the frozen web of abstractions. Real life is elsewhere. And Eva had gone back to Martin's apartment and, no matter what took place between them, had never run away again.

Eva herself had stopped going to her classes almost immediately after moving in with Martin. The old life no longer had anything to do with her. She had thought briefly about attacking the caked-on squalor of Martin's rooms, strewn with beer bottles and apple cores and old newspapers, crawling with meaty cockroaches. At least, she had thought, she would wash up the souring contents of the kitchen sink. But the *Hausfrau* mood quickly passed. She felt a little guilty about the neighbors, who must surely suffer from the run-off of roaches. They were mostly, however, students, and nobody ever came to complain. Perhaps their housekeeping habits were not much better.

Mostly she thought about her body, which, though no longer feeling like her own, had become an object of great interest to her. The only times she left his rooms were when she went down to the discount drugstore on the corner, where she would browse among the aisles, studying the various things that were offered for the care of the body. She conceived the desire of making her legs and arms completely hairless, and experimented with various depilatory methods, eventually settling on a pumice stone and a pair of tweezers. As soon as Martin left the apartment she'd settle down to work, using the stone to rub the surface of her skin raw so that every little hair follicle was exposed, and then plucking out the hairs. It was enormously satisfying. She thought of nothing but the task at hand, submerging herself so fully in it that she was invariably surprised to hear Martin's key in the door, and to realize that three, four, maybe even five or six hours had fled by unregistered. It was the only period in her life when she didn't suffer from the thought that she might be wasting time, didn't struggle with the wings beating violently in her face.

She was filled with a silent certitude. It was not just desire she was experiencing like an involuntary process of the body. Belief, too, was no longer a matter of deliberation, of conscious manipulation, but rather coursed through her like the blood in her veins. She knew that all that was happening had to happen, and thus was absolutely right. No events surprised her, even those which might have seemed startlingly coincidental. The structure of events is sealed against the possibility of chance.

Martin's name, for example: Weltbaum. Something deep within Eva had responded to that name immediately, there on the steps of Low Library, though it took a while for the buried association to surface.

The world-tree, the Yggdrasill. When Eva was a girl her father had given her a very beautiful book about the German gods and goddesses. She must have been ten at the time. The book was, all through her later childhood, her very favorite possession. Her father and she would often read it together in the evening, up in her room. The pictures were dazzling, filled with action and detail, so that she could study them for hours and still find things she had not noticed before. There was a diagram as a frontispiece, showing the Yggdrasill. The German gods and goddesses lived at the very top of the world tree, in Asgard. Great heroes were brought there when they died. In the middle of the tree was Midgard, where mortals lived, and, beneath, the Unterwelt, part of which was ruled over by the goddess Hel, in a place of coldness and shadows, where non-heroic mortals dwelled after their death. As long as the branches of the Yggdrasill were blowing, the cosmos would last. In the end would come the *Götterdämmerung*, as inevitable as the death of the flesh, and the tree would burn down.

Eva had made up a game for herself and her friends, which they played all the summer that she had received the book. The giant *Esche,* the ash tree that grew in the churchyard, was the Yggdrasill. Someone would count to fifty, slowly. Those who made it to the top could be the gods of the Aesir, the German pantheon, whomever they chose, the highest choosing first. The gods set tasks for the mortals, those children who were clumsier, younger, or too timid to scramble upward to the thin branches. Whoever failed to complete his assignment, or whoever lost his footing, died and was delivered over to Hel.

Papa had been amused by this game of hers.

"What happened among the gods and goddesses today? Any wars?"

"No wars. But Maria and Margit had a fight. Maria was Idun, and the blackberries growing near the cemetery were her golden apples, the ones that keep all the gods young."

"Ah yes." Papa had smiled. "That is good."

"And Margit was her husband, Bragi."

"And did Bragi sing?"

"That was what the fight was about, Papa. Margit said she had to sing all the time because she was the god of singing, but Maria said that Margit's singing was spoiling the whole game."

Papa smiled. "Ah yes. I have known such arguments."

"So Maria wouldn't give Margit any apples. And Margit grew older and older. We rubbed white dust on her face and hair. And finally she lay on the branch and was dying. Margit always dies very well. And then, at almost the last moment, Maria popped a berry into her mouth. Then we had a celebration, and we let Margit sing."

Again Papa smiled. "And who were you? A god? No mere mortal, I hope."

"I was Wotan, Papa."

"Again Wotan. You like to be the most powerful."

"Sometimes. Not always. Sometimes I like to be Loki and make trouble, and sometimes I like to be Ull, just because it's funny to go around looking angry and friendly at the same time."

"Show me how that looks."

And Eva had shown Papa the face she wore as the god of winter, her eyes screwed up with anger while her mouth smiled.

"And how did you look today? Show me. How does mighty Wotan look?"

"He looks like you, of course. Just like you, Papa."

At this, Papa had looked unaccountably angry. He had scowled and his eyes had darkened, and all the warmth was gone. Papa! Papa! He had gone off to his study, leaving her quite desperate to correct her error, if only she knew what it was.

The tree had been a *Schutz*, a protection; and the few childhood memories she had were scrimmed with its shade. Now, in these days with Martin, she felt almost as if she were enfolded once again in the softly umber world, held safe in the spread of those thick branches.

When she was a young child she had known what she had to

]77[

do, because there were her parents to tell her, whom she knew to always be right. Papa was like the world-tree, her *Schutz,* and she had been able to live, at least for a time, with very few questions. The time that the questions had come had been a bad one.

But now it was she herself who carried the precious elixir of certitude within her, she who had stilled the questioning voice. Actions came to her ready-made, bearing so complete a sense of necessity that it was almost as if they had already happened, as if the present had hardened over into the finality of the past; and that what was happening now was just an echo or a shadow, a flickering and pointless concession to the illusion of passing time. This sense was, of course, never articulated within her; barely anything was. But it was all-pervasive, and it induced a sort of careless inattention to the possibilities of the moment (since really there were no possibilities). On those rare occasions when she left the apartment to go to the drugstore, she didn't even think to look before crossing Broadway. Nothing could happen, or it already would have, and she wouldn't be there now, doing what she was doing.

And so it was that she was well into her pregnancy before she noticed it. She had not considered the possibility, because it was not supposed to happen.

She had been examining her breasts, gently squeezing the nipples, testing their swollen painfulness, and a small droplet of thin, bluish-white liquid had gathered itself at the tip and slowly run down the inside of her breast and onto her bloated belly. She squeezed the other nipple and the same thing happened. She stared at the wetness on her belly, for a moment baffled, but then suddenly understanding what it signified. The instant the thought occurred to her she knew it to be true. And after a few racing moments of confused terror, the sense of certitude had come coursing back through her and she knew that this baby, too, was final, necessary, and right.

But then terrible things had happened.

"Bitch!" Martin had screamed, his eyes gone wild, his face

almost purple. "You fucking bitch. Couldn't I even trust you with that?"

She remained quiet, completely still, while he screamed, which was surprisingly brief. He broke off, shaking his head in disgust and making a strange noise in the back of his throat. He turned abruptly for the bathroom. She heard the toilet flush, and then he was before her again. She hadn't moved. Strangely, as she thought about it later, he didn't beat her, didn't lay a finger on her.

"You find out what to do about it, how to get rid of it. And then, bitch, I want you out."

The black terror came flooding back, and she spoke from out of it: "But, Martin, can it be you don't understand? That this baby was meant to be?"

And he had looked at her and laughed softly, with that calm child-sweet expression she dreaded more than any other.

"You really are completely mad. Did you know that? What, exactly, do you expect? That I'll marry you? Take you up to the Heights to present you to my parents? Here's my bride. I'm afraid she's slightly soiled. And, one of your darkest fears: she isn't Jewish. But you haven't heard anything yet. Wait till you hear about the in-laws. Wait till you ask her about Papa's high-minded theories. I, your only surviving child, am presenting you with a nightmare that not even you two tormented souls could have dreamed during this endless night your lives have been—since he and his kind had his way with you and your kind."

He was crying by the time he finished the words, sobbing with the sounds of his sleep. She had been so wrong. It was she whom he had hated all along.

III

Eva had come to the conclusion that there *was* something seriously amiss with her book. It was for this reason that the final chapter remained unwritten. Some part of her must have known that the work was not ready for completion. She must go back and rethink everything.

That original ambiguity had spread, was seeping through all the closely reasoned lines now. She had pretended that it wasn't there, had built her argument over it and deceived herself into thinking all was firm.

Time, Eva now thought. It was time that contained the ambiguity. She had not come to terms with the concept of temporality in her book. She had not shown, had not even taken up the question, of how the systems of Plato and Spinoza, which presented reality as eternal and changeless, held by tenseless logic in the stasis of necessity, could accommodate even the notion of passing time. How is it that our sense of the flow of time, which so dominates our experience of this world, can arise? To say that it is ultimately an illusion does not solve the problem. How can there be room for even this deception in such systems as these?

Time, Eva now saw, was at the heart of reconciling the sense of contradiction that had always lurked beneath her fragile sense of understanding of these philosophical systems. It was the problem of accounting for the participation of the timeless Platonic Forms in the passing flux of particulars. And it was the problem, too, of explaining how, in Spinoza's system, God and nature can be, as he claimed they were, two alternative conceptions of the same fundamental reality, *Deus sive Natura.*

She had known instinctively that time posed problems that might well overwhelm her, unravel the tight little pattern of her ideas. She had ignored it because she had not understood it. It was her minotaur, and she had built a system of labyrinths to try to contain it. It had been an act of intellectual cowardice. She now had the truly terrible thought that her entire book might be such an act.

She would have to come to terms with time.

But now it was nine o'clock, and she must listen to Michael's program.

Eva had woken up happy, the thought already in her head that it was Friday.

Michael came bounding into her office, alight with his joyful energy: a golden shaft of sunlight.

He was excited today. He had read William James's *The Will to Believe* and was ready to challenge all of Spinoza on its basis. All of epistemology.

"Maybe James is really right. Like if you keep asking for reasons to believe, you're just going to miss out on truth altogether. And maybe like missing out on truth is worse than making mistakes. These guys, all these philosophers, they're so terrified of being wrong, you'd think that was like the worst event that could befall mankind. And they're so afraid of ever possibly being wrong that they make these impossible demands on belief. It's like love."

"Like love?" She smiled.

"Somebody could be so impressed with the possibility of being hurt in love that they just don't take the risk. Or they ask for these impossible assurances. But then they're like sure to miss out. That's what all these epistemologists are like. They're so afraid of being wrong that they don't risk believing. But then they're definitely going to miss out on the truth. I think epistemology is a disease. And it ends in death, the death of skepticism. Just like the other disease ends in the death of loneliness."

"But if one doesn't ask for good reasons to believe, how is one to know?"

She had been too charmed by the energy of his raw enthusiasm (how many of his contemporaries could get so worked up about ideas?) to argue with him in the way that she ought to have.

"One simply knows," he said, throwing his arms open, the dazzle of his smile blotting up every shadow of the room.

"One simply knows." She smiled. "And if one person simply knows p, and the other simply knows not-p, then what?"

"Then like maybe they're both right."

"Oh no." She laughed. "If you're going to throw out logic too, there's no point in going further. Even if I demonstrate the inconsistency of what you say, it won't have any claim on you. That's just logic, you'll say. You think some more about what you're arguing, think out its consequences."

"Okay, I will. I'll think about it all week until I see you again. But since there's no point talking to me about it anymore now, let's go swimming."

"What?" She laughed.

"Swimming. It's midsummer and you're as pale as a ghost. That's what all this epistemology has done to you. It's a glaring mistake. I have to correct it."

"But of course that is impossible."

"Why impossible? Logically impossible? Even if logic is as absolute as you want me to believe, like I don't see any contradiction at all in the proposition: Today Professor Mueller will go swimming."

"I don't even have a bathing suit."

"So run home and get it. I have all day. I promise to sit here and think out my confusion until you get back."

"I mean I don't have one at all. I don't own one."

"You've got to be kidding." He stared at her as if she had announced she had once committed mass murder. "You mean you never went swimming in the gorges? Swimming in the gorges is one of life's ultimates."

"No." Eva shook her head, smiling at how deeply her revelation rattled him.

"Oh, maybe you don't know how to swim." This he spoke with a certain delicacy, as if he might possibly have stumbled on some hidden and hideous deformity.

"Yes, I know how to swim. I used to be rather a strong swimmer."

"Yeah, you don't look like the type that wouldn't know how to swim. Then why don't you own a bathing suit, for godsake? I mean, I know like swimming isn't as important as philosophy. But still. Not *once?*"

"You sound almost angry."

"I *am* almost angry. I mean, like even if these guys did have their hands on Almighty Absolute Truth, which I sort of wonder, but even if they did, you can still have a little fun. Even sanctimonious Benedictus—whose initials by the way are B.S.; did you ever notice that?—I mean, like even he says it's okay to have some pleasure consistent with the life of reason."

Eva quoted: " 'Assuredly nothing forbids man to enjoy himself, save grim and gloomy superstition.' "

"Exactly. So, Professor Mueller, let's go get you a bathing suit."

"You're teasing me, of course."

"I've never been more serious in my life, and I'm a very serious person. Let's go downtown to Fairbanks' and get this woman a little pleasure consistent with the life of reason."

"No, no," she said, but smiling. She had not been able to stop smiling since the moment he started in with his anti-epistemology lecture (although really, she now thought, she ought to have come down harder on such dangerous foolishness). "Not today. Perhaps another time. Now show me what you've brought me to read. Have you written something on the *Ethics,* or have William James and the midsummer sun completely addled your brain?"

It was difficult for Eva to wait for the next Friday to come around. Of course she had his nighttime program to listen to, and that helped. It was wonderful now to hear him exuberant over the music he loved so, to take in the warm happy flow of his voice. There were still times when she found him childishly silly, but this, too, now charmed her.

Eva was also coming to find things to enjoy in this music, Michael's music. She had been quite mistaken in thinking that it all sounded the same. She now had her favorites, others that she listened through impatiently. But what held her in such fascination was not so much the individual songs, not even hearing

Michael, but something else, hard to describe. It was a way of apprehending life, of what it is all about, that the music represented to her, a way she associated with the boy. Something tight and constricted within her opened up, in a powerfully welded fusion of pleasure and pain, as she listened to the breathless rush. She did not enter into this rush but viewed it from outside, as from the distance of memory. And she remembered.

On Wednesday, Eva went down to Fairbanks' and purchased a simple blue one-piece suit. It had been hard to find something appropriate, for they were all cut so impossibly high on the leg. And yet, Eva had thought with some satisfaction, she did not look bad in those revealing suits.

After making her purchase, she took the escalator up, on an impulse, to the beauty salon on the second floor. She had never been inside. A hard-looking woman, unsubtly done up, was at the desk, and said that well, usually one couldn't just walk in like this without an appointment, but that, as it happened, Norman was free now and could take Eva.

Eva sat down on the chair, tensely on its edge.

It had been years and years since anyone had done her hair. She trimmed it herself.

Norman, a long-haired, slight, Oriental youth, came over and fingered her hair gently, making Eva tense up all the more. He smiled softly.

"Do you know what you want to have done, Eva?"

On another occasion the familiarity of his address might have offended her. After all, he might even have been a student on a summer job. But Eva was feeling so uncertain of herself in this unknown territory that she thought nothing at all of his calling her by her first name. He, after all, was the authority in this relationship, the one with the superior knowledge.

"No," she said. "I really don't know."

"You're just ready for a change, right?" He smiled.

Yes, she agreed, shaking her head a bit in assent. A change.

"But nothing too drastic, right?"

Yes, she agreed again. Not too drastic. But definitely a change.

"Well, then, why don't we just shape it a bit in the front, make it softer and more flattering, maybe some wisps coming over your forehead, like this?" He arranged her hair gently to try to give her some impression of what he had in mind. "And I think we should trim it a little, to gain a little fullness. How does that sound?"

"Yes," Eva said. "That sounds good. That sounds just right."

The boy worked without speaking, for which Eva was grateful. She slowly relaxed, leaning back and closing her eyes, even enjoying the feel of his hands moving through her hair. At one point she opened them and asked him what other beauty services they offered in the store.

"Oh, everything, really." He laughed gently. There was a wonderfully soothing air about him. Eva felt that he knew that this pampering she was undergoing was very unusual for her. There was a tone of sympathetic understanding. And although this made her feel slightly exposed and childish, she was also grateful for his intuition. "They have girls here that do manicures, pedicures, body waxing. They even have someone who does facials. Are you interested in any of those things?"

"Yes," Eva said, closing her eyes again. "I think so."

"Which ones?" he said. "I can send Martha over to make appointments."

"All of them," Eva said.

Martha, the hard-looking woman at the counter, came over to Eva as Norman was blowing out her hair and persisted in her air of slight disapproval, trying to impress on Eva that usually this place was very busy and you couldn't expect to just walk in off the street and be waited on. (Where else but from off the street? Eva had silently queried.) But, as it turned out, everything that Eva wanted could be done to her that afternoon. So, after her hair, Eva had a manicure, a pedicure, a facial, and a leg waxing, the discomfort of which induced a certain grudging respect for those frivolous stoics who voluntarily undergo such torture regularly. The woman who had applied her makeup after the facial had been the only one to service her who had been intent on making conversation. But by this time Eva had been lulled into a state of sleepy relaxation and did not wince at the woman's inconsequential chatter.

Eva hadn't really looked in the mirror in the beauty shop. She was self-conscious about examining herself before the eyes of strangers. She had simply nodded her head and smiled, murmuring something like "Very nice" to Norman and the others, hoping that the handsome tips she bestowed on all would make up for any deficiencies in her verbal assurances.

But once home she ran to her bathroom mirror, throwing on the light switch and staring at herself. What she saw was quite impossible. It was not herself she saw. The cold blue eyes, made colder still by the elaborate shadings of silver and gray, the mouth made hard and assertive by red lipstick, and the prominent cheekbones accentuated by highlighting. It was the face of her mother.

Eva watched as the face in the mirror raised itself, so that the chin pointed outward, the head tilted a bit to the side. She watched a smile form itself on the lips, while the eyes remained staring coldly. It was exactly as her mother had held herself, had smiled.

Eva tore off her clothes with such violence that she ripped two buttons from her new silk blouse. She turned on the shower full-blast and stepped in.

It was very late. Michael's show was long since over. The night wore on, so slowly, so oppressively close and still. Normally, the town, cradled by its mountains, enjoyed indulgently comfortable summers, coddled by cooling breezes blowing off the lake. But these had been days of pounding heat and airless nights.

Eva usually enjoyed her vigilance in the dead of night. She had taken pride in her ability to get by on so little sleep and not much food. But tonight it saddened her to be up alone, thinking that all the rest of the world slept. Michael, too, must have arrived home long ago and be fast asleep. She was strongly tempted to call him, just to hear his voice and make certain where he was. She would not say anything, just listen to his voice, filled sweetly with his sleep . . . She began to dial but then hung up before reaching the last digit, her impulse snuffed out by the thought that the silent nighttime summons would perhaps frighten him.

Four o'clock.

How hot it is. I am parched. I am parched past all memory of moisture, beyond all bearing of water's weight. I am reduced to a fine white powder, ready for the wind to scatter.

But those are not my words. Whose words are those, and why do they come to *me?*

She should get up, take a shower perhaps. What was the point of sitting here and doing nothing, assailed by random thoughts not even her own? But she could not muster the will to stir, so heavy on her soul was the silence of this night.

She had made herself a life of perfect solitude; and now she sat paralyzed in her rocking chair, contemplating it with mounting horror. It seemed, somehow, a distinct presence, at once sinister and pitiable, like a child without innocence. Ashen white, a cinder stench that burned her nostrils and filled her throat with dryness.

How have I borne it? How have I borne it all these years?

She shook herself, forcing herself to get up, willing her body to move. She walked over to the tall French windows, throwing them open to the night. All was silence. She longed for a sign of life out there, an indication that someone besides herself was awake to the awful darkness of this hour.

And then, like an answer to an unvoiced prayer, it came. The music of the nocturnal flutist. He had been absent for several weeks now, sharing perhaps in the collective unconsciousness. But now he was here once more, here for the night and for Eva. And, as if as another sign of grace, he was playing one of Eva's favorite pieces, Bach's Air for the G String, sounding surprisingly perfect transcribed for the flute.

Mein Gott. Mein Gott, wie schön. She listened, transfixed, to the impassioned logic of the piece. For it was logic, of course, though not tenseless and static. But logic all the same, each measure following with necessity from the one before. So that one knew with certitude that it was right and nothing about it would bear changing.

There rose up to meet the music that nameless something within Eva that had been pushing to emerge over these long summer days and endless nights. It is longing, she thought quite suddenly. I am filled with longing. And putting a name to it, knowing at long last the nature of the creature growing within her, infused it with new strength; so that now Eva herself could hear the wild beat of its life.

I will break. I am breaking.

And it rushed forth from her, a great wailing throb of longing, out into the night, beseeching.

She was crying now, bent double in her rocking chair, her head in her lap, sobbing as a child sobs who has no hope of being heard. And in between, again and again, the words "That is what I had meant. That is what I had meant all along."

It was one of the memories she never allowed herself.
Martin had given her the money. Of course she
hadn't asked him to. He called one evening, abruptly
putting forth his offer, hanging up before she could stammer out
her surprised gratitude.

They were to meet in front of the college subway station on
116th Street and Broadway. She came very early, at least an hour
before, anxious not to miss him. He arrived precisely at the ap-
pointed moment. Her searching eyes had spotted him, his familiar
slouch, coming from College Walk. He didn't glance her way but
walked straight up to her, holding the white envelope awkwardly
in front of him, away from his person, jerking it forward, thrust-

ing it into her fumbling hands. Before she could thank him —she was slow again, waiting for him to look at her—he had turned and was walking away.

She opened it. Five bills: four hundreds and a fifty. And, laid on top, an index card, with the name of a doctor printed in block letters, as if he could not bring himself to associate even his handwriting with her mess.

The doctor's name? Irretrievable. Her mind slammed shut . . .

She had spoken to him on the phone. He had an accent of some sort.

But she could not forget that his office was in Washington Heights.

It was on the second floor of a large brick building. On the first was a Jewish bakery. She passed two middle-aged women speaking German on the street. She thought, One of them could be his mother.

He had scheduled her for mid-afternoon. She walked into a waiting room which was windowless and shabby, but crowded with women. Most of them were observably pregnant, their softened bodies melting over the sides of the chipped wooden folding chairs, their heavy bulk contrasting with the quick flowing Spanish they spoke between themselves. She was the only Caucasian woman there.

The hands of the women lingered over their tumescent bellies. A girl no more than fifteen sat beside Eva. She was obviously in an advanced state. Her skinny, childish legs in cheap sky-blue summer pants dangled down from her engorged womb. Eva stared in disbelief at the bulge of it. The thing quivered, and the girl giggled at Eva, making a motion of swimming. Eva fought down the surge of acrid sickness, averting her eyes from the sight.

She sat all afternoon, as women came and went. There was no receptionist; patients were called in by the doctor himself.

Finally, there was no one in the waiting room. She had been there for five hours. She had looked at her watch only once. She didn't wonder why, if he hadn't intended to see her until everyone had left, he had scheduled her for mid-afternoon.

Technically speaking, she had been awake for the procedure.

She knew that. The doctor: what was his name? how did he look? She could not remember. There was a blank between her handing over the white envelope and her sitting up on the table, a vague soreness within her.

"Get dressed."

He had not left the room. He had stood there, watching her as she slid off the table—it hurt!—and slowly walked to the place in the corner where she had left her clothes in a crumpled heap. She remembered she had thought, but without any personal involvement, He would like to deepen my humiliation. And she had felt—it was the sole thing she remembered feeling—a slight satisfaction at the thought that she was cheating him out of part of his expected fee. She had handed over the eight hundred —he had upped the price when he learned how far along in the pregnancy she was. But he wasn't getting her humiliation.

She had felt nothing as she walked past the bloodied plastic basin he had left on the floor, not bothering to remove it from her sight. She had thought only, He does not love women, this doctor. He does not do this for love of women.

Over the years she had heard, and even taken part in, any number of philosophical discussions about abortion. She had given thought to the debated criteria for personhood: the ability to survive independent of the womb, a human appearance, self-consciousness, the capacity to acknowledge to oneself the desire to live. She had considered the proposals dispassionately, objectively, never once thinking to herself, I am in a special position as regards this question. I am a woman who has had an abortion.

Dr. Korab. He was a Filipino. Short and pudgy, with fat stubby fingers. He had smiled as he stood with folded arms, leaning against a cabinet, a wide mocking-man smile as he watched her slide bare-assed off his table.

That Friday Eva slipped the new bathing suit into her leather briefcase. She felt a little silly, thinking that by now Michael would most likely have forgotten his impulse. But she was also excited at the thought that perhaps he had not, that they might really go swimming.

As it turned out, she hadn't needed to buy the suit, and she never told him that she had. For he arrived that morning, his face even more aglow than usual, holding out to her, in his right hand, a few typed pages, and in his left, a bag from Fairbanks'.

"This is for your mind," he said, handing over the pages. "And this is for your body."

She opened the bag. Curled on the bottom was something not very large and intensely pink. Eva put her hand in, unconsciously registering the silky softness of the thing. She pulled out a bathing suit. She immediately recognized it as one of the inappropriately revealing ones she had tried on, although at least not a bikini. She felt almost dazed for a moment, not taking in the significance.

"What is this?"

"A bathing suit." The grin he had been wearing suddenly left his face (so sudden and complete a change, the sun going in). "I hope I haven't like offended you, Professor. I mean, I hope I haven't overstepped the bounds or anything. I'm very bad at seeing bounds. But I figured if I didn't buy you a suit you'd never go swimming. And I couldn't allow that." He looked at her uncertainly.

Eva was still in a state of confusion, although something very much like happiness was beginning to stir within her.

"But I can't accept this from you. It is an act of very great kindness, and I'm truly grateful, but really I cannot accept it."

"But why not? Show me the proposition in the *Ethics* that forbids it." The joy had returned to his face. "Do you like it? I went crazy trying to figure out which suit to get you. God, there's so much choice when it comes to women! But I love the color. Will it fit you? I held it up and pictured you in it to try to get the size right."

"It's a lovely suit, a lovely color." A color Eva had never worn in her life. She glanced at the label. At least two sizes too small. "And yes, it will fit. A very wise choice. But I must pay you for it."

"No, no, please, don't take away my pleasure. Especially since it's consistent with the life of reason. At least I think it is. Maybe I'll like change my mind when I see you in it." He laughed, again a little uncertainly.

"But how can I accept a present from you?"

"It's a birthday present, okay? There's nothing wrong with a student buying his favorite teacher a birthday present. Or end-of-semester present. I never bought you one. When I was in elementary school my mother always bought my teachers presents at the end of the school year. Call it whatever you like. When is your birthday, anyway?"

"Well, actually, as it happens, at the end of this month."

"When? What day?"

"The twenty-seventh."

"Really. God, that's completely amazing. Mine is the twenty-seventh too. Only the twenty-seventh of February. What a mind-blowing coincidence."

"Well, not so mind-blowing as all that." She laughed. "Let's see, the odds of any two people having birthdays on the same day of some month are . . ."

"Roughly one in thirty," he answered quickly. "The odds of our both having it on the twenty-seventh are one in nine hundred."

"Clever boy." She laughed. "You did that very fast."

"Do you really think so?"

"Think what?"

"That I'm clever." He looked anxious. She marveled at the mutability of his face, how wide open and easy to read it was. What perfect trust in the world it implied.

"But of course I think you're clever. Would I be wasting time discussing the *Ethics* with a boy who was not clever?"

"You don't know how happy that makes me," he said, but she of course did, by looking at his face, which spoke the truth of what he said. "You just can't imagine what those words mean to me, coming from you."

They smiled at one another, again a smile of shared knowledge, as in that smile of several weeks ago. Only this time Eva did not pull herself back from its perceived impropriety, did not feel it to be a dangerous tunnel leading to something unknown and forbidden. She simply savored it until its end.

"Anyway," he said at last, "I hope you like the stuff I wrote for you as much as you like the bathing suit. I have to confess I actually spent more time on the bathing suit."

"Bad boy," she said, smiling.

"Yes, I am. I *am* a bad boy."

"But also very serious, you said last week. So you must be seriously bad."

"Well, I don't know about that. I'm not sure like that follows."

"You're right. And I'm glad to see you have returned to the jurisdiction of logic."

"Well, yes," he said. "Maybe I went a little too far last week. I'm like not sure. But I still think there's a lot in what James says. And I'm still very suspicious of just the whole thrust of Spinoza. I think maybe he's too scrupulous, you know, overscrupulous about belief, about living in general. He's killing off something important by being so . . . so . . ."

"Ruthlessly rational?"

"Yeah. Right. That's it exactly."

"What is he killing off?" For some reason she was grinning at him.

"Fun." He grinned back.

Fun, she thought to herself, mentally shrugging her shoulders. No longer even the pursuit of happiness, the self-contained abiding stillness deep beneath the flow of time. But fun, the plash of a few moments. They hardly even qualified as hedonists, these students, not even taking their pleasure seriously.

"But, as you yourself quoted last week, Spinoza says that pleasure that's consistent with the life of reason is good and should be pursued."

"But that's not the kind of fun I'm talking about. I'm talking about fun that *isn't* consistent with the life of reason, and it's fun *because* of that. The letting-go kind of fun. The what-the-hell-I'm-just-in-it-for-the-ride kind of fun. You know?"

"No," Eva said, shaking her head. "Letting go can be very dangerous. They were right, these men."

"Men. Notice that you find only men saying all this stuff about the life of the mind."

"You mean as opposed to women? I'm afraid that you don't find women saying very much of anything at all."

"Maybe because they're the ones who really know what it's all about. They don't *have* to say anything."

Eva smiled. "That, I seriously doubt."

"But you. Haven't you ever felt it, the pull of the irrational?"

"Yes. I have felt it."

"But you don't like it, right? You never give in to it."

"I don't like it. That is right. And I believe it to be very dangerous. I know the underside of that will to believe which William James so naïvely trusted." (The naïveté of an *American* thinker, determinedly blind to the abyss.) "You see, Michael, the egoism of our hearts is so very great, and the forms of self-deception this induces so very varied and ingenious, that our only hope lies in what you call overscrupulousness. But why are you smiling like that?"

"Oh," he said, coloring slightly, "nothing. Well, if you really want to know, it's just that that's the first time you ever used my name. It just kind of gassed me to hear you say it. I wasn't even sure you *knew* it."

She had to laugh at him. Such a mingling of the little boy in the man.

"I'm sorry," he said, still grinning. "I didn't mean to change the subject. I mean, what you were saying was like really important. You're telling me you're really committed to this."

"To this?"

"The life of the mind."

"Well, yes. You can put it like that."

He stared meditatively at her for several seconds, finally giving a barely perceptible shrug. "Well . . . I guess that's the way it ought to be. I mean, a professor of philosophy and all."

"Yes. That is the way it ought to be." That *is* the way it ought to be.

"But you'll still go swimming with me, right?" he said, breaking out once more into his full smile. He didn't seem to know how to smile halfway.

"Yes, of course." She smiled back at him. For it was entirely impossible not to.

When they left the building the sun was blazing high overhead.

"Listen, if you don't mind walking a little bit, I know a really great place to swim. It's less crowded than the other places because the water's much wilder. But you said you're a good swimmer."

"I said I used to be. But anyway, I'm game."

"Great. Also, this place is sort of shaded, which is probably good for you. I mean, you look like you wouldn't take the sun very well. You're so fair."

Eva felt herself blushing by the nature of this attention. Silly woman, she chided herself, but with a little less than her characteristic vehemence.

"And it's pretty private. Sometimes I don't even wear a bathing suit when I swim there."

"Ah, yes." She smiled. "I know. You are a bad boy."

He laughed. It was very easy to make him laugh. He seemed always ready.

It was a pretty little spot which Eva knew from her walks. There was a ledge in the wall of the gorge from which some girls and boys were diving.

"You can go change back there," Michael said, nodding to a large rock, his warm smile on her. As in the beauty salon, with the boy Norman, Eva again felt the shift in the authority relationship. This was Michael's domain, and she had the feeling he would take care of her.

As she undressed behind the rock she saw, quite suddenly, a living scene: herself as a child with flaxen hair, getting ready to go swimming in a brook to which her father sometimes took her on long summer days. Then, too, she would go behind a rock to get into her suit. And, always, when she emerged, her father would lift her high high, so high in his arms, and carry her to the water so that she would not have to step on the sharp rocks.

"But don't they hurt you, Papa?"

"Not so much as they would you, *meine kleine Fee.* Your feet are more tender. Mine have stepped on many rocks in their time and have grown tough."

"But how will my feet grow tough if you are always there to carry me, Papa?"

He didn't answer her, but smiled gently into her face and pulled her head a little closer to him . . .

Eva slipped on the suit, pulling the tight straps up onto her shoulders. My God, she thought. I'm glad there is no mirror. But she stepped out bravely. He was standing there in his blue suit, lean and brown. He was blonder too, she now noticed, than he had been before the summer, the long hair which fell into his eyes now streaked with gold. He was frankly looking her over.

"Wow! You look great in my suit! Philosophers aren't supposed to look like that!"

She laughed, surprisingly unselfconscious under his scrutiny.

"Okay. You said you were game. The water's going to be pretty icy. We should go in first and get adjusted to it a bit before diving. Once when I dove in straight off I just froze. I mean, I was literally paralyzed. I barely made it back to the rocks."

"It's deep enough to dive?"

"Oh yes. It's deceptively deep. It only looks shallow. Like me." He laughed.

She laughed too. "Better than being deceptively shallow. Only looking deep."

"Yeah, I agree. That's the pits, in people and in diving. Well, come on, here goes."

He took her hand, and they waded in together. The coldness of the water came as a shock, but a distant shock. Eva's attention was fixed on the warmth of his hand around hers.

"Under we go," he shouted.

In a daze she bent her knees, feeling the water close over her head. Now that he had let go of her hand the coldness invaded her.

"We better start moving. Come, let's swim. Head out this way, under the rocks, where it's really deep."

She followed him, her eyes fixed on his golden head. He swam in strong, smooth strokes, only breaking his rhythm now and then to look back over his shoulder at her. Eva was able to keep up with him.

He pulled himself up onto the rocks, and then reached out a hand for Eva. He was looking at her with a gentle smile, his eyes brimming with something Eva did not try to name but which skimmed some of the chill off her.

"You *are* a strong swimmer. And after all these years out of water."

Eva herself was surprised at the ease with which she had assumed the old motions. Her attention had been so focused on Michael that she hadn't thought about her own swimming, and the knowledge had simply returned.

"Are you very cold? My God, yes, look at you! You're shivering."

This too Eva now realized with mild amazement. Was she really so cold that her body should tremble so?

"Gee, I wish I had a towel or something to put around you. I meant to bring some towels. Here, give me your hands."

He took her two hands in his own, rubbing them briskly. Her hands looked very small and white, almost bloodless, in his.

"Ice," he said, laughing. "Is it helping? I always find if I can like get my hands warm the rest follows along pretty quickly. Here." He brought her hands up to his open mouth, blowing on them, alternating that with his rubbing. Slowly, the shivering stopped.

"That's better," he said quietly, gently returning her hands to her.

They sat together for a few minutes, not talking, watching the girls and boys diving from the rocks.

"It doesn't look very safe," she said.

"Oh, it's great. In fact, I think I want to go over there now and do some diving. What about you?"

"No," she said, turning to him with a smile. "I'll watch you."

She could see the movements of his muscles, the smooth, sliding working of them as he climbed the slippery rocks. The wet blue trunks clung to him like a second skin, so that she could see

beneath them too his muscles' rhythmic contractions. He waved
to her when he reached the top, the sun behind him, in a quat-
trocento halo about his head. And then he dove, in a long and
liquid motion, his body in a perfect arc, hitting the water straight
and smooth. He swam underwater, resurfacing far from the
rocks, laughing at the surprise on her face. She watched him as
he swam back to dive again, the strength in his arms and legs, the
sunlight and shadow sliding over him in a moving chiaroscuro.
You could see in his body how he was enjoying himself, like a
rousing young pagan.

Eva watched as he dove and swam, and again climbed the rocks
in his strong youth. There was some quotation playing itself out
in her mind, but only the metered structure of it, without the
content itself emerging. Curious. She gave her attention to it for
a brief moment, trying to call forth the words, and then gave it
up.

Once again surprising herself, she joined him on the rocks,
diving, not from the top as he did, but rather from a niche much
farther below. They dove in unison, laughing when they met
together in the icy waters.

After a while they went back to the flat rocks to stretch out in
the last of the sun's rays.

"How different you look now."

Eva opened her eyes. Michael was lying on his side, his damp
golden head propped up on his palm, looking down at her.

"I can hardly believe it's Professor Mueller."

The manly voice had deepened still more in his reclining position.

"And why not?" She too rolled over onto her side, her head
supported on her open palm, and smiled back.

"Look at you!" He laughed his child's easy laugh. "You look
so much less . . . I don't know . . . Spinozistic."

She laughed, settling down on her back again.

"I think Spinoza himself would have trouble maintaining his
look of high-mindedness, stretched out on a rock in a pink bathing suit." Several sizes too small, she added to herself.

Again his ready laughter poured over her, like a thick and

heavy unguent sinking in. "It would have done him good. It's certainly doing you good."

"Do you think so? I wonder."

"Don't tell me you're feeling guilty?"

"Guilty?" She looked over at him quizzically.

"For wasting time."

"Ah yes, wasting time. It is a grievous sin."

"It is a grievous sin *never* to waste time." He mimicked her accent very slightly.

"Bad boy." She smiled.

"Bad girl." He smiled back.

It was time for Michael's show. He was in very high spirits tonight, as he had been when he had left her earlier in the evening. The first song he played was "Bad Boy," making her laugh aloud. And then he played what he introduced as some "golden oldies." This too made her smile. She knew how "old" was used in the context of Michael's music. The Top 40 chart should perhaps replace Heraclitus' river as a more timely metaphor for the transience of earthly existence.

"Now I'd like to do something I've never done before. I want to play this song for a very special woman, who probably isn't even listening. In fact, I'd be pretty shocked if she was. But here it goes anyway:

I watch your moves
You're in control
You're picture-perfect
You're picture-cold

I can't see
What you're feeling inside
I just can't see
When there's so much to hide
There's no denying
That you know a lot
But there's no use lying
That there's something you forgot.

Don't you remember love?
You must have known it in the past
Don't you remember love?
Why do you put it last?
Don't you remember love?
You forgot the one thing we know that's true
Let me give it to you.

You're gonna wake up
One morning in the cold
You're gonna wake up
And, baby, you'll be old
You've got a chance now
Don't push it all away
You're gonna need love
You're gonna need it on that day.

Eva's emotions passed in rapid, explosive succession. When he first spoke of a "special woman" she imagined some doughy contemporary of his, and felt, there was no denying it, something spiked and pitiless crushing down on her, making it difficult to draw a breath. But as she listened to the words the thought occurred to her that he was not playing this song for some gooey little girlfriend, but rather for herself, Professor Mueller. It was consistent with the tone of the teasing jokes he so often directed at her, the gently pressing challenge that underlay so many of their exchanges. And then there had been the strange intimacy of this shared afternoon. For a fleeting moment there was a breathless rush of relief, feeling almost like happiness. But this was quickly followed, upon a moment's more reflection, by a little flurry of annoyance. For really, it was too stupid. This was the medium he chose in which to deliver his considered judgment? Was he trying to reduce her life to something that could be refuted by the shallow lyrics of a rock-and-roll song? A child of his generation. And she? My God, of what had she been thinking? She had let him get too close, and now he was taking unpardonable liberties. She must remember who she was. She switched off her radio as the female singer was still ululating over the word "love." Eva had no desire to hear any more special messages for a special woman.

She awoke that night with a start, listening. All was silent without. Not a note entered from the nocturnal flutist. What then had awakened her?

She sat there, breathing hard, her pulse racing. And then she heard the words, the words whose rhythm had resonated within her earlier that day, now pushing themselves forward:

"When one who is fresh from the mystery, and saw much of the vision, beholds a godlike face or bodily form that truly expresses beauty, first there comes upon him a shuddering."

It was the *Phaedrus,* of course, the dialogue that speaks deep out of the divided soul of Plato, joining philosophy with the richly stained madness of *erōs.* Socrates, grown philosophically indifferent to the simplest needs of his body, so that he can easily do without sleep or food, and in winter walks barefoot over the ice, follows the beautiful and gifted boy Phaedrus, whose name means "Sparkling," out of the city and into a green place where wild spirits lurk. It is the only time that Socrates chooses to leave the city limits of Athens, where the intellectual conversation he delights in abounds.

The two lie in the grass on the bank of a flowing stream, while Phaedrus recounts for Socrates a certain dry and maddeningly rational discourse he has recently heard from a renowned suitor, arguing the practical wisdom of choosing as one's lover someone who is not himself in love. When the boy finishes, Socrates himself delivers a speech developing this same theme.

They are about to depart when Socrates is stopped by his daimonion, who always intercedes when Socrates is about to do wrong. He has offended a divinity, *Eros,* and he must, like the poet struck blind for failing to do justice to the beautiful Helen, "recover his sight."

And so it is here, in this green moistened place, at the hottest hour of the day, beside the wild water where once a satyr had carried off a young girl, and in the company of the receptive and sparkling boy, that Socrates is himself carried out beyond himself and, in speech transformed into lyricism, describes the ascent of the philosopher in the most erotic of terms: How it is that the soul once had wings, and dwelled in that place where Truth is; but how it lost its wings, "burdened by a load of forgetfulness and wrongdoing," and, falling to earth, became fastened to a body.

But when one who is fresh from the mystery, and saw much of the vision, beholds a godlike face or bodily form that truly expresses beauty, first there comes upon him a shuddering and a measure of that awe which the vision inspired, and then reverence as at the sight of a god, and but for fear of being deemed a very madman he would offer sacrifice to his beloved, as to a holy image of deity. Next, with the passing of the shudder, a strange sweating and fever seizes him. For by reason of the stream of beauty entering in through his eyes there comes a warmth, whereby his soul's plumage is fostered, and with that warmth the roots of the wings are melted, which for long had been so hardened and closed up that nothing could grow; then, as the nourishment is poured in, the stump of the wing swells and hastens to grow from the root over the whole substance of the soul, for aforetime the whole soul was furnished with wings. Meanwhile she throbs with ferment in every part, and even as a teething child feels an aching and pain in its gums when a tooth has just come through, so does the soul of him who is beginning to grow his wings feel a ferment and painful irritation. Wherefore as she gazes upon the boy's beauty, she admits a flood of particles streaming therefrom —that is why we speak of a "flood of passion"—whereby she is warmed and fostered; then has she respite from her anguish, and is filled with joy. But when she has been parted from him and become parched, the opening of those outlets at which the wings are sprouting dry up likewise and are closed, so that the wing's germ is barred off. And behind its bars, together with the flood aforesaid, it throbs like a fevered pulse, and pricks at its proper outlet, and thereat the whole soul round about is stung and goaded into anguish; howbeit she remembers the beauty of her beloved, and rejoices again. So between joy and anguish she is distraught at being in such strange case, perplexed and frenzied; with madness upon her she can neither sleep by night nor keep still by day, but runs hither and thither, yearning for him in whom beauty dwells, if haply she may behold him. At last she does behold him, and lets the flood pour in upon her, releasing the imprisoned waters; then has she refreshment and respite from her stings and sufferings, and at that moment tastes a pleasure that is sweet beyond compare. Nor will she willingly give it up. Above all others does she esteem her beloved in his beauty: mother, brother, friends, she forgets them all. Nought does she reckon of losing worldly possessions through neglect. All the rules of conduct, all the graces of life, of which aforetime she was proud, she now disdains, welcoming a slave's estate and any couch where she may be suffered to lie down close beside her darling; for besides her reverence for the possessor of beauty she has found in him the only physician for her grievous suffering.

The next Friday he brought her a fine little essay on Plato's and Spinoza's treatments of the problem of *akrasia,* or weakness of the will.

For both philosophers there is a difficulty in explaining how it is possible that we should sometimes know what is right but end up, through want of will, not doing it, because for both philosophers virtue is knowledge: there are ethical facts, and the discovery of these facts is both necessary, *and* sufficient, for ethical conduct. To know the good is straightaway to do it. The conclusion of the practical syllogism is an action. But then, how is akratic behavior possible?

Michael's paper laid out the problem very clearly, showing precisely which assumptions underlay its formation in the moral systems of Plato and Spinoza. When it comes to the solution they offer, there is, first of all, the imputation that passion is partly to blame: "Human infirmity in moderating and checking the emotions I name bondage; for when a man is prey to his emotions, he is not his own master, but lies at the mercy of fortune; so much so that he is often compelled, while seeing that which is better for him, to follow that which is worse," Spinoza had written.

But the aspect of the solution to the problem of *akrasia* that most interested Michael in his paper was the part played by the concept of time, particularly the distinction between the present and the future. We are misled into wrongdoing not just because we are prey to the passions but also because we irrationally weight the present more heavily than the future, so that a present good means more to us than an even greater future one. The rational person, according to both Plato and Spinoza, stands aloof from the temporal phantasmagoria in making his choices. It is in the nature of reason, Spinoza said, to view things *sub quâdam aeternitatis specie.* "In so far as the mind conceives a thing under the dictates of reason, it is affected equally, whether the idea be of a thing future, past, or present."

"Very good." Eva looked up from the essay with a smile. "A fine paper."

"Yeah, well, I wanted to do something that would work well for both Plato and Spinoza. Seeing the way you feel about both of them."

"Well, it works very well. I like it."

"Yeah, like I thought you might."

"Well, I do."

"I'm not sure I really do."

Eva arched her eyebrows in response. "How do you mean?"

"Well, I guess I treated their solution with more respect than I really feel. Like out of respect for you maybe. I don't know. But the more I think about it, the less I really like what they say about putting yourself outside the stream of time. I mean, like how can time's passage, even if it is, in some sense too abstract for me to grasp, really an illusion, not *matter* to us? I mean, even if it *is* just subjective, like we live our lives inside that subjective time. Is it not supposed to matter to me that I'm twenty? Should my actions be exactly the same whether I'm twenty or forty or sixty?"

"Well no, I don't think Plato or Spinoza would demand that of you."

"Well, then time's passing *does* matter. And why shouldn't it? The present is where we live. And it's because we keep losing it, because it keeps slipping away into the past and taking so much with it, that life has that . . . that zap of poignancy." He was speaking with great earnestness, and on the last phrase he snapped his fingers.

Eva smiled. "I don't think Plato and Spinoza approve of poignancy."

"*I* don't think Plato and Spinoza approve of life."

Eva's smile widened. "You will persist."

"Yes," he answered, uncharacteristically not returning her smile. "I will persist. By the time these philosophers of yours get through examining life, like there just isn't any. It's like, I don't know, vivisection."

"The unexamined life is not worth living," Eva said quietly.

"You really believe that, don't you? I think it's the examined life that's not worth living, at least what these guys call the examined life. *Sub quâdam aeternitatis specie.*"

"So you prefer the existence of those pathetically chained prisoners in Plato's allegory of the cave?"

"At least they're chained *together*. The philosopher who makes his way outside the cave makes his way *alone*. And when he comes stumbling back inside, with all those pretensions about enlightening the others, he doesn't even know how to live in their world anymore. He can't even see in there. For him it's all darkness and shadows."

"That's because it really *is* all darkness and shadows in there."

"Not for the others. Not for the ones who are chained together. They can see."

"But *chained*, Michael! Think! So unfree that they don't even know they're unfree. So foolish they have no idea they are fools."

"I'm not so sure who the fool is in this story."

Eva sighed. "What a perverse reading you give to the allegory."

"I'm not saying that that's what *Plato* meant by it. That's his mistake."

She raised her eyebrows again. The engorged hubris of them, the heedless crashing arrogance. The less they knew, the faster and freer flowed their easy, groundless opinions.

"So you think the fact that they are attached to one another transforms their bondage into a blessing."

"Yeah. I think I do."

"But viewed from outside, from the objective point of view, these attachments between people count for nothing."

"I don't believe that. And I don't believe you do either. I don't believe any woman does."

"Ah." Eva smiled slightly. "So it is back to philosophy as gender again." She shook her head, but not with the detonatory impatience she had experienced on similar occasions. "It is offensive, I think. I, at any rate, am offended by this claim that it is not natural for a woman to pursue the examined life."

"The claim is that it's unnatural for *any*one, and women just like instinctively know it."

"Instinctive knowledge is highly suspect, if indeed it exists at all. And I can assure you that I do not find the life I lead unnatural."

He looked at her, silent for a few long moments, and then he half whispered, almost as if in defeat, "Okay." And then he was grinning. "Anyway, I'm glad you liked the paper. I wanted to write something that would really please you. For your birthday."

"My *birthday?*"

"Yeah. Tomorrow. Like don't tell me you forgot."

"No. I haven't forgotten. I'm just surprised that you remembered."

"Of course I did. I never forget my friends' birthdays. Do you have any plans?"

"Plans?"

"Yeah, for tomorrow. For your birthday."

"No. I have no plans."

"That's awful! You have to do something really special on your birthday!"

"It's not at all awful!"

"I guess you don't like count birthdays particularly. I mean, given the illusion of time's passage and all."

"Even without that particular illusion I've never much seen the sense of celebrating the day on which a person was born."

"Any excuse for celebrating makes sense to me." Michael laughed, and she, unable to resist the pull of that laughter, joined him. "Listen," he continued, "why don't you meet me tomorrow evening at the Red Herring. Just one drink, to mark the occasion."

"Okay," she agreed, against her better judgment, but induced to follow in the flow set in motion by their shared laughter.

Eva entered from the bright outdoors, where one of those splashy sunsets for which the town was famous was just getting under way, into the noisy darkness of the Red Herring, a crowded, friendly bar much favored by the students. She was rather elegantly turned out, in a dove-gray dress, silk and sleeveless, and a single strand of very good pearls. Momentarily blinded by the suddenness of the change in light, she looked around in confusion, unable to make out anything, feeling herself very clumsy and out of place. Then she saw Michael motioning to her from a large round table toward the back of the room, where he was seated with several other people. Eva felt her confusion deepen. Why had she ever agreed to such an inappropriate suggestion? She had no business being here.

She made her way uncertainly to the back of the room, hating the noise, the smoke, the thick palpable blackness filling her eyes.

"Surprise." Michael laughed up at her when she reached his table. "Instant party. These were all the people I could round up on like such short notice. And in the middle of the summer too."

Eva looked around the table. There were three students who had been in her class together with Michael that last spring: two girls, both indifferently dubbed *tabulae rasae,* and a boy who had revealed a rare precocity in pedantism and whom she had mentally christened "the young Wittgenstein," a philosopher he was much given to quoting. There was also present, incomprehensibly, a fellow faculty member, one for whom Eva felt a distaste bordering on the passionate. Her name was Sasha Moskowitz, and Eva considered it a scandal that the woman was even allowed to teach, although, like Eva, she was one of those professors deemed a "must" undergraduate experience. There happened to be two others in the university who shared this dubious distinction: a sarcastic and bitter libertarian economist (fanaticism —no matter what the persuasion—tends to make for preceptorial popularity, the students irresistibly drawn to the singularity of a professor actually professing) and a scholar of religion, once quite erudite, but whose dip into senility had as yet gone undetected by his faithful flock.

What drew the students to Sasha Moskowitz was not fanaticism. She was a feminist, but her lectures weren't drenched in her viewpoint. She was a member of the English Department, and also had some sort of formative connection with the infant (and, to Eva's mind, imbecile) interdisciplinary program in Women's Studies. (Women's Studies indeed! A scholarly cheat at best, and a nasty insult to all women who toil and reap in legitimate fields of research. The entire concept, and the display of administrators and faculty members gyrating and salaaming and prostrating themselves before it, had thoroughly sickened Eva several years ago when the program—against which Professor Mueller had consistently voted—had been under active debate.)

"Hello, Sasha," Eva now said to her stiffly.

"Hi there, birthday girl," Sasha answered with a grin and a slight raising of her full and vermiform eyebrows. My God, how Eva hated her at that moment! Well no, not hate, of course, which was never a justified reaction, but, rather, reasoned disapproval. "Why don't you come sit here between Michael and me." She indicated a seat. "We're all drinking beer. Okay?"

"Fine," Eva answered, barely moving her lips, feeling herself constricting in the presence of this overflowing woman. Everything about Sasha Moskowitz was invasive: her musky scent, her husky voice and unrestrained laughter, the general assertiveness of her physical presence. She was a tall woman, of generous proportions, thick in the jowl and full in the lips—and hips —with dark frizzy hair fanning about her face in a great lion's mane, beneath which inevitably dangled a pair of oversized earrings. Her skin gave the impression of being rather oily; in fact, all of her seemed activated by a glandular vigor more suitable to an adolescent than to a woman in her mid-forties. And, as if this overstatement of her person were not already sufficient, she tended to wear large billowing dresses, capes, and scarves. She was in some sort of ankle-length Indian getup this evening, made of flimsy purple material, with great yellow flowers embroidered across the amply stuffed bodice.

"I like figured you two must be friends," Michael was saying. "I mean, the two best professors in the whole university. I had Sasha last semester also," he explained to Eva. The woman had the reputation of assuming very egalitarian terms with her students, so it didn't really surprise Eva that he called her by her first name; it didn't surprise her, but it did, unaccountably, bother her —just the tiniest pinprick of unreasonable chagrin. Friends! How idiotic he could be. Eva's mind was only on getting away.

Eva had, in fact, undergone only one face-to-face encounter with Sasha Moskowitz before this moment, but it had been more than enough to plant within her the desire never again to cross paths with her esteemed colleague. They had found themselves seated beside one another at a faculty meeting, and afterward had walked a short way together, talking about their enthusiasm for undergraduate teaching, a preference which distinguished them from the great majority of their colleagues. But, as it soon emerged, their enthusiasms were fed by quite divergent sources.

Both were agreeing on how enlivened they felt by their contact with the undergraduates.

"I relive the excitement I felt when I came upon these questions and these answers for the very first time. And then when one sees it happen, sees them move over the edge, into true abstract thought."

"Of course," Sasha said, in her great booming voice, "one has to be aware of how much of the sizzle and crackle generated in the classroom is sexual in nature."

"Sexual?" Eva had stared at her.

"All those young bodies." Sasha had laughed. "And one just knows what their minds are occupied with most of the time. Marc Epstein, over in the Psychology Department, actually once did a survey. In the middle of a lecture he just stopped and had everybody write down exactly what they were thinking about at that moment. Maybe seven percent were thinking about the lecture. Something like eighty-six percent of them had been thinking about sex."

"Well," Eva said dismissively, "in a psychology class."

Sasha laughed. "I'd be willing to put it to the test in my Methods in Literary Criticism. Or in your Seventeenth-Century Rationalism. *I'm* thinking about sex most of the time. Why the hell shouldn't those juiced-up kids be?"

"Do you really think of them in that way?" Eva had asked, genuinely curious.

"How can one help it? They're so strong-brewed and brimming with it. I sometimes look at these dorms"—she gestured sideways with her head to some huge brick dormitories they were just then passing—"and I imagine that if one could just ply off the roofs and look down into them, all you would see are rows and rows of those cubicle rooms of theirs, every one of them containing squirming fornicating young flesh, maybe with a few poor schmucks just getting it off by themselves. I always think of the fundamental problem of teaching as: How can anything I say to these kids in the classroom seem as interesting to them as what they're doing outside the classroom? Basically, I think it can't be."

And this perversion of pedagogy actually attracted a campus following rivaling the famous "Mueller numbers"!

"Boy," Michael was exclaiming. "Sasha on Mondays and Wednesdays, Professor Mueller on Tuesdays and Thursdays. Like nothing else in college is ever going to be able to match that."

"Nothing in life!" boomed Sasha.

Of course, there was Michael's fatuous laughter, always on tap and ready to pour. My God, the boy would laugh at anything! He had no discernment whatsoever. "You mean like I've peaked at twenty?"

"We *all* peak at twenty," Sasha intoned dramatically, fleshy hand clutching empurpled bosom. Almost unconsciously, Eva moved her chair away.

The conversation now turned to where they should head next. Various names were tossed about. Eva heard, for the first time, the chirping auditory projections of the two attending *tabulae rasae*. They had never had anything to say in class, but apparently enjoyed well-founded beliefs concerning proximate hot spots. Eva allowed her attention to drift, the words of those at the table merging with the general din.

"So, is that okay with you?" Michael's voice broke in.

"I'm sorry, Michael. Were you speaking to me?"

Michael grinned. "The Brink of Destruction. It's a new place. About twenty miles down the lake. None of us has been there yet. Okay?"

"No, I'm sorry, Michael. I really hadn't planned on this. I only signed up for one drink, you remember."

"But this is your party! We're all here because of you. You

]124[

can't just abandon us." And as he spoke, his hand reached out for hers at the side of her chair and gently pressed it.

"Okay." She smiled at him, feeling all her granite resistance going molten within her. He gave her hand another gentle squeeze before releasing it.

Sasha laughed. "What powers of persuasion the boy enjoys. And against a mind sharpened on the rapier logic of Spinoza."

This time the woman's words, and Michael's prompt antiphonal laughter, had no effect on Eva. She still felt the gently stirring warmth where Michael's hand had pressed hers.

They left the Red Herring soon after, emerging into early twilight. Michael's motorbike was parked right outside, Sasha's little red Audi halfway down the block. One of the girls climbed onto the back of his machine, and, for the first time, Eva examined her somewhat more closely.

Eva had never noticed her as one of the really pretty girls in class, and, God knew, there was no reason to attend to her qualities of intellect. She was rather too chunky for Eva's spartan tastes. Eva's eyes passed mercilessly over the bulges in the seat of the girl's jeans. And her face was much too wide, with all her features—somewhat delicate features, that much must be acknowledged—crowded too closely into the center. Rather an impractical utilization of available space, Eva thought. Why not spread the eyes—lackluster brown—a little farther apart and give the mouth—at the moment pressed into a rather stupidly smug smile—a little room to move away from the nose? Eva felt slightly queasy as she watched the girl put her arms around Michael's chest and lean her head against his back, her fleshy knees pressed into his thighs. Was there some sort of romantic relationship between these two? It had never occurred to her that Michael might be involved with any of these contemporaries of his. He seemed so separate from them.

"A cute couple," Sasha said, as they walked off to her car.

"Are they a couple?" Eva asked.

Sasha laughed, shrugging.

"Well, sort of," the girl who had been left behind simpered. "They've like kind of gotten involved this summer."

This summer! Eva was unprepared for the cruel gash these words cut through her. While he had been working with her on the *Ethics*, a task she had thought was absorbing the greater part of his attention, he had simultaneously been developing a "sort of" involvement with this little nothing of a girl—not even one of the brighter students in the class! Perhaps *she* had been his reason for tarrying in town during vacation. It was unusual for undergraduates to remain on campus through the summer months. Perhaps they had planned it together, she too outwitting her parents for romantic considerations. (The misguided guardians would have done better to pack the child off to a Weight Watchers summer camp.) After all, what other kinds of considerations existed for such a girl?

"But you know Michael." The girl went on: "I mean it's great while it lasts, but don't like go start picking out your china pattern or the names of your kids or anything."

There were only three of them left now; the young Wittgenstein had pompously excused himself from the remainder of the night's festivities. The three of them spoke very little on the drive out along the lake. Conversation was not easily accomplished between an Eva Mueller, a Sasha Moskowitz, and a *tabula rasa*.

They found the Brink of Destruction quite easily. It turned out to be on the side of a slight promontory overlooking the lake, a strange shack of a building, looking as if it were about to plunge downward into the water. Eva thought, in fact, that this must be the meaning of its name. But when they got out of the car and approached nearer, Eva considered that the name was meant to connote more than mere physical precariousness. The people congregated outside in joyless silence were among the most grimly repulsive Eva had ever seen. She was of course aware of the latest trend among the young, to adorn themselves in a way that assaulted all aesthetic sensibility. She had had students with irradiated hair in every color, or with thin tails lying limp and eel-like between their protruding shoulder blades, even a bald-headed girl or two. But the sheer bulk of hideousness now displaying itself before Eva's unwilling eyes was truly staggering. *Nibelungen,* Eva thought to herself, searching the hollowed eyes, the unwholesome pallor, the defeated slouch. There was a terrifying sameness underlying the feeble attempts at individuality. They did not look as if they were enjoying themselves. Were these possibly students? It was difficult to believe. But where had they come from, and why were there so many, here, in the middle of nowhere?

It seemed that even the dauntless Sasha was mildly daunted. She looked up at a crudely hand-lettered sign, reading aloud, " 'No spiking, no slam-dancing, no stage-diving.' " She turned to Eva in mock consternation. "So, what's left?"

"Shall we go in?" Eva asked her doubtfully.

Sasha shrugged. "They're probably inside already. I suppose we have to."

They had to pay a surprisingly hefty sum for the dubious privilege of entering. Where, Eva wondered, did these children even get money like that . . . if children they were. There was the agelessness of despair clinging to them.

They entered a darkened cavernous room, with a large video screen on the far back wall. The inhabitants were seated on the floor, huddled together in small groups, watching the flickering images in heavy silence. On the screen a woman in a garish negligee, the same shade of purple as the ugly bruise stretched across her cheek, was cowering in a corner, a look of mounting terror on her face, as the shadows around her loomed nearer and larger. Suddenly, just at the point when whatever approaching horror it was was surely going to reveal itself, the scene faded out. Now one saw that same woman in a tight black evening dress and incapacitatingly high heels, wobbling up a decrepit flight of stairs, knocking at a door with peeling paint, slowly pushing the door open. Was this the sequence leading up to the one they had just seen before? Was there any relation at all? The woman was in the room now, examining her scar in a mirror, delicately picking at the scab with her inch-long purple nails.

What ghastly horror. Eva's group was standing at the side of the large room. She looked around at the lumpen humanoid forms, sitting hunched and silent, their unblinking eyes on the meaningless images. Why?

"Let's try and find Michael," Sasha was whispering.

The three of them walked about the periphery of the room, searching.

The screen suddenly went black, and slowly the hulking masses were rising to their feet, in silent obedience to the rituals of the cave.

Some very loud music, unlike anything Eva had heard played by Michael, began to thrash the air around them, and the dwellers started moving. It wasn't dancing, or at least not like any dancing Eva had ever witnessed. A circle formed, motionless; and within people ran, their heads down, their arms pounding the air. Occasionally one of them charged into the encircling ring (slam-dancing?), knocking down bystanders, none of whom uttered a sound, whether of protest or of anything else.

"I think we should go," Sasha was saying into Eva's ear. "I've just walked all around this place again. They're definitely not here."

"But how can we leave? Certainly they'll show up."

"Look, I don't know, Eva. We've already been here close to two hours."

"Surely you're mistaken. We've only been here about ten or fifteen minutes."

"Take a look at your watch, Eva."

Eva squinted at the face of her watch, finally making out the position of the hands in amazement. Apparently, the incoherence into which she had stepped upon entering this place had completely dislodged her sense of time.

"But what could have happened to them?" Eva asked as they left the building, making their way through the group still waiting in silence. There seemed even more of them now. For what were they waiting?

"I guess they like changed their minds about coming," the girl said with an unconvincing little laugh.

"That's not possible," Eva said sharply. "I am afraid something must have happened to him. Those dark roads, that little flimsy motorbike he speeds around on."

"Take it easy, Eva," Sasha said. "I'm sure there's some non-catastrophic explanation. It never pays to worry." She gave a little laugh. "You never struck me as the Jewish-mother type."

But Eva remained tense. As they rode back to town in silence she was expecting to confront at any moment the pulsing strobo-scopic lights and siren screams that signal disaster.

The phone was ringing as she entered her apartment. It was Michael.

"Where *were* you?" he was saying.

"Where was *I*? In that place, that terrible place you sent us to. Waiting for you to show up."

"You're kidding!" He was laughing. "We were outside, waiting for you guys."

"I don't understand. Why didn't you go in?"

"I guess we were kind of stupid, come to think of it. But we were pretty sure that we had gotten there first. I mean, like we left first, and I took a shortcut I know through the back roads. At least I thought it was a shortcut." He laughed. "It just like never dawned on us that you might be inside."

"I still don't understand. Why didn't you come in anyway? We were supposed to meet in there, weren't we?"

"Well, I mean when we drove up and saw the kind of place it was, you know, we figured it was too weird. We couldn't picture you in a place like that. Sasha okay. But not you." He laughed again, the raucous noise of it pelting her already pound-ing head. What a truly awful laugh he had. He had the soul of a hyena. "Pretty funny that you were actually in there. Anyway, we just figured we'd like wait for you outside and then go some-where else."

"But when we didn't come, you didn't think to go in, just to check?"

"No. It just didn't occur to us. Anyway, we didn't want to go in there."

"I see. You didn't want to pay the entrance fee merely because we might have been there waiting."

"No, no. That came out wrong. I didn't mean it like that. If it had occurred to me that you might be there, of course I would have gone in, if only to rescue you guys."

"But then why didn't we see you when we came out?"

"Gee, I don't know. How long were you in there?"

"Almost two hours."

"God! Why did you do *that?*"

"Do what?"

"*Stay* there for so long?"

"Were we not entitled to the assumption that you were coming?"

"Yeah, well, I guess so. I guess like we just weren't as patient. After a while we just figured that you had changed your minds, gone somewhere else."

"Gone somewhere else? When such an act would leave you stranded?"

"Well, yeah, I don't know. I mean, like that's what we ended up doing."

"Ended up doing?"

"Yeah, when you guys didn't show, after a while we just left and went someplace else. In fact"—he laughed—"I'm calling you from the Ritz. You know, I just thought I'd check and see if like maybe you were home."

"I see." So while she had been scanning the roads for his mutilated young body, he was off with his overyeasted little girlfriend, ritzing.

"Wait a minute. You're not *angry,* are you?"

"Haven't I reason to be?"

"I don't know, do you? It just seems like a mammoth mix-up to me. These things happen. I mean, are you like angry at *me?*"

"Well, really, Michael. I was very concerned. I didn't know what to think. I couldn't come up with any rational explanation for your non-appearance. I certainly wasn't thinking about going someplace else and having a good time. Even though it is *my* birthday." (*Her* birthday. But it was that puffy little nonentity who had him with her now.)

"I'm sorry. Like I really figured that that's what had happened. I mean, I just always assume that people operate the way I do."

"And how is that, Michael?"

"Well, I guess trying to make the best of any situation. You know, like not wallowing in it."

"And that's what you're doing now. Making the best of it."

"Well, yeah." He laughed again, but this time a little uncertainly. "I guess so."

"Okay."

"God! I can't believe it! You still sound angry. I mean, I'm really sorry if I did something wrong, if I was insensitive or something. I really wanted to give you a good time. I *really* did."

Eva sighed, suddenly weary to the marrow of her bones. "Look, okay, Michael. Let's end it. All I want now is to go to sleep and get those terrible images away from before my eyes."

"What images?"

"Those ghastly videos they were showing. And then the dancing of those people. The violence of it. I was trampled on, practically knocked down. What *are* those people? What do they mean by their behavior?"

Michael laughed. "Punk, I guess. Pretty awful, huh?"

"My God, yes." Eva shuddered. "Such a feeling of, of . . . I don't know . . . mindless menace. What is their point?"

"Oh, I don't know. A kind of nihilism, I guess."

"Nihilism?" (*Der Nihilismus,* here? For Eva the word carried a particular and penetrating stench. What could American boys and girls know of nihilism?) "But, my God, that is a most serious proposition. I cannot believe it. Truly, it is for nihilism that they groom themselves so?"

"Oh, look, I don't know. Nihilism is probably too pedantic a word for it." There was a note of exasperation in Michael's voice that penetrated her hearing with a long, thin sting. "I mean, like you're not supposed to take it all so seriously. It's just a way they have of, I guess, feeling a part of something. I'm sure you had your ways too when you were young."

"I see." Silence. Then: "Good night, Michael."

"Good night. Look"—he paused—"I'm sorry things got messed up tonight. I really did want you to have a good time."

"Yes," Eva said, and hung up.

The next few days were very bad. Any thought of work was impossible. But why, she continually asked herself, why such dense despair?

She tried taking long walks, resisting the dead-weight sluggishness wrapping itself about her. How strange, she thought, as she walked the campus, the town, the surrounding hills. I have so few memories attached to this place in which I have lived for so long. It is because I have felt so little that I now remember so little. It is as if those years have never been. I did not register time's flight. My mind was . . . elsewhere. And yet it has flown, registered or not, away into the irretrievable past. Years have gone—as many as he has been alive. Like that song that he played the other night. "The night sounds are lonely/ As you toss in your dreams of chances left behind/ Time ticks by slowly/ When you're chasing the shadows that dance in your own mind." Only time does *not* tick slowly—but quickly, so quickly. Who would ever have believed so quickly?

Chasing shadows? Can it be? And so they turn and look at you now, these pagan youths who think they can ride time's crest and never fall; they turn and look, with horror splashed across their vacant faces. Yes, horror. That boy's eyes had shrieked with it, and then he had turned and fled.

All of life's poignancy. He is right.

But there was work, important and ennobling, lifting me up beyond the passing and pedestrian.

And that idea of freedom? Have I been free . . . or asleep, dreaming of freedom?

I have not given myself over to that insidious spread of triviality claiming the lives of most women. Specks of pettiness, the dreary details of eating, dressing, housekeeping, shopping; blotting up whole hours and whole days; until they are no longer the minute particles they were meant to be, but rather the soggy substance of these lost paludal lives. No, I have not partaken of such an existence.

And those lives from within: the airless tight little space confined by narrow self-concern; alive with black swarms of feelings, reeling about in the random frenzy of dust motes in Brownian motion. I choke to think on it!

And what is there to show at the end of such a life? Progeny, perhaps. But what does that come to, in the end, when the lives of these children and grandchildren will almost assuredly add up to no more than the lives of the parents who begot them?

Relationships. That is what they would say I have forgotten. Personal relations, they chant in glorious unison. Holy! holy! *sursum corda!* And I put it to them: How can the *relating* of things of such meager importance issue in the existence of the significant?

You don't think much of men, do you, the Athenian of Plato's *Laws* is asked. Sorry, he answers, I was thinking of the gods. The gods. Yes, the gods. I too have been thinking of the gods.

Twenty years. When viewed through the long sight of reason, they are as nothing. And yet, when sliced from a human life, what a mortal gash they leave. And when that life is a woman's, and the twenty years are bounded at one end by the passing of fecundity? Goethe, she remembered, says somewhere (Papa had made it a strict rule that they read at least a page of Goethe every day) that for a woman mortality does not knock gently, but rather crashes down the door. In the old days she would think, with her small self-contained smile, Yes, that is true—for *some* women.

No memories, no memories. As if the years never were. A few faces. Students. No names. Never known, never touched. They have flowed past me, over me, and away.

Eva concentrated hard, allowing the stream of faces to pass before her. A few at first, recollected with difficulty, but then coming faster. Hundreds and hundreds of them had made their way through her existence, listened to her exacting exegesis, spinning out the precious strands of her arguments. The premises are these; the conclusion thus; Q.E.D. Everything hangs by a thread. But the thread is woven of the strongest stuff: of logic, pure and simple. They had taken their notes and asked her their questions. What had she meant to them? Anything at all? For as tentative as her brushes with them had been, there had been no others.

This one, so earnest, who argued with me that logic was not absolute. He made a very subtle point, drawing the analogy to the discovery of non-Euclidean geometry, demonstrating that geometry too was but empirical, the appearance of necessity unreliable. Wrong, but subtle. And that one: she asked me whether I thought Descartes had been on drugs when he wrote the *Meditations*. My God. That was one who took my words away!

And this boy: always sitting at the front, his eyes so intense. And how soft his voice when he asked me his question. I leaned nearer to him, to catch his remark, and I heard him draw in his breath. So sharp it was almost a gasp of pain. Oh my God! Did he care? Did he love? Oh . . . I am sorry for him! I should have noticed.

And had I noticed—what would I have done, what could I have done? And yet . . . a little warmth breathed into that distance between us. It could have been.

No memories, no memories.

Only when she went to sit on the rocks from which she had watched the boy dive did she feel the quickening of recollection.

She saw him again, poised on the crest, his arms stretched overhead, the sun splashing full on his hair, running dulcet down his shoulders and the tapered slope of his back. How remote he was in his happiness, how remote and unfathomable. The glint on the surface shone too brightly for her to see beneath.

Happiness was something, she now realized, of which she had no understanding, none at all. If she had given it any thought in the past, it was as a state without any positive attributes of its own —as simply the absence of pain, as rest is the absence of motion, and silence the absence of noise. It was sorrow, in all its examined variety, that she had thought of as with a texture and a depth of its own. It had never even occurred to her to take seriously those who had not suffered, as if they too might be bearers of a special knowledge.

But now, as she sat with the picture of the tensed body of the boy before her, or felt again the spreading warmth of his hands on her own, she wondered about happiness, wished that she too might be drawn into its secrets. And it seemed to her that the boy, who dwelled within those secrets, was the only object worthy of reverence. But the recognition of this, and the great span of distance it revealed between herself and the boy, was felt as a terrible pain, as if something had torn within her, followed by the deep, deep ache of incompleteness.

My God, it was from precisely this that I have tried to render myself free and invulnerable. And I have been right in my desire; for this is . . . unbearable.

I will wait it out. These fearsome moods move in, massive and ponderous, like the shifting of the continents. They take hold of one so that one thinks that they will never let up. But they do. They always do. The important thing is to wait. To remain perfectly still and to wait. And above all, not to act. It will move on. And then all will be as if it never was.

I have only to wait.

"Why, it's Eva Mueller. May I join you?"

Eva was in the faculty cafeteria, dawdling over her last cup of coffee. She slowly turned her head in the direction of the baritone voice and smiled. It was Frederick Simmons, the amorous chairman of the English Department, toting his tray carefully before him.

"Hello, Frederick," Eva responded, gathering her own things together to make room for him.

"What a pleasant surprise this is, Eva. I so rarely see you in here."

"Yes. I usually don't take time out for lunch."

"Oh my, you make me feel rather the glutton." He nodded at his crowded tray, among whose more conspicuous items were two cardboard containers of chocolate milk and a plate heaped with ice cream of six different flavors. "I can see by your face that lunch isn't all you've been doing without, Eva my girl."

"Excuse me?"

"The sun. You're white as a ghost. We need a little sunshine on that pretty face."

"You're looking very fit yourself, Frederick."

"Freddy, please. All my friends call me Freddy, you know."

"Freddy, then." She smiled.

"How is your work going?"

She shrugged. "I seem to have reached a bit of an impasse. And your work?"

He too shrugged.

He was anywhere between fifty and sixty-five. His body was arranged with deliberation: the stomach sucked in, the head poised with the chin slightly ascending. Upon receiving Eva's observation of his apparent physical well-being, the abdominals had tightened still more, as a restrained glee flitted across his face. This was clearly a species of flattery that fell sweetly on Freddy. But he was a good-looking man still, over six feet, with a full head of (touched-up?) brown hair, a becoming tan, and the bright eager eyes of a sniffing pup. His rather thin lips looked as if they had just been licked.

"You know, you've always intrigued me, Eva."

She laughed. "Ah yes. That seems to be the reaction I generally elicit."

He smiled. "Well, of course. A beautiful woman. Is there anything more intriguing?"

"I don't know. You tell me, Freddy."

"Nothing. Unless it's a beautiful woman who seems totally unapproachable . . . and turns out not to be."

Eva turned her head toward the large picture window beside which they were sitting. The faculty dining club was perched beside a vigorously gushing little waterfall. She didn't know how to respond to Frederick's—Freddy's—attentions. She was not adept at this sort of exchange. And yet she did not feel inclined to discourage him . . . entirely. She turned her head back from the sight of the small gush and smiled at him. He smiled back, his nostrils undulating, and then took a sip, through the straw, of his chocolate milk.

They chatted a bit about university matters, agreeing about nothing. They stood on separate sides of all the issues presently before the faculty.

"You're really a bit of a reactionary, aren't you, Eva my girl?" He smiled.

"I suppose by your standards I am. Do you think that wrong?"

"That's not a word I ever use. I never make judgments." His smile was smug. Eva was trying hard not to despise him.

"Is that not itself a judgment?"

"Oh no." He laughed. "I'm not about to engage in a match of philosophical logic with the likes of you. Here, let me share some of this." He had begun to attack the ice cream. "My will simply dissolved at the sight of all those flavors, each lusciously waiting to be chosen. As you can see, I live by Oscar Wilde's *bon mot:* 'I can resist everything except temptation.'" He laughed, delighted at his, or Oscar's, wit—though how much pride can one take in one's familiarity with a *bon mot* which has been displayed on T-shirts and picnic hampers?

"Well, just a taste."

"A taste of each. Believe me, they're all ecstasy. Allow me to give you a sampling of ecstasy."

Why not? Eva thought. If I am in such dire need of it, which it appears I am, why not a man like Freder . . . Freddy? A man more or less my own age and experience. He is apparently well-bred. And, more to the point, he is clearly eager. Perhaps a night with Freddy, a night of demystification and reduction, would put me to rights, shake me out of the path of this darkening obsession.

"Okay, Freddy"—she smiled over—"I will follow Wilde's and your lead."

"Oh goody," he said. "Let us go where the wild Wilde leads."

]140[

It did not further Freddy's designs that the wet-lipped smile with which he handed over his plate of ice cream brought with it the image of the weepy girl as she had sat in Eva's office, with her damp smell of intimacy and her muddled tale of woe. I wonder if she's still in the picture. Oh, what does it matter? I hardly desire a meaningful and sustained relationship with this man.

She looked at the beaming Freddy, who was watching her closely as she sank the spoon into the mound on his plate. My God, what an old fool. If I must have a fool, let it be the young one.

"Well, was I right?"

"Right?"

"The ecstasy," he said in a low throaty voice, into which an unfortunate gurgle intruded. "Is it happening?"

"It's quite good ice cream."

"That's all?"

"That is absolutely all." And she stood to leave.

By the time Friday came, Eva's head had completely cleared, so that she could calmly look out at the boy from within the imperturbable tranquillity of her philosophical detachment.

Now, what was all that nonsense? she asked herself when he had left, after discoursing none too coherently about Spinoza's explanation of falsity and error. He had not been at his best today. He looked uncomfortable, and was not concentrating as he ought to have been. The little boy who has offended an authority, trying to assess exactly how seriously.

Eva had to smile. More at herself than at him. What had she

been trying to make of this child? A very nice child, to be sure, and not without some pleasing qualities and a few scattered grace notes of talent. But he looked about as right with the form of the mythically large imposed upon him as would a little boy dressed up in his father's suit, arms lost in the dangling sleeves, tripping about on the dragging soiled trousers.

How very stubborn foolishness is. One starves it, for years and years withholding all nourishment. And it shrivels up so that one thinks it is quite done and gone. But let some few random droplets of human kindness fall and it swells up with that rank throbbing assertiveness that is its nature, demanding its due. One can never relax one's guard. To be human is to wrestle forever with the condition of foolishness, the multitudinous forms of self-deception suspended above us, like iron cages, always waiting for their chance to descend.

And now that she was free from the cirrus trifles that had been overhanging her vision these past few weeks, she found her way once again into the main argument of her book, held firmly in her grasp the precious intuition of which she had begun to lose hold. Yes, yes, it worked; it all hung together. That man in New York was dead wrong. And she saw now what she must say. It was so simple, so staggeringly simple. For it all lay within the infinitely generative powers of the logical relationship.

How exquisitely small and simple truth is. Not something loud and large and showy, but quiet and self-contained. Here it is. The relation of logical entailment. Concepts entail concepts, propositions follow from propositions. And from this emerges the truth entire, indestructibly forged of logic locked into the necessary facts of existence. It was this structure that Spinoza called *Deus sive Natura*. And it rises up beyond the corrosive tides of time that wash over all that is conditioned and contingent, including us, our own poor bodily selves. It rises beyond, and yet—the gift of it!—within our reach. Our minds, in grasping the logical entailments, can take possession of it, can apprehend it and claim it for our own. And in this way we too can partake of eternity.

Eva lost herself in the wordless wonder of it all, and in her gratitude for the saving grace of reason. For what is *a priori* reason but the faculty of apprehending the relation of logical entailment? And where else can we seek our salvation?

And what a salvation it is! *Acquiescentia animi*, Spinoza called it: the almost perfect tranquillity and peace of mind, short of death, that is the state of human blessedness, and is one with the knowledge that there is no chance, no choice, no brute contingency or perplexing plurality of possibilities. It is logic alone that determines the world: and all that happens, happens necessarily.

She returned to the *Ethics*, rereading the section "Of Human Bondage" with a renewed and recleansed understanding. The Master writes: "Again, it must be observed, that spiritual unhealthiness and misfortunes can generally be traced to excessive love for something which is subject to many variations, and which we can never become masters of. For no one is solicitous or anxious about something unless he loves it."

She had been right: to gather herself up within herself. She had been right: to keep her soul her own. It was this that made the task of being human completable, that reduced the pain of existence to the blessed level of endurance.

And once again she felt the force of the vision: of the crystalline structure of logic, incomparably bright, lit by the frozen flame. And in this vision all desire is purged . . . save that of becoming one with this very structure.

She knew she was healed of her infirmity when she found herself without the slightest inclination to listen to his nighttime program. In fact, a certain queasiness rose up in her at the very thought.

That music of his: was it not an ugly symptom of a hideous degenerative disease? Worse, did it not express a perverse and morbid longing for its own state of unhealth? When she thought now of his music she compared it in her mind to a ward of the terminally ill, moaning and shrieking and gasping in a concerted and horrifying harmony.

For what is romantic love but a spiritual malady?—more often than not involuntarily contracted, so that the most unworthy of objects can play the part of the beloved. And thus the myths: of capricious Cupid's arrows and love-inducing potions; sip, and like Tristan, one will be overcome by a fatal passion for the very first person upon whom one's eyes chance to fall.

And, again like physical disease, which can the more easily invade an already weakened body whose immunological defenses are not functioning as they ought, so the spiritual illness claims the feeble soul.

Invalid and lover are each dead to the world, can attend only to his or her own state of unnaturalness, dwell with*in* that state, so that every flicker and flutter of it is acutely present, while the world *ab extra* goes unheeded. The phenomenology of recuperation is the same for both: the all-absorbing symptoms recede and the presence of the world asserts itself once more. Truly, falling in love is more a rupture than a rapture.

Rapture indeed! What manner of perversion to mistake this pain for pleasure? The very language of love is the language of disease: one is enfevered and weakened; pierced by desire, one aches for the beloved. Those are the standard clichés, scooped up in bulging fistfuls by the handicapped poets of pop.

Oh, those lyrics: I need you. I want you. My body burns for you. I will have you. Yes, I will have you. I will find a way and I will have you. Not much effort expended toward sublimation there. Did the consumers of these products actually end up speaking to one another in such words, simply handing over their raw desires and primitive passions, unrefined and unexamined?

It was altogether ghastly: to celebrate this empyemic lesion, to squeeze out of it, as from a suppurating sore, a vision of beauty and salvation.

Truly, mediocrity is a nasty proposition.

"I have to speak to you. Could you meet me at the Red Herring? Please."

"You must be joking, Michael."

"Why? Why is that such an unreasonable request?"

"Well, for one thing, I don't like that place."

"Really? Oh, I'm sorry. I had no idea."

"No. You have no idea."

"Okay, then where? Name the place. Only I have to speak to you."

She sighed. "Okay, Michael. If it is so very urgent."

"Can I just come over to your place? I mean, like that would be the simplest. I'd invite you here, but like . . ." He laughed.

Was she supposed to understand that laugh? It was his "bad boy" laugh. Perhaps it meant that there was a girl living there: that flaky little piece of puff pastry, heavily greased with conceit, who had been sticking to him that night two weeks ago at that fiasco of a birthday party? Or had he already moved on to another? She remembered the words of that other silly girl who had been there that night, how it was great while it lasted, but don't start picking out the names of your children.

So his love of women was like the love of his music, of those songs that flit their way through the chart. They completely occupy his mind for as long as they do. And then they are gone, as silent as a song that is not played, never thought of, never regretted. He lives within the transparency of the moment, unthickened by the sense of the past. Perhaps this is the open secret of the happy, their possession consists precisely in their privation. What they gain in happiness, they lose in humanity.

But she would have thought that he would at least display more subtlety and refinement in his choice of women. Eva had happened to look over the bluebook of that bulky bimbo-in-training. Jan de Witt. A ludicrous mess of an exam. Hideous. Hardly the idea of an idea had filtered through, not a flickering shadow of what it is all about. And she had not even managed to get her conceptual confusion into grammatical English. Could Michael really care for a girl who promiscuously mixed her modifiers, viciously split her infinitives, and, after an entire semester of seventeenth-century rationalism, could not spell Descartes?

And Eva had reviewed the girl's behavior at the Red Herring, which she had only half-consciously attended to then but which she was now able to recall in surprisingly lavish detail: the way the girl had looked only at Michael as she simpered sweetly; how she had opened her eyes artificially wide and arched her back, so that her already more than ample breasts protruded still farther. Her every gesture was an unaccomplished approximation to some already impoverished celluloid vision of feminine allure. She was the portrait of banality, clumsily framed in affectation. She would not have expected that of the boy, that he would be taken in by talents so shoddy and thin. But really, what

]147[

did it matter? What was he, or his sexual preferences, to her?

"Yes," she answered him. "You can come here. If that is what you wish."

"Great!" She could envision the released smile washing over his face. "Is now okay? I mean, is it okay if I like just come right now? I'm not far. I'm on campus."

"Yes. I suppose that's okay."

Slowly, her movements weighted by her thoughts, she gathered up the remains of her dinner, a boiled egg and toast, which had been left lying for several hours as she read. She looked around at her home, trying to see it through the eyes of another, through the boy's eyes. It had suddenly occurred to her that it was perhaps rather remarkable that she had never invited anybody to her place. But whom could she have invited? However, the absence of any probable candidates did not, perhaps, count against the present hypothesis of her peculiarity.

Was she an eccentric? She'd never really thought about it before. She considered the question now, with dispassionate objectivity; for the answer, positive or negative, would touch her about as deeply as the discovery, say, of her zodiacal sign.

What did it mean, "eccentric"? She supposed she was quite different from other people, at least in terms of the thoughts that occupied her, the desires that stirred her. But how could it be otherwise, when she had devoted herself all these years to the educating of both her thoughts and her desires? Yes, of course she was different, in the most fundamental sense possible, from the vast majority of others. From her own past self. This distinction had been her very end.

But did such difference as she enjoyed qualify her as a genuine eccentric? The category was a behavioral one, she thought. And, so far as she could tell, she was pretty much like others as far as outwardly observable behavior went. She didn't dress outlandishly, or sleep on the floor, mutter to herself or forget to take baths. She had furniture, just as other people did. She looked about her apartment, trying to detect any indications of her posited singularity. Her place wasn't terribly neat, of course. But then people living alone were rarely scrupulously tidy, were they? Too much fastidiousness, in her circumstances, would constitute the greater erraticism. And really, everything was in its place, although that place might be her dining-room table and chairs, the radiator, the corners of her floors, and the kitchen counters and cabinets—all of which were stacked with papers and books.

She heard a knock on her door—the doorbell had broken several years before and she had simply taped it over—and went to answer it. There he was. It was somewhat strange to see him in her living room, standing in the middle and looking around with unconcealed curiosity. She was glad that it was dark outside. She liked her rooms so much better when no light from without entered and they were illumined only by the gentle glow of her little scattered lamps, the shadows dancing on the walls and ceiling.

"So this is where you live," he finally said, with a small smile.

She didn't know what information that was meant to convey, and so answered nothing.

"You've got a lot of books here too," he said, walking over to the bookcases she had in her dining room. "You have so many books in your office, I like figured that's where you kept them all."

"Those are my English books. These are mostly German. Also French, Italian, Latin, some Greek."

"Yeah," he said, "I see that now."

He looked at her, his eyes glowing, as they so often did, with some sort of emotion that Eva could not identify. Was it admiration? Could his wide-eyed wonderment possibly be provoked by her having English books in her office and German books at her home? How very strange these students were!

He examined her books for several more minutes, then asked if he could sit down.

"Yes, of course. I'm sorry. Please sit down."

She watched him settling himself down at one end of her pale blue couch, leaning over to place his motorcycle helmet on her wooden floor. It was strange, almost alarming, to see her familiar surroundings radically shifted by the mere addition of his presence. Why was that? Why did the simple act of his seating himself on her couch hold the phenomenological depth she was now perceiving, as if her entire world was tilting and sliding away from her?

"Perhaps I can get you something to drink?" Even her voice did not sound quite her own, was too loud or too soft or too something or other. She cleared her throat.

He grinned up at her. "That would be great. I'm like really dusty from the ride over. It's been so long since it's rained, the roads are just covered with this fine white dust." He suddenly stood up. "Oh, God, I hope I'm not getting your couch all dirty. My mom gets like really furious with me, makes me go and beat the seat of my pants before I'm allowed to sit down on her precious furniture."

"No, no." She smiled. "Go ahead and sit down. I shall not require a beating."

So he referred to his mother as his mom. She continued smiling.

He sat back down, relaxing into the pillows, and laughed. "My friends back home used to really tease me about it, say that my mom and me were like into S-M and all. But she's not as interesting as that. I mean, like that might be interesting, having a pervert for a mother."

"A little too interesting, I think."

"Yeah, maybe." He laughed. "But you know the kind of person that my mother is, like you know, really conventional and materialistic, in the way that only Southern California can breed them, it really kind of scares me."

"Scares you? Why? Have they power over you?"

"Yeah, I guess you could say that. The worst kind of power. I may be just like them. I may really *be* them, like in one of those ultimate horror movies."

"And that's what you're afraid of?"

"Terrified." But he grinned.

"But then," she said, returning his smile in spite of herself, "the identity can't be complete. If you fear it."

"Not yet, it's not complete. But like I don't know about the future. Of course, if I do become just like them, then it won't bother me anymore. But that doesn't stop me from fearing it now. Like death."

"Death?"

"Yeah, well, I mean that when we're dead like in all probability it's not going to bother us much. I mean, discounting immortality, which is a pretty shaky proposition, we're just not going to exist when we're dead, so how could it bother us? But like that doesn't keep us from fearing death now."

"Yes, I see now what you mean." Eva had sat down at the other end of the couch. She was not really in a mood to continue this line of conversation. She still had much work to do tonight. "Tell me why you needed to speak to me so urgently."

"Well . . . okay. I will." His face immediately transformed itself, lost its look of easy relaxation. He leaned forward, toward her. "It's like this. I still feel like you're angry at me. Things just haven't been the same between us, since that stupid foul-up the night of your birthday. Before that I sort of felt like we were becoming friends. And that made me . . . very happy. But now, I don't know, it just all seems destroyed. I feel this real coldness coming from you. I keep thinking how ironic it is, how bad things can go. I mean you do something just to make a person happy and they end up hating you."

"Michael, how absurd. Of course I don't hate you."

"Yeah, of course. What's that line in the *Ethics* that forbids hatred and derision and all that bad karma?"

Eva promptly quoted: " 'He that rightly realizes that all things follow from the necessity of the divine nature, and come to pass in accordance with the eternal laws and rules of nature, will not find anything worthy of hatred, derision, or contempt.' "

"Yeah, that's the one. I knew you'd have it handy." He grinned at her.

"Now why is it that I sense *your* derision?" she said, but gently.

"No," he said, quite seriously. "It's not derision. It's . . . I don't know what to call it. But anyway, we've got to get back to what we were talking about. We've got to get this thing settled between us."

"Isn't it settled? I thought it was. I told you I don't hate you, I am not angry with you. It's all quite ridiculous, all this fuss about nothing."

"No, it isn't ridiculous and it most definitely is not nothing. Okay, like maybe you don't hate me, or anything unseemly and undignified like that. But I've really felt a change. I mean . . . I think we're friends. And I want us to be better friends."

What courage the boy had. Once again Eva felt an awed reverence passing over her. She could never imagine that she herself would have the courage to go before another and solicit his affection. She felt something inside her moving, relenting, and with that a growing warmth suffusing her, a warmth she sought to articulate in the words: How dear he is. How dear to me he is.

And to him she said: "Yes, Michael, we are friends. And we shall be better friends still."

He had been leaning toward her the whole time, his face and body tense. Now he leaned back, smiling, but still holding her gaze.

She opened up and looked at him, seeing through the deliberately abstract image of him she had hung before her, tagged with the title "unworthy." She took him in, full in the face, the sight of him, hard and thick with detail. It entered her with a shock, grabbing breath, in waves of pain and pleasure.

"God, I'm happy," he was saying. And it was a wonder to see it, to see how completely his happiness took him over, the light of it spilling out of his eyes. "But also tired," he said with a slight smile. "Boy, I feel really spent." He sighed. "That took a lot out of me."

"Well, it's over now." She had the urge to smooth his golden hair. She wished she had some treats to offer him. Cookies or chocolates or something.

"Oh my," she said suddenly. "I never got you your drink." They both laughed. "Can I get you some wine?"

"That would be great. A drink of celebration. Oh, wait a minute." He glanced at his watch, his face instantaneously becoming distressed. "Oh, God, I've got to leave. Better just give me a glass of water. We'll celebrate another time."

Another time, she repeated on her way to the kitchen. He gulped down the water she brought him.

"Do you want another glass?"

"Please."

When he had finished that, he stood to go.

"This was great. Really great. The conversation, I mean." He laughed. "The water was pretty good too. It's a shame I have to rush off now."

"Another time," she said.

"Right. Look, I want to tell you where I'm going. I've like really wanted to tell you for a while. You see I have this show —on W____—from nine to midnight, every weekday night. It's basically rock and roll. I guess you think that's pretty asinine."

"Asinine? Why asinine?" (She did not say: Yes, I know. I listen to you every night. And your songs play in my head all the day.)

"Well, that kind of music. Caring about it so much. And I really do. I love that music. It like goes right to my . . . core. I bet you think that means I have a pretty wormy core." He smiled. "But actually it's more complicated. I've really wanted to talk to you about this. It's like there are these two halves in me, warring with each other. There's the really rational intellectual half that studies philosophy, and then there's this *other* half."

"And what does it do?" Eva smiled.

"You wouldn't want to know," he said, smiling back, shaking his head slowly from side to side. "You really wouldn't. I mean, like that side of me is attracted to some pretty degenerate stuff."

"Degenerate?" She smiled skeptically.

"Yes, really. Degenerate. It's important that you see that."

"But degeneracy is so ugly."

"I don't think so. If you're attracted to it, it's not ugly. And it's so much more interesting. Or at least that's what half of me thinks. It's pretty bizarre, isn't it? I mean being so divided."

"Not really. Plato described it very well, as part of the human condition. Have you read the *Phaedrus?*"

"No. Tell me." He had been standing, but now settled himself halfway on the arm of her couch and looked up at her, prepared to be instructed.

"Well, Plato uses the metaphor there of two horses, one good, one bad, both trying to take control of the driver. Here." She walked over to a bookcase, pulling out her Greek copy of the dialogue and finding the place quickly. " 'In the beginning of our story,' " she translated, " 'we divided each soul into three parts, two being like steeds, and the third like a charioteer. Well and good. Now of the steeds, so we declare, one is good and the other is not, but we have not described the excellence of the one nor the badness of the other, and that is what must now be done. He that is on the more honorable side is upright and clean-limbed, carrying his neck high, with something of a hooked nose.' "

Here his irrepressible laughter broke through. "*Hooked* nose? Oh yeah, I guess the smart one is Jewish. Hey, did Plato even know any Jews?"

"Hush," Eva smilingly admonished him, and then continued: " 'In color he is white, with black eyes; a lover of glory, but with temperance and modesty, one that consorts with genuine renown, and needs no whip, being driven by the word of command alone. The *other*' "—she paused and looked at him with mock meaningfulness—" 'the other is crooked of frame, a massive jumble of a creature, with thick short neck, snub nose, black skin, and gray eyes; hot-blooded, consorting with wantonness and vainglory, shaggy of ear, deaf, and hard to control with whip and goad.' "

Michael laughed again. "I love it. Especially the whip and goad. Pretty kinky. Only of course I wouldn't call them the *good* and *bad* horses."

"No." She smiled. "I suppose you wouldn't."

"And I certainly wouldn't want to like totally tame the wild one either. That would be completely boring. I *like* the feel of the tension between them. I think I *like* the human condition. But I've *really* got to go now."

He started to the door, and then abruptly turned back. "Oh, I almost forgot." He reached into his helmet and pulled out a somewhat crumpled brown paper bag. "This is for you. I was going to give it to you the night of your birthday. I've been waiting for the . . . right moment."

And then he was gone.

Eva opened the bag and pulled out a multifaceted piece of crystal, about seven inches long. Wrapped around it was a piece of white paper on which he had scribbled: "Nothing is pure and simple—not even sunlight. Michael."

Eva sat down on her couch, the prism on her lap, looking around at her apartment, which was still recovering from the disturbances set in motion by the presence of the boy.

Eva hung the prism in her office window and watched all day for the light to enter. It happened toward late afternoon, right before the sun began to set. It was quite wonderful: the room bathed in the loveliness of those colors, splashing across Eva herself, her clothes, her hair, her skin. She wished for Michael to be there. She could give him a short lesson on Spinoza's one scientific work, published ten years after his death: *Treatise on the Rainbow*.

Spinoza says that in the move toward understanding we shed all the painful emotions: hate, fear, anger, regret, remorse, even pity. There is no room for any of those responses once we understand that all facts are logically determined.

Love, which is a pleasurable emotion, is not lost along the road to rationality. In fact, the highest state, *aquiescentia animi,* can be described as a state of love: the intellectual love of God, he calls it. So the rational do love. But it is *Deus sive Natura* which is loved, the structure of truth. Attachments to anything less, to things and to people, are every bit as irrational as hate, anger, and fear.

For if hate toward individuals is unjustified, so must love be. Hate is unjustified because all that happens, happens of necessity. There is always an explanation, and to grasp the explanation is to see how that which is explained could not have been otherwise, how it is entailed by the logical structure of truth. And thus to understand the actions of a person is to see how he could not have acted but as he did. How then can we hate, even if the actions in question bring us pain? But, congruently, how can we love, even if the actions in question bring us pleasure? And this is one way of removing the rational grounds for loving.

Spinoza doesn't emphasize this congruent line of reasoning. It is not as pressing to rid ourselves of love, which is pleasurable, as of hate, which is painful. But still, the conclusion is there, whether Spinoza underlined it or not. Eva had drawn it for herself.

The love that Spinoza *was* intent on purging is that love which grows excessive, and in so doing bears a poisoned pain; such love as hinders the godlike goal of freedom. For we are to become like God, we who would be rational, to become like God in being free, in determining, as much as is humanly possible, the facts about ourselves. The project he sets before us is that of asymptotically approaching the state of *causa sui*. Unlike God, we finite and conditioned beings cannot determine *that* we are. But we can, with ever increasing power, determine *what* we are, by determining what we think and what we feel. The only power that we have, but then the only power that we need, is the power to change our own minds.

The implication of this claim of reason is that others cannot mean too much to us. Otherwise, we become the helpless hostages of their inconstancy. We ought to devote ourselves to that over which we ourselves have control, viz., the progress of our understanding, itself fixed on that which does not change: the timeless relations of truth. And that, and that alone, is what we must love. To love anything less is to open ourselves up to the pain of passivity.

And for both these reasons: the one, that we who are rational are moved only by justifying grounds; the other, that we who are rational have given ourselves over to the *causa sui* project; for both these reasons, then, we rationally do not fall in love. Q.E.D.

This is odd.
I think of you,
And not of God.

Though all Spinoza said is true,
Instead of God,
I think of you.

Falling in love *is* a fall. A dizzying descent from reality. All the world outside, and only passion within. A madness, Plato said.

And if love for individuals is in general unreasonable, just consider this particular specimen. Who is this boy that I should so care? Is he worth such an all-out expenditure of emotion? What do I know of him? When his soul makes its stretch after the sublime, what it comes up with are the songs of the Top 40! And it is into *such* a shallowness that I would pour myself empty?

He has not the horror of mediocrity. Does he even perceive the distinctions? Does the boundlessness of his enthusiasm derive from his inability to differentiate? He embraces it all: the heights, the depths, and the vast and dismal stretches of the middle ground, where Jan de Witt reigns in a blissful absence of reflection, enshrined on her rippling throne of flesh, the smile of possession forever smeared across her lips. How can I take any pleasure in the boy's warm regard for me when I consider the other objects that delight him? A delight so easily awoken, a laughter always ready to flow; what does it signify?

And that girl! Again and again, in a feverish intensity of pain, Eva's thoughts returned to her. What was the nature of this pain? Surely it was not jealousy. Eva was not the sort of woman who would stoop to so demeaning a pose. And, even more assuredly, that girl did not have what it took to draw envy from Eva. What should Eva envy her? The fleeting fancy of that fatuous boy?

Both characteristics—the fleetingness of the fancy and the fatuity of the fancier—could be deduced from the very fact that it was *this girl* who was fancied.

Fatuous, yes. And vain as well, although his manner, so boyishly eager, seemed at first glance to belie the presence of arrogance. But there *was* a vanity to be inferred, all the more extensive perhaps for being merely inferable. She had occasionally heard him produce statements, especially on the air, which indicated that he was very much given to making comparisons between himself and others, comparisons which left him with a very smug variety of pleasure. So absurd in a person at his elementary stage of development, a toddling abecedarian of cultivation. And approaching dangerously close to this absurdity is she who would take him seriously! If he was so vain at this stage, imagine how swelled up he would become when he had nibbled at some actual success. It was a dubious proposition that his charm would outlive his youth.

And he was selfish as well. He had indicated that the night of her party. What did "making the best of it" mean other than pursuing one's own pleasure, even if that means refusing to think about the possible unhappiness of others?

Yes, it was true: the surface glowed. But perhaps surface loveliness was all that it was. Perhaps—here was a thought!—it was his very *mediocrity* which had excited her wondering awe, so unfamiliar had she become with such a sight. She had dwelled for so long on high ground, untouched by any seepage from below.

Yes, the surface shimmered. But were one to subject this shimmer to analysis, would it not reduce to a happiness that was selfishness, and a confidence that was vanity? And what is more commonplace than selfishness and vanity? The world is full of those who are full of themselves. What had such a person as this to teach her?

No: not *golden;* not forged of the brilliant stuff of the philosopher's one noble lie. A cheat, rather: mere fool's gold. And she, to her disgrace, had been beguiled by that cheap dazzle.

Was it for this that she would wound herself so deeply? For

this, rupture the tissued walls of her self-containment—so that she must go through all her waking hours wondering where he was, what he was doing. Whether he was with another. So that she should make of herself so abject an imbecile and slave that she must walk by his house several times a day, checking for the motorbike in front. And yes, occasionally surrender to the shabby impulse of calling without saying anything, just to hear his voice and know for certain where he was for the moment. (Twice a girl's voice had answered, tinkling bright, and Eva had dropped the receiver as if burned.) So that the fact of his separate existence must bear down upon her stripped soul like a whip and a goad. And she must suffer his inadequacies and incompleteness —*why* had he not better taste?—as her own.

Was such a fool's passion to be the final fruit of all her philosophy?

Eva had been walking through Collegetown earlier that day, the part of town occupied by most of the students who lived off-campus. The houses, when they had been privately owned, had maintained a certain degree of middle-class respectability, but gradually the neighborhood had changed. Landlords had bought up the clapboard houses, subdivided, and rented to students; and the whole neighborhood now had the character of that false poverty—false because bounded at either end—so beloved by those on the threshold of adulthood, perhaps, so that when they finally do move on they can look back and gloat on how far they have come. It is an appearance of progress they deliberately, if unconsciously, build into their lives.

It was in such a house that Michael had his apartment. Eva had passed by it. The motorbike was not parked in front. Out. Again. So much of his life escaped her grasp, was pursued far from the range of her knowledge. The weekly hour that was for her the focus of life was for him, no doubt, a relatively minor affair. And why did she actively seek the torment of reminding herself of the asymmetry?

Eva noticed a woman approaching from the opposite direction. Even before she had drawn near enough for her features to be discerned she had attracted Eva's attention. Something about the emphatic way in which she walked suggested a crackling vitality. There was some drama of which this woman was a part, or in any case believed herself to be.

She was rather chic, Eva saw, as they drew near one another. Her skirt was a richly brocaded velvet, and she wore a cashmere sweater that took up one of the browns of the skirt, suede boots in the same shade. She was not young. She was significantly older from up close than she had at first appeared; in her late forties, Eva would guess, about Eva's own age. But there was an element incongruously young on her face. Her features were rather heavy, resulting in a face more striking than beautiful. Her hair was an improbable shade of red. Her expression was so animated as to suggest that she was responding to an unheard remark —or God's inaudible music. Such a vibrancy of anticipation to encounter on a street!

Eva glanced over her shoulder as the woman passed. The woman had not noticed Eva at all, so intent was she on whatever it was that was provoking her expression. She turned in toward a house, a fine example of Collegetown decrepitude, quite similar to Michael's. She climbed the sagging steps onto the porch and knocked sharply, apparently already aware that the bell did not work. Eva did not stop walking, although she had slowed her pace, and now looked back in time to see the boy, dark and rather exotic, who opened the door in bare feet, a slow smile beginning on his lips and in his eyes.

I shall not need him. I shall not allow my love to become a need. It would be the height of absurdity, to ask of him . . . to ask what? That he love me? And love me as what? As a woman? But I am no longer even a complete woman. I can bear no children. He who is just becoming a man; and I who am no longer fully a woman.

He will want children. He will want it all. It is his due. All of life's colors, the brilliant spectral dazzle released by the crystal prism.

Why should I feel this: that in this passion I can reclaim my lost years? That if I cannot appropriate him through love then it is all for nothing. Nothing.

Only love me!

No. I shall not need him. I will love him, because I must. But I shall love with nothing asked, nothing even said. There could be no wrong in that: to love without need, as a mother loves her young child, as I myself would have loved . . . Yes: as I would have loved my baby.

There can be no wrong, and no pain either. It can be turned back. It *must* be turned back.

It will not be allowed. I shall not feel this: that there can be no life without him.

Any knock on her office door made her breathless with the thought that it was he. But this morning it *had* been Michael, come to tell her that he had read the *Phaedrus* the day before and hadn't been able to wait until Friday to tell her how "swept away" he had been.

"We should be studying *that* this summer. The two of us stretched out beside a running stream."

"There should be no problem finding a suitably watery place on this campus." She smiled.

"I mean what *happened* to Plato? I thought he was just another old prude. The *original* old prude. How did he ever come to write something as wild as the *Phaedrus?* Was it some sort of mid-life crisis, or what?"

"Some have speculated it was his relationship with Dion of Syracuse. The dialogue seems to have been written around the time of his second trip to Sicily. You know he had hopes, which he shared with Dion, of converting the tyrant of Syracuse, Dionysius the Younger, into a philosopher-king."

"Like in the *Republic.*"

"Exactly."

"And did it work out?"

"Plato barely escaped with his life."

"And Dion didn't even do that, right?"

"That is right."

"And Plato loved Dion?"

"Plato loved Dion. Or so some of us think."

"Wow! Good old Plato. I would never have thought he had it in him. So he *did* finally see the light in the cave!"

Eva smiled, shaking her head very slightly.

"How old was he when this happened?"

"In his sixties."

"Wow! Outta sight!"

(His speech with her had considerably loosened; his slang, which she very much enjoyed, was more in evidence than it had been at summer's start, though it never reached the level of his nighttime deejay self. How, she wondered, did he talk to his peers?)

"And what about Spinoza?" he was asking. "Did he go and fall madly in love with someone, too?"

"No. Spinoza was consistent to the end."

"God, that sounds awful! Poor old B.S.!" He laughed.

And then, when he was leaving her office, standing by the open door beside her, their eyes almost at the same level, he had asked, in an offhand tone, but glancing at her sideways in a way so characteristically his, "How many years have you been teaching here?"

She had paused only the briefest of moments. "Twenty."

]165[

His pause was only slightly longer than hers, and his voice only a shade less somber. "Wow. That's like as long as I've been alive."

She had reason to chastise herself over the turn their tutorial had taken. She certainly was not holding up her end as she ought, as she acknowledged to herself when she stepped out of the magic circle of his presence and sought detachment as a countercharm. She was so openly receptive—much too openly receptive—to his words, which were each so perfect because so perfectly his. To her, he was stunning: literally. The pleasure she took in him stunned her. She was no longer able to play the authority with him, the teacher, to inflict those gentle prods in the direction of recollection. It was he who stirred the memories, the simple sight of him.

Yes, he was simple. She reveled in that simplicity, the absence of the dark dimension pocked with secrets. A word like "degeneracy" rolled sweetly out of his mouth. And yet there are things in him of which I haven't a notion. A whole swarming life of intimate pleasures. The disc jockey who would know Spinoza!

"I think I *like* the human condition." Oh my God. I am lost.

He went off the air at midnight and usually arrived back at his place in Collegetown between twelve-twenty and twelve-thirty. Sometimes he went out after his show and didn't come back until the full light.

In the dark, across the street from his house, she stood and gazed at the sight of his bright window, behind which he moved and lived. She waited until the light went out, and she knew then that he slept.

What a house of illusion we live in, a long hall of mirrors, distorting, blurring, magnifying.

Spinoza, having supported himself through all the years of his dangerous heresy by grinding and polishing lenses for spectacles, telescopes, and microscopes, had been fascinated by the refractory properties of light. His early death, at the age of forty-four, from tuberculosis, was probably hastened by the dust of those lenses.

He had thought about refraction and written of rainbows. Eva was thinking now about the treacherous deceptions of light or, rather, the psychological analogue of light, which is *conatus*: the necessary endeavor of each thing to persist in its own being and to increase its power of doing so.

Conatus is, according to Spinoza, the very essence of each finite conditioned existent; that is, of all things less than the *causa sui*, God. One's *conatus* is the light of one's internal view, the medium through which one sees. Very rarely does it itself become the object of one's sight. And so it is that one seldom thinks even to ask the question of whether one is sufficiently significant to be worth the effort. It is entirely natural to make too much of oneself —and, by extrapolation, of one's own kind, seeing in our species all variations of mystery and beauty. These delusions of a grandeur adhering to both ourselves and others are a by-product of the very process of internal illumination, by which we are what we are. To see ourselves unradiant among the unradiant indicates a severe malfunctioning of the system.

So a bit of self-deception is demanded by the situation. The interesting cases are those which arise when one's *conatus* becomes intensely focused on some external object, which gathers it up as in a lens, producing a dazzling display of special effects. From such optical tricks arise all the varieties of romantic hallucination, from the relatively innocent delusions of sexual love to the full thrashing horrors of the false hero, the awaited savior, the frenzied masses shouting as one voice.

The glare of significance created around a chosen individual makes it next to impossible to see anything else, makes it almost impossible to see the very object upon which it is fixed: bouncing off his every word and gesture, endowing every aspect with the appearance of dimensions that are not there. So that what one beholds is a kind of mental hologram, a projection which gives the illusion of a depth . . . into which one longs—so futilely

—to step. And how profound the sense of betrayal when the beam of brightness shifts, the glare dissipates, and one sees the chosen for what he really is: a creature like any other, his truth no deeper than one's very own. Such a shift suggests a sight we none of us ever fully apprehend: what one's own self would seem, unlit by the light of its *conatus*.

There could be no possible reason for selecting one such being, in essence no different from any of the others, and loving it. So that all that one is is gathered up into one great rush of longing, streaming outward to that bright point. And all that one asks is that he receive it . . . and love in return.

What a house of illusion. How much we make out of beings so very small and inconsequential, seeking in that flimsy nature we all share our truth and our salvation.

A madness, Plato said. But a madness coming in two forms. And one of them a divine disturbance, provoking *anamnesis,* the recollection of a world long lost.

He must think of me as over the hill, out to pasture, grazing in near-senile insensibility. Forty-seven, when one is twenty, is beyond the most extravagant reaches of the imagination.

How does he regard me? As the radiant prototype waiting at the end of the long hard haul to rationality? Perhaps even as the whip and the goad meant to prod him up along that vertical climb. But then why does he buy me a bathing suit and play me a song like "Don't You Remember Love"? For surely the song, and the earnest overture he had spoken to it, had not been meant to convince that simpering schoolgirl, thrusting out her bosom and making goo-goo eyes at him.

The passion of a woman no longer young. A rather good place in the spatio-temporal manifold from which to view one of its most striking features. The contingency, inconsistency, and chaos that offend and madden our rational selves beget both humor and pathos. Only now was she beginning to see how very funny it all is, which is not at all incompatible with its being so very sad. She had been so totally sunk in the glumness of things that she had not taken in the equally universal comic aspect. This less than ideal realm we inhabit is every bit as risible as it is tragic; and it is largely a matter of temperament, but also partly of choice, that we are moved to laugh or to cry.

(Only this afternoon Eva had found herself softly chuckling in her office over an interview in the college daily newspaper with a punk performer who, in trying to get across just how deviant the "psychotic bisexual animal" that he plays is, describes how he "kicks the shit out of an eighty-five-year-old man and seduces a forty-five-year-old woman," both acts obviously equally indicative of the presence of far-gone lunacy.)

The world apprehended through pure reason is indeed lovely to behold, and the sight of it can only enhance and ennoble our small lives. But the perfection of it can provoke neither our human pity nor our equally human laughter. And is it not the case that in these two responses we may also manage, on occasion, to break through to the other side?

The inner life of Spinoza must have been rich beyond compare. How many mortals can lay claim to the belief that they have deduced *a priori* the structure of truth entire? But so far as the public externals went, he hastened to decline drama whenever possible, as he declined the various professorial posts he was offered, choosing instead the quiet freedom of the philosophical quest.

Yet there are times when a bit of drama itself follows from the philosopher's rigorous adherence to the truth as it emerges. And given the lack of understanding from the world at large that he can expect, the action is likely to be nasty. Socrates' death, for example, the event that so lastingly shaped the outlook of the young Plato.

And so it was for the young Spinoza, who at the tender age of twenty-four had been forced to suffer the whole rain of curses from Deuteronomy to fall down upon his head in the solemn enactment of the rite of excommunication. The Portuguese-Jewish community of Amsterdam, itself insecure with the memories of the Inquisition not long ago, fled, and not wishing to enrage the somewhat begrudgingly hospitable Christian authorities by harboring a dangerous heretic in its midst, had issued a series of warnings. The young man, however, would not desist, questioning, for example, whether Moses wrote the Pentateuch, whether Adam was the first man, and whether the Mosaic law took precedence over natural law. And so, on July 27, 1656, the youth was excommunicated:

> The chiefs of the council make known to you that having long known of evil opinions and acts of Baruch de Spinoza, they have endeavored by various means and promises to turn him from evil ways. Not being able to find any remedy, but on the contrary receiving every day more information about the abominable heresies practiced and taught by him, and about the monstrous acts committed by him, having this from many trustworthy witnesses who have deposed and borne witness on all this in the presence of said Spinoza, who has been convicted; all this having been examined in the presence of the rabbis, the council decided with the advice of the rabbis, that the said Spinoza should be excommunicated and cut off from the Nation of Israel.

Then he was anathematized, and all members of the Jewish community were forbidden contact with him.

How had the title of outcast felt to the philosopher? To be officially and ceremoniously cut off from one's community; it must have tasted bitter. Bitter, too, for Plato, the state's execution of the beloved teacher Socrates. Two noble youths, so deeply and cruelly bruised. But they rose out of their pain, rose forth as few others have managed; and in their rising they bequeathed to the world the path of escape.

For there *is* salvation in the liberation of the self from the self. Sink one's sight in what *is*—austere and remote—and one's attachments to the particular—the personal and the petty—will wither away. This is the attitude of high-mindedness, the ethics of detachment. Detachment from others, and from one's own minute but aggressively potent and feverishly industrious ego: throwing up its images, bright and beguiling, against the opaque back wall. So that one cannot see outside, so that few even think to see outside.

We are most of us cave dwellers to the bitter end. Even when there is pain in the dark, we simply substitute another reel of images. Only the few, led by the Masters, can break through to the other side.

The idea of the girl caused her pain. Dimpled white, the bouncing buxom bountiness of her, fattened on sweet mother's milk.

And what species of regression *was* this? After the years devoted to the educating of her thinking and desires, was this the place in which to be: here on the desolate plane where a sorry specimen like Jan de Witt could assume the form of formidable opponent—could, by virtue of qualities of no account, get the *better* of her?

It was not fair, of course, to hate the girl; hardly the attitude of high-mindedness befitting the student of philosophy. And yet Eva did hate. She acknowledged the inglorious passion as her own. She hated the girl, who was so plush and plump on the possibilities of her youth.

Eva was not young. No. Time's snatching fingers had never ceased: pulling, plucking, mauling. What was the nature of their work, ravage or revelation—slowly dissolving the filmy spume of birth (we are a long time being born) until the true face is unmasked? Faces no longer young can be among the most captivating ever created. But since the creative act lies largely in the life that precedes, very few of them are. Eva saw the changes in her own face—no, it was not the face of twenty years before— but could not read their message for herself.

The human face; the soul's thin membrane.

Oh, but my God. Papa's face when he lay dying. The mouth twisted into that open snarl, the filthy secret shamefully showing itself. Like those corpses that were always making trouble, that surfaced in reservoirs and woods, plowed fields and rivers. Until finally, in desperation, the authorities constructed crematoria and ordered all bodies burned.

And how I longed to cover those features—for love of him . . . still. Bury it! Fill those eyes with heavy dirt, the ugly gash of a mouth. Bury it!

IV

As an older child Eva had never known what to do with the infant pictures that had the feel of memories but could not be.

They reached far far back, beyond her recollections of the cruelty of a child's empty stomach. Those memories of hunger she understood. That was the war. Papa was away, in Berlin. Mama and she were in the countryside, where it was safer. Away from the terrifying firestorms, the awful drone of the airplanes. Mama and she were in the fields, searching for food. She understood all about that, could connect those recollections with the present.

But the other pictures could not be made to fit. For most of her childhood she had simply regarded them as the powdery residue left by some receding dream of long ago. Meaningless *Traumbilder*. What else could they be, when they were so unlike anything else she knew?

The house in which she lived with her papa and mama was a place of quiet and order and moderation. There was always a kind of hush, almost palpable, muffling the sounds within. Of course, there was music. Papa's violin, Mama and Eva's piano. And they had a record player as well. Bach and Beethoven and Brahms and, most especially, Mozart. Musical notes were the only sounds permitted to pass through the walls of any room.

People's voices were never raised, neither in anger nor in laughter. Papa's voice was quiet, low. There was a sort of huskiness or hoarseness to it, a permanent suggestion of tiredness. Mama sometimes scolded Eva, if her school assignments were not written neatly, or she had not practiced her piano sufficiently long or well, or her hair or clothes were untidy. But Mama would never have raised her voice. She too spoke low, almost in a whisper.

Excess of any sort was unthinkable. Everyone moved softly and slowly on the well-oiled wooden floors.

But Eva's *Traumbilder* were full of tumult and loud noises. *Loud noises in the house.* Of parties with laughter, and shouting too, but most especially of the thump! thump! thump! of footsteps, echoing all the way up to her room high on the fourth floor of the very old house, the beautiful and large house on a quiet back street she had never been able to find.

She knew that the old house had been destroyed by the bombs of the Americans or the British. She knew that much of Münster had been laid flat. But now it was all restored and so beautiful. The gabled houses and twisting streets, the ancient colonnades of the Prinzipalmarkt, hung with overflowing baskets of flowers in the spring and summer, and unspeakably lovely at Christmas time, with thousands of white lights dancing in the darkness.

Papa had told her much about the history of the city, so much, in fact, that for Eva it was as if there were still ghosts hovering about, revenants lurking from that great drama of the Middle Ages that had been played out here. For it was in Münster, in the sixteenth century, that the fanatical Anabaptists had founded their "kingdom of a thousand years." Papa had told Eva all about them. They were baptized when they were adults, which was a crime punishable by death in those days; a second baptism, only they didn't think of it as a second but as a first, because they believed that infant baptism counts as nothing. Babies don't know the difference between right and wrong and, therefore, can't be punished for their sins.

They came to Münster with their "king," John of Leiden. They took control of the city. They were sort of like Communists, Papa said, they didn't believe in private property. And also, the men had many wives. Their "thousand years" lasted a year. Münster was recaptured, and John of Leiden and two of his accomplices were put to death. The really interesting thing was that the iron cages where their bodies were exhibited were still hung high on the façade of St. Lambert's Church, right in the center of town. Eva loved to stand on the street with Papa, holding his hand, looking oh so far up to the great Gothic tower, at those two suspended cages, while Papa told her again about the zealots who had died there.

Eva was already quite a big girl, fourteen years old, before she connected two of the most vivid of her *Traumbilder*, the one auditory: of the loud footsteps banging on wooden floors, stamping up and down the wooden staircases; the other visual: of the heavy black glossy boots that her father, and other men who visited the house at that time, used to wear.

It must have been her perspective, so near the floor, that accounted for the great detail lavished upon her memories of those boots. She could remember the leathery smell of them too, reminding her of horseback riding in the Teutoburg *Wälder*. They reached all the way up above the knees of the wearer. When she grew up she would wear pretty high-heeled shoes, like Wilhelmina wore on her day off.

]179[

Sometimes, if the man was tall, his boots reached higher than Eva's head. Not Papa's, though. Papa was not very tall for a man. Mama, although just a little taller than Papa, was tall for a woman. Eva was tall, like her mama. People said she looked like her mama, and sometimes Eva would stare in the mirror, making expressions like her mother's.

When Eva, walking home from *Gymnasium*, book bag on her back, thinking of something entirely different, had made the association between the noises of loud footsteps and the heavy black jackboots, she had stopped walking and stood for several moments on the sidewalk, letting others walk around her. She had stood there, blinking, in the bright September sunlight.

She knew she could not go to her parents, not even to Papa. She had seen the look darting between them across the dinner table when questions about the past arose, even about the old house which had been destroyed. She set about her work of corroboration discreetly and cautiously.

How is it that a child's mind will choose some undistinguished moment—an outing to the park no different from countless others, a music lesson or a morning's awakening—to preserve in memory, while the rest is washed away in oblivion?

Eva had such memories. Of lying awake in the very early morning: The sun is falling onto my bed, a little wooden bed, with sides on it, so that I can't roll out in my sleep. I must lie here quietly and wait for someone to come to me. Oma.

Oma is very old, with gray hair she wears in a bun. I watch her comb it out at night, long gray hair falling all the way down the back of her white nightdress. I think that she looks then like a witch, *eine alte Hexe*. I tell her, and she laughs. But she has a nice laugh, not at all like a witch's.

"Like Baba Jaga?" she asks me. "Do I look like Baba Jaga in the story?"

"Tell me! Tell me!" I beg her.

And she sits down near my head and tells me again the story

of *Die Verzauberten Brüder,* the two enchanted brothers, who are turned into trees by the bad Baba Jaga. They grow right beside the house of their mama, who spends years and years searching for them. They are always calling out to her, but she isn't able to hear them.

Oma is a wonderful cook, much better even than Gaby. I am so happy when I see her showing Gaby out of the kitchen. I know that there will be wonderful things to eat for dinner, like *Goulashsuppe* or sauerbraten and maybe, for dessert, *Apfelstrudel* or *Rote Grütze,* cold and creamy, with vanilla sauce!

Oma has a nice soft fat lap. She bounces me up and down, singing *"Hopa, hopa, Reiter!"* Or sometimes she sings songs in the funny language of the place she came from long ago, when Papa was a little boy. I love to hear her singing.

And then there were memories of someone named Wilhelmina. She must have been a housemaid. Eva is very fond of Wilhelmina. Wilhelmina is up in my room. She often comes to me. We're standing at my window looking out into the street far below. There is a parade. Wilhelmina and I are excited. She laughs and claps her hands. I do too. Her cheeks are pink and her eyes dance with lights, like the colonnades at Christmas. She's very pretty.

The marchers are shouting together, so loudly we can hear them all the way high up in the top of the house where my room is. Wilhelmina and I march around the room and shout together too, just like the people outside: "Germany, awake! Jews to the stake! *Heil! Heil! Heil! Heil!"*

Oma comes hurrying in, looking very angry, and speaks sharp words to Wilhelmina.

There was the excited air of Christmas trembling over the *Traumbilder.* Often, when she pulled them out to look at them she would seem almost to smell the yeasty *Stollen* and spicy sweet *Pfeffernüsse.* The pictures shimmered in a special light, as if they were reflecting the glow of colored foil paper.

It was when Eva was reading her first history of the Third Reich (she was to read many, so many, more) that she came upon the name of Dr. Joseph Goebbels, the Reich's Minister of Propaganda, and a memory was jarred loose, bringing with it the explanation for that strange reflected glow. And with it, other memories came tumbling out.

Mama's face has a spot of pink on each cheek, and her eyes have points of light. She looks younger, pretty like Wilhelmina. Soft like Oma. It makes me so happy to see her like this. That is why I laugh, and not because of the little chocolate eggs wrapped in colored foil paper that she holds out.

"Look at what Dr. Goebbels has sent you for Christmas." Her voice is so happy, almost singing, and her eyes shine. "Take them, take them! They are yours." She is pushing them into my hands. "Because of your papa."

Eva knows of course that her papa is a great man, a professor at the university. He wrote a very important book. Yes, very important. It is because of this book, perhaps, that all of the happiness and excitement of Christmas is in the house. Because Papa is so good, people come to the house, and there are loud voices from downstairs, many parties, happy sounds. And Mama too is happier; her face is not so white and her lips not so straight. She gives many performances now. Her fingers are long and very white. Eva stares at those fingers.

Mama practices at the piano for hours and hours every day, and we must all be very quiet and not to bother her. Such beautiful music coming from her hands and running all through our house. Her music can be soft, like Oma singing to me while she holds me on her lap, or big and booming, like the parades that pass outside on the street. Only I am never allowed to go out and watch the parades. Very very bad people come there, people who are the enemies of our country and of our Führer. And of Papa. And then the brown police must come and there is fighting. These people are so bad that they would not even care that there is a little child who could get hurt from all the trouble they are making.

We even had a performance in our house. It was on a Sunday afternoon. The drawing room was filled with people. And I was able to sit right in front, next to my papa. I was very quiet and good, and I kept one leg crossed over the other like a big lady. They made a fuss over me, the ladies. I was too excited to really hear the music, to feel it all around me and in me, the way I can when I listen to my mama by myself, or my mama and my papa playing together at night. Mama on the piano, darling Papa playing his violin. But I could tell that everyone loved it. They love the way Mama plays. And they love Papa's great book. The good people do.

There are very bad people and Papa must make sure that they cannot play music anymore. They used to be allowed to play. They fooled many people. But not Papa. They wear masks, I think, like at carnival, like on *Rosenmontag*. And they have many names so that they can confuse people: Jew and Bolshevik, more names too. It's hard to remember them all. But of course Papa can, and that is why they can't fool him. It used to be that only these bad people could make music, and that is why people like Mama could not play. I am so happy that my papa is so good.

Her initial emotion when she began to read the books was of almost joyful relief at discovering the key to unlock the perplexity of her *Traumbilder*, to be able to clear up their mystery at last, and appropriate them for herself as genuine recollections. It was the pleasure of fitting the pieces together to form a finished puzzle.

Books. Whatever books she could get her hands on that concerned *das Dritte Reich*. She read them voraciously that year dating from her moment in the bright September sunlight of her fourteenth year. For months and months she gorged herself on this material, until she was a walking encyclopedia of those twelve years that were meant to be a thousand.

The first book she read was *Bis Zum bittern Ende*, published in Zurich in 1946. She happened on it almost by chance, randomly selecting it from the stacks in the library of the Westfälische-Wilhelms Universität, to which she had gained admittance through the position there of her father, Dr. Herbert Mueller, professor of musicology. It was written by Hans Bernd Gisevius, who had started his career in Hermann Göring's Gestapo, but who had gone on to become a leader of the very quiet and subterranean opposition, and had ended up participating in the abortive plot of July 20, 1944, to kill Adolf Hitler. He was one of the few who was able to escape Hitler's retaliatory wrath, slipping away to Switzerland.

Much of the book was incomprehensible to Eva, for she didn't yet possess enough of the story. But there was still much to stir the quickening of recollection within her. Most importantly, she found a way to grasp the reason why these reclaimed memories of hers clashed so violently with the reality she now knew. Reading it, she could see how to go about fitting together the long-ago loud noises, of pounding and shouting, laughter and singing, with the muffled hush, the shrinking away from all excess, the almost neurasthenic exhaustion of the members of her family.

Abruptly men's spirits changed. A wild national jubilation broke out. Banners, garlands, testimonials, laudatory telegrams, worshipful orations, changes of street names, became as commonplace as parades and demonstrations. Victory celebrations, community appeals, followed one another in rapid-fire succession. The glorious sensation of a new fraternity overwhelmed all groups and classes. Professor and waitress, laborer and industrialist, servant girl and trader, clerks, peasants, soldiers and government workers—all of them suddenly learned what seemed to be the greatest discovery of the century—that they were comrades of one race, "*Volksgenossen* " [yes! she remembered that word]. Above all, youth, youth was getting its due. The dreary past was forgotten, even the oppressive present was hardly noticed in view of the transcendent future of this new, this Third Reich, which was at last being established.

No wonder that the popular rejoicing verged on the ecstatic. Serenity vanished, all rational thinking, all inner restraint, were abandoned. In the end there remained nothing but black and white, good and evil; the whole world was divided into rascals and heroes, the past and the eternal, centuries of ignorance and a thousand years of salvation. Everything ran to superlatives.

If today, a radio program consisting of phonograph records from those days were played, I rather think that our people would not believe their ears. They would be unwilling to believe that they had listened to so much trash and had themselves participated in such raucousness, such singing, such idiocies.

Raucousness! Yes! Singing! Yes! That is what she remembered. Idiocies? She could not say at this point. She knows it had all seemed like Christmas to her then, back before the time of the firestorms and then the bottomless hunger; that Mama, who now always stared ahead coldly and unsmiling, had once had pink spots on her cheeks and had laughed like a schoolgirl.

"Look at what Dr. Goebbels has sent you for Christmas." Her voice is so happy, almost singing, and her eyes shine. "Take them, take them! They are yours." She is pushing them into my hands. "Because of your papa."

It was in this first book that Eva came upon a reference to Joseph Goebbels's children. Gisevius made a passing, cynical reference to the presence of the Goebbels children at one of those fêtes the Nazis were such masters at creating, Hitler's fiftieth birthday party perhaps. "There were the inevitable Goebbels children, trotted out once more for display." Yes, she could remember them. There had been six of them. They had been pointed out to her once, at some sort of celebration, very very large. Perhaps it had even been that massive birthday party for Hitler! They had been standing on the podium, beside their mama and papa, dressed all in white. She could not really remember how their famous papa had looked. She had only stared at the beautiful children, the six shining specimens of Aryan perfection.

"Look," Mama had said, "look at how beautiful and good they are."

It was several books later that Eva learned the fate of the Goebbels children. All dead, together in the bunker with Hitler, their mama and of course their papa as well, who had described the death of his family as his "final act of propaganda" for the sake of the German nation.

The image Eva first arrived at of Hitler and the others, Himmler and Heydrich, Göring and Goebbels, was not very sinister. They seemed almost like buffoons, characters from a comic opera: Hitler flying into a foaming rage at the slightest setback, suffering a nervous breakdown before every major decision. And Hermann Göring! The descriptions of him almost made Eva laugh. The would-be Nordic Renaissance tyrant who loved to play dress-up, always strutting about in a different fantastic uniform, each more magnificent than the last. The indications Gisevius gave that these men were something else, something dark and truly horrible, Eva simply could not take in. She was able to follow the intricate twists and turns of the plot to overthrow the government, but could not understand much of Gisevius's story. There were references made to "horrors," "atrocities." What did it mean?

At the Nuremberg Trials all the leading defendants, led by Göring, the founder of the Gestapo, and Kaltenbrunner, its last chief, swore that they had not only been innocent but ignorant as well of the atrocities. When I testified at the trial . . . I took the liberty of admitting, in the name of our oppositional group at least, that we had known about all the horrors—that, in fact, these had been the chief reason for our taking action.

Eva felt her stomach lurching in a sickening way when she came across words like these in the book. She knew that the writer was not just referring to the undermining of principles of democracy. She knew that something darker lurked behind these words.

The enemy was first alleged, as we have noted, to be Communism. Then it was—somewhat more generally—Marxism. Later the limits were extended—reaction. And —always—it was the Jew. But names meant nothing at all. All had their turn, of course—the men of the Red Front, the Social Democratic functionaries, others whose political color was not brown, and the Jews.

. . . And they have many names so that they can confuse people. Jew and Bolshevik, more names too. It's hard to remember them all. But of course Papa can, and that is why they can't fool him . . .

Eva had gone on to read more. She found the books that filled in the details, told the stories of the horrors and atrocities. With these books she had entered the work camps, the death camps, until finally the entire picture was before her.

But "picture" is not really apt. For here was a curious thing. Although Eva came to possess a vast store of facts concerning the twelve years of the anomie that had swallowed up her country and so large a part of the world, her knowledge was composed almost entirely of words, with very few images. In particular, she could not see the victims. She managed, with concentrated effort, to visualize the trains that carried them eastward, the camps that awaited them, with the brick watchtowers and the electrified barbed wire. But the ghettos, the trains, the camps, and the crematoria were always uninhabited for her.

She knew the numbers: Poland: 3,000,000; the Ukraine: 900,000; Rumania: 300,000; White Russia: 245,000; the Baltic countries: 228,000; Germany/Austria: 210,000; Russia: 107,000; the Netherlands: 105,000; France: 90,000; the Protectorate: 80,000; Slovakia: 75,000; Greece: 54,000; Hungary: 45,000; Belgium: 40,000; Yugoslavia: 26,000; Italy: 8,000; Norway: 900.

And three million of these dead had been children, her age and older, many many younger; for what means did a child have to protect himself?

Eva knew the numbers in her sleep. But try as she might, she could never picture to herself a single victim. She could even conjure up an image of the black-and-white striped pajamas they wore. But they too hung limp and empty.

Well no, not always empty. In the grotesquely cruel and mocking joke her mind sometimes played on her, she would see a face above the prison clothes, staring out, dazed and vacant, from between barbed wire.

The face was her father's.

After the light had been turned off, he would sit beside Eva on her bed, no longer the little wooden one from long ago, from the shiny, noisy time of the pretty Wilhelmina and of Oma's cooking and early-morning singing. Wilhelmina had been killed by a bomb, and Oma had died from typhus. Münster smelled of fresh plaster, paint, and tar.

In the dark, he would sit and talk to her. Only not to her, because his voice was not the one he kept specially for her. He would use long and grownup words, and she knew she could not interrupt and ask him what they meant, as she could, as he wanted her to, at other times, daylight times. Sometimes she would fall asleep and wake up to find him still there, his voice alone in the dark.

There was so much of it she didn't understand, so much she had slept through, so much she had willfully forgotten. And yet she retained a good part of it, the long story weaving in and out of her sleep and her years. Once upon a time, there was a little boy growing up in green mountains in a place called Moravia.

The little boy was named Herbert. He had a mother, named Olia, who loved him very much. Olia; say it aloud. Does it not sound like a song? Olia loved Herbert, her only child, even more than she loved the green mountains where she herself had played, and her mother, and *her* mother before that. Do you know what that is, Eva: to leave the place in which your mother's mother's mother was born? But because Olia loved the boy so much, they left the small village in the beautiful green mountains.

They left because Olia wanted everything for Herbert, her dream child. His musical talent was clear from the age of three, as, flaxen-haired and somber-eyed, he trailed her from room to room and out to the small kitchen garden and the chicken coop, reproducing every twist and turn of her improvised melodies. She had managed to find someone, a schoolteacher, several villages away, who was able to give the boy violin lessons. Herbert had been playing since he was seven, and he had already surpassed what the schoolteacher could offer.

Olia herself was like a songbird. Songbird was what Herbert's father called her. She was the daughter of the innkeeper there, in their little row village lining the steep mountain road. But there was something so fine and quick and bright that ran through her, her hair pale as glass when she undid her thick braid at night —a something that his father, shy and awkward and uncomfortable with words, pictured as a circle of light, as sometimes bounced off the metal of his tools, darting here and there on the dark walls and ceilings of his small cluttered shoemaking shop. Sometimes, in the middle of his work he would see such a light dancing about, and he would stop and stare, suddenly sunk deep within the sweetness of his image of pale Olia, dressed in the local costume that so suited her, the full black skirt and brilliantly embroidered blouse, cut low so that the white beauty of her showed, the little gold cross lying just beneath her neck.

And the boy was just like her. His father would listen to their music with a child's simple delight, his wife singing in the full round richness of her mezzo-soprano, like a bird calling in the deep of the forest, and the trilling, pure notes of the boy. Ah, that boy! Bringing such beauty and sadness out of that fiddle of his, music such as the most aristocratic of fathers would burst with pride to hear. The father never could get over the wonder of it, that he, great big black Slavic peasant that he was, had sired the fineness of that little fellow with the shock of flaxen hair.

His father had agreed, though with unvoiced trembling and a wrenching longing in his heart—oh, the thickly forested mountains! the foaming blue-green streams!—that they must leave the ancestral village and emigrate to Germany, where the opportunities for little Herbert would be so much greater. The mother —and so the father—burned with the dream that Herbert would become a musician.

But I regarded music only as my beloved hobby. When I first went to the university, the very famous and old University of Marburg, I chose to study mathematics. It seemed a much safer decision.

All that changed abruptly in my twentieth year, my third year at university. Quite abruptly.

There was a young man at university. His name was Ernst Brouwer. He too was studying mathematics. I didn't know him very well, but he invited me to come with him to Bayreuth, to attend the Wagner *Festspiele.*

Bayreuth is a small town in a remote part of Bavaria. It was here that Richard Wagner, after the years of Sturm und Drang, *had finally come to rest, building his home, the somber stone mansion* Wahnfried, *and the theater hall, the* Festspielhaus, *specially constructed to accommodate all the demands of the towering tone-poem dramas. When Wagner died in Venice, in February of 1883, Cosima, his widow, had his body brought back to Wahnfried. In 1913, Cosima was still in black.*

Cosima Wagner was a most extraordinary woman. She too was touched by the hand of genius. While her husband lived she had accepted his verdict that "woman has nothing to do with the outside world." But since his death she had taken upon her female frame the full mantle of that great legacy. No tampering was to be permitted, not with a single element of the Meister's vision—the almost mystical intuition of which had been vouchsafed to this woman alone— from the backdrops of the scenery to every gesture of the performers. Wahnfried had waged a battle to restrict performances of all the dramas to Bayreuth, where ein Gipfel der Menschheit, *a pinnacle of humanity, had stridden the earth and gone about the labor of his immortal creation; Bayreuth, where alone the ideal world enveloped within the physical is revealed, and the archetypes, which everywhere else exist only in the abstract, rise up embodied before one's astonished eyes. But ultimately even the superhuman determination of Cosima had been powerless to prevent the desecration of having the Meister's music flung willy-nilly about the globe, unto the heathen reaches of New York City, where* Parsifal *had been performed by the Metropolitan Opera in 1903, an event that Wahnfried justifiably decried as a "rape of the Holy Grail."*

This fellow, Ernst Brouwer, was a passionate Wagnerian, having made the pilgrimage to Bayreuth every year since he was sixteen. I was hardly on intimate terms with him. In fact, I believe I had spoken to him before on only one occasion. So I was somewhat taken aback by his proposal. And then, when he actually offered to help defray my costs, after I had intimated that for me the cost of the tickets was . . . rather steep; well, I was overwhelmed!

He was a mysterious fellow, this Brouwer—without a doubt the most brilliant student of mathematics then at the university, head and shoulders above all the rest of us. I myself was nothing more than adequate, for all my diligence. I was constantly at my books and had no time for the sports or the student clubs that so absorbed the others.

Brouwer too was a loner. There was something about him that discouraged contact, no matter how passing. Sallow-complexioned, tall, and rail-thin, he looked as if he might bend with the wind. I remember that his eyes were very clear and a somewhat remarkable

steel-blue. His hair was black, rather long. He had a way of uncon-
sciously sweeping it up off his forehead, with his long, nervous fingers,
and then tapping his forehead three times, very gently. Other strange
mannerisms as well, such as lifting one shoulder toward his chin and
making a low gurgling noise in his throat. The other students, includ-
ing me, I must say, were all a little wary of him, and also resentful
of his soaring talent, which left the rest of us looking as if we were
plodding along on feet of clay.

I can see him still. Strange, when I can recall so few faces from the
past. It is as if those steel eyes have cut through all the intervening
years . . .

It had been Herbert who first approached Brouwer, driven by
his search for illumination concerning a question in topology that
his professor had suggested to him as a suitable subject for his final
paper. He had been fitfully circling the impenetrable thing for
more than a month now. He had even begun to dream of the
problem, which, in these dreams, took on a physical form: cobalt-
black and gleaming menacingly, with sides smooth and cold as a
crystal. In one of his dreams he reached out tentatively to brush
it with his fingertips and received a startling sensation of pain, as
had once happened when, as a little boy, he had touched a frayed
electric cord with damp hands and had run terrified into his
mother's open arms.

He wanted only a hint from Ernst, a suggestion as to how to
begin to pry open the formidably dense object. He posed the
problem, looking up into those steel-blue eyes as he spoke, for
Ernst was at least a good half a head taller. In physical type
Herbert was the very counterpart to young Brouwer: milky-fair
and dolichocephalic, rather small, with a very good form, trim
and compact, suggesting a certain robustness and even subdued
strength, where the other's drawn-out height bespoke only a
gangly awkwardness. Herbert had been, like nearly everybody
else, slightly consumptive in his boyhood, and this had left him
rather nervously careful about his state of health. His real weakness, however, was his eyes. His unceasing study had left him
extremely nearsighted and he had worn glasses, gold-rimmed and

scholarly, since the age of twelve. Behind the lenses the blue eyes wore a rather high-minded expression. His blond hair was smooth, parted, and slightly oiled. He was already, at the age of twenty, beginning to bald, a sign of maturation which had caused him no few pangs of vanity, although, in fact, the presentation of his frontal pate to the world increased his appearance of manly sobriety and reflective intelligence, and would conspire with other attributes of his person to conduce to his early success, in matters both personal and professional.

Herbert was amazed by the alacrity with which young Brouwer had responded, the generosity with which he had offered the gift of his insights. They had come pouring out, as the two young men walked the narrow cobbled streets of Marburg. Once Ernst started in, he seemed unable to quit. As it happened, he had not considered this particular problem before, but he quickly saw that it belonged to a class of problems that went beyond the topological, to which he had given some thought. And once one saw this, well then, the solution was pretty straightforward, wasn't it? Ernst had talked on and on, so that when Herbert finally left him more than two hours later, his head was literally spinning, and he ran all the way back to his rooms in order to jot down what he could recall.

The next thing he knew, Ernst was proposing that they meet that July at Bayreuth for the festival. They would travel separately, for Herbert would be remaining in Marburg, studiously taking courses through the middle of July, whereas Ernst was required to pass his summer months at his family home in Frankfurt am Main. Herbert received the impression, though from nothing directly said, that the Brouwer family was quite well-to-do; and this fact, together with the rather offhanded way in which it was indicated, served to increase Herbert's awed reverence for his new acquaintance. Poverty was a grimy, almost sordid, fact of life.

Herbert experienced the weeks of that first *Festspiele* as a quasi-religious awakening. He was, of course, reasonably familiar with the works of Wagner, which by now were commonly recognized within Germany as the truest expression of the national soul. But, truth to tell, it had not been this composer's work which had commanded Herbert's greatest passion but rather that of the beloved Mozart. He had attended a number of instrumental concerts of Wagner's music but had never had the wherewithal, nor the driving interest, to see one of the dramas performed. He was certainly not prepared for the transports which were to seize him that summer.

The atmosphere at Bayreuth was indescribable. The infectious emotionalism, the fervent, wildly beating love and camaraderie that bound the audience together, with one another and with the spirit of the immortal genius who seemed almost present. The press of oneself against these others was so great as to be capable of almost obliterating the sense of one's distinct identity, the maddeningly incessant drone of one's own inner *Stimme*.

Herbert and Ernst attended six performances of *Parsifal*, Wagner's last work, which was performed every year at Bayreuth, and which, perhaps more than any of the others, captures the yearning desire for that spiritual regeneration which lay at the heart of the "Bayreuth Idea." And, in the all-absorbing embrace of that yearning and that vision, entranced by the mystical brotherhood of the Grail of which this opera tells, the elation of the audience, and the heady beauty of the mixture of music and poetry, Herbert felt himself happy as never before. He felt, for the very first time since emigrating to Germany as a boy, not like the gaping outsider, the shabby uninvited guest at the groaning banquet board, but rather as one with this most noble of all people . . . this race of Parsifals.

Lifted up by the swelling longing of the music, he at last allowed himself to feel what he had been for so long resisting: the full dimensions of his love for this country. Here was the incarnation of all the nobler instincts of mankind. The genius—intellectual, aesthetic, and, above all, spiritual—that in other races ran weak and thin was in them—oh, Goethe, Schiller, Beethoven, Brahms! oh, Wagner!—distilled and refined, burning with a pure, clean flame! It is true that he himself had, up until now, suffered to a certain degree from his feelings of separateness, of self-despised distinctness. In admiring those around him he had to wonder whether he himself could be absorbed into the grace of being one with them. Oh, he would have cut off his right arm to have been born a German—although, he was quite certain, his mother's people, blond and blue-eyed Alpines, must surely have originated in Germany. And even his father's side: the name "Mueller." The Czech lands were such a racial goulash.

The festival's closing address was given by the internationally famous Houston Stewart Chamberlain. The *Festspielhaus* overflowed that night, so that people actually had to stand out in the street, there in the dreamy moonlight. Ernst had warned Herbert, so they had come very early and were able to find a place standing in the back of the hall. Herbert had almost swooned with the ecstasy of it, not just because of the content of the inspiring speech. The very fact that it came from this man was the ultimate proof that racial distinctions were more a matter of inner character, of moral criteria, than inherited blood. For this man, who was *not* German-born but rather *English*, was the living avatar of the truest Teutonic type. He had long ago, when in his twenties, found his spiritual home in Bayreuth, becoming a member of the magical inner circle, the *Zauberkreis*, surrounding Cosima, and had become the most famous spokesman for the "Bayreuth Idea." Only five years before, in 1908, he had himself become, once removed, a Wagner, wedding Eva, the youngest daughter of Cosima and Richard.

But Chamberlain was an important personality in his own right, one of the most influential thinkers then alive in Germany. He was not a bloodlessly sterile academic type whom nobody reads. His books were read by the thousands, and generated the excitement, the enthusiasm, and yes, of course, the controversy as well, that is a sign of the living written word. He was the author of the renowned masterpiece *The Foundations of the Nineteenth Century*, published in 1899, which had demonstrated, using the most sophisticated scholarly methods available, from the findings of Charles Darwin to the modern techniques of historiography, the undeniable facts of race: the division of the world into distinct and antagonistic racial types, and the racial conflict which is the reality underlying all historical events. The *Volkerchaos* which has resulted from the evils of miscegenation, the mixing of noble and ignoble bloods, has so weakened the peoples of the world that they have, for the most part, been reduced to a state of confused decadence, in accordance with the Darwinian principle that "crossing obliterates character." There are, in fact, only two relatively pure types left, Teuton and Jew, forever destined to oppose each other. For whatever the Teuton is—noble, idealistic, mystical, and trusting to a fault—the Jew is not.

The fundamentals of the theory of race had by then been accepted by almost every thinking German, and any respectable university had its scholars devoted to racial research. It is quite amazing how all this has been buried in forgetfulness, the reams and reams of scholarly papers now gathering dust in buried archives. Present consciousness would have it that something quite novel and inexplicable seized our Europe, that we were all swept up into a kind of temporary madness. But the principles of race were not the abrupt eruptions of fevered brains but of the most sophisticated techniques of science. Precision had been attained in 1840, when the Swedish anthropologist Anders Retzius had introduced the cephalic index, a figure computed from the length and breadth of the head. Two major types were identified: the dolichocephalic or longhead, to which classification the Aryan belonged, and the brachycephalic or broadhead. Already, by the end of the nineteenth century, scientists had gathered a wealth of anthropometric evidence, involving the measuring of millions of skulls, in addition to the observation of other racial characteristics, such as hair and eye coloring, general countenance, and complexion. One experiment alone, commissioned by the German Anthropological Society, and completed by 1885, had involved 15 million schoolchildren in Germany, Austria, Switzerland, and Belgium. Jewish children were given a separate classification. The evidence from this enormous undertaking was able to demonstrate the groundlessness of the vile slur propagated by the

French after their defeat in Sedan in 1870 that the Prussians were racially distinct from other Germans, not blond and blue-eyed dolichocephalics but culturally inferior brachycephalic Finns or Slavic-Finns. The scientific findings also laid to rest the fear that the Germans in the extreme east of the Reich were being polluted by Slavic types.

But it was the nonacademic scholar Houston Stewart Chamberlain who was able to present one of the most important results yet obtained in the field of racial theory: the conclusive proof that Jesus of Galilee was not a Jew. This fact had, of course, long been suspected, since the Saviour manifested all the character traits typically Teuton or Aryan, none of the Jew. But the final, the *scientific*, argument had awaited Chamberlain, who had shown that the Galilee was inhabited mostly by non-Jews, by Greeks, Phoenicians, and even some Indo-Europeans. Their looks and speech (they had difficulty pronouncing the Aramaic and Hebraic gutturals which every Jew is born to utter) alone proclaimed their racial distinctness.

Chamberlain strode to the lectern, fair-haired and dignified. (A fleeting, disturbing thought: Was it not the case that the German and the Englishman were more consanguineous than the German and the Slav?) He had a rather high-pitched voice, but refined and cultivated, without a trace of an English accent. He was no longer young but a man in his fifties. However, it was clear to all, once he began to speak, from the animated expression on his face to the stirring throbs in his voice, that he was still fired by the enthusiasm of his mission. The audience gave him the thunderous applause that had sounded repeatedly in the *Festspielhaus* throughout the weeks of the festival, and then, within seconds, quieted down in fevered anticipation. And among the packed bodies, holding their breaths so as not to miss a single syllable, stood the young Herbert and Ernst.

Chamberlain spoke first on the great success of this year's festival, the perfect harmony that had descended upon one and all, performers and visitors, under the unfailing guidance of the Wagner family.

And then Chamberlain spoke, briefly but beautifully, of the basic ideals that ensoul these performances, the "Bayreuth Idea": that of the spiritual regeneration and redemption of the German *Volk* through the uniquely German genius for art. The apotheosis of art attains its fullest expression in *Parsifal*. It is art which expresses the underlying reality of things, which alone can penetrate the outer crust of false appearances, revealing the living realm of freedom, the Kantian *Ding an sich*. It is through the divinely immortal dramas of Wagner, above all, that the German can, in that experience which combines all the dignity and bliss of which the human soul is capable, confront the nature of his own true self.

"The German's existence is quite different from that of other men. In him self-awareness and the feeling of his own worth have reached their high point. He is both artist and practical organizer, thinker and activist, a man of peace *par excellence* and the best soldier. He is a skeptic and the only man who is really capable of belief.

"But, as always, the greater the natural gifts, the greater the responsibilities which go with them. Germany's role is a tremendously difficult one, and if she is to fulfill it, the whole nation must recognize the task and strive together as one for its accomplishment. Not only does Germany have so much to perform and develop, but in the meantime, she must preserve herself against the animosity and misjudgments of all Europe. If one is not caught up in all this, but can observe the course of things from afar, the question often arises: 'Will Germany be able to fulfill her alloted task? Will she accomplish it?' And though one may love Germany with all one's heart without seeing any overhanging clouds, still one must reply: No!—if the fundamental corroded moral relations are not improved. And they will not stay as they are; if they do not improve, then they will deteriorate. No! —if the whole nation does not understand that purity is the greatest strength of a people.

"And so, while the future of Europe depends on Germany, Germany herself can have a future only if the roots of the present condition are attacked and if morality is raised aloft as the principal weapon against the rest of the world. If Germany does not understand this, then she too must fall—fall prey to the barbarians without having fulfilled her role.

"Ah, you beloved German nation! Will you never discover your exalted role and see that your ordained path is not to be that of the other nations?"

These words of Chamberlain falling upon his soul, which had already been seared wide open by the performances he had attended, produced an enormous effect upon Herbert. Never in his life had he felt this. The truth had fallen on him like a pelting hail of fire. He had been a vain and silly boy until now, taking far too seriously his mother's overblown estimation of him. His all-too-easily-wounded ego, the out-of-proportion anguish he suffered from the insults of others, his feelings of never quite belonging. Now he could see they were as nothing, so much dust in the wind.

He felt all his doubts vaporize in the pure Bayreuthian atmosphere, and he himself burned flame-like from that moment.

Only one discordant note had broken into the perfection and completeness of Herbert's first visit to Bayreuth, and this had occurred later in that same evening. Both Ernst and Herbert had been in a state that precluded the possibility of sleep. Tirelessly, they walked the quiet streets of the town, the fragrant park surrounding the *Festspielhaus*. They hardly spoke to one another, for they were both too full of feeling for words.

And then the singular event had occurred. Herbert suddenly became aware that Ernst's pace had slackened and that he was several feet behind now, was in fact standing still in the waning moonlight, for it was almost morning. The young man was weeping into his open hands. Herbert waited at a discreet distance, and after about ten minutes Ernst again caught up with him and they fell once more into their silent strides.

After a short while Ernst began to speak to Herbert. As it had been in that first conversation between them in Marburg, when Ernst had talked on and on, seemingly unable to stem the flow of his insights once they had gotten started, so it was now. Only now it was of his inner torment, the anguished grief he suffered for the tragic flaw of his birth, that he spoke.

Herbert looked at him in astonishment, asking him what the deuce he was going on about.

"Surely you know I'm a Jew."

No, Herbert had not known. He was so isolated from the other students, like Ernst himself such a loner, no word of Brouwer's racial identity had ever reached him.

Ernst had smiled sadly. "Ah, now I understand why I never sensed it in you."

"What? Sensed what?"

"That fastidious shrinking back, that slight hesitation, always there, before they speak a word, before they reach out to return a handshake. It had amazed me that you were so free of it."

Herbert had simply continued to stare at the young man. It was amazing to be witness to such a transformation. From being something of a wonder in Herbert's eyes, an *Übermensch* whose talents had left Herbert and the others looking rather dwarfed and defeated, Ernst was deforming to something rather commonplace. He was very much the mere mortal, perhaps . . . yes, perhaps even something somewhat less. How odd.

"You, Christian that you are, can't possibly know what it is that I suffer. The self-hatred coursing through my blood like prussic acid. Knowing that I myself am a carrier of all that I most abhor, of that which is in opposition to the very ideals to which I would devote myself, the purity and chosenness of this nation that generously tolerates the presence of my kind.

"You can't know what it is to be so torn apart, a divided self.

]203[

For surely it is only natural to love oneself, to want to preserve oneself from harm. And yet my other half, my better and truer half, can wish only for my own annihilation. Yes. I do not shrink to use the word. *Ausmerzung.*

"Our only hope is war. That is the possibility I pray for nightly, hourly. That Germany at last will rise to its full strength and stature, arouse itself and answer the insults of the insufferable England! Seize that empire which is rightfully its own! And that we Jews will overcome our characteristic cowardice and die in droves for the Fatherland. This blood, and only this, can possibly wash away the stain of our guilt."

Herbert listened to the outpouring of his companion, himself feeling somewhat divided, while he tried to grope for some words by which to comfort the young man's grief. For there is no doubt about it, Herbert did feel a certain measure of sympathy for Ernst. First of all, he had felt quite a warm intimacy with him through the course of the festival. Yes, he could not deny it. He had felt a spiritual kinship. And of course he understood only too well the sentiments being voiced.

He now offered Ernst the very insight by which he had sought, with varying results, to assuage the pain over the tragic flaw of his own Slavic birth.

"Surely, Ernst, you must have considered that according to many theorists, including Chamberlain himself, the truest indicators of race are not of the blood but of the spirit. And certainly the pain you feel, and the great *Innerlichkeit* of which this speaks, must convince you that in reality, despite the accident of your parentage, you are not completely a Jew."

Nor I a Slav. But even as I spoke these words to Ernst I had thought to myself that I did not really believe them, at least not as applied to this young man who now walked beside me, fallen back once more into the brooding darkness of his silence. For really, would a true Teuton display such sniveling self-pity and unmanly unwillingness to face up to one's destiny?

Perhaps Brouwer, gifted as he had once seemed to be, was a true Jew after all.

Herbert had not seen much of Ernst Brouwer that next year at the university. He hadn't deliberately gone about avoiding him. It's just that he moved in a different circle now. Herbert was no longer a student of mathematics. He had switched his field of concentration to musicology, and was deep in study of the Wagnerian dramas.

It was a time of great happiness for Herbert; a time, as always, of intense study, but now lightened and sweetened by a greater degree of companionship. He had not realized how much he had longed for the touch of sympathetic fellowship, until now, when he was privileged to feel the clasp of these good fellows' hands upon his shoulders. His musical labors brought him into contact with a new group of people, with whose interests and passions he had everything in common. He even joined one of the *Studenbunde* in Marburg which was devoted to the music of Richard Wagner. It had ties with Wagner societies all through Europe.

It was on a visit to Vienna, to hear Houston Stewart Chamberlain speak once again, this time at the Vienna Academic Wagner Society, the largest and wealthiest of the Wagner clubs, that Herbert first made the acquaintance of Elsbeth Hansler, the daughter of a prominent member of the society. The Fräulein was an aspiring pianist, studying with one of the finest teachers in Vienna, Harriet Wasserman, who had herself been a student of Franz Liszt.

As a guest from the famous German university, Herbert had been introduced to the charmingly cordial and urbane Herr Hansler. They had spoken a short while about Chamberlain's *Foundations,* which by now Herbert had studied in depth, finding themselves in harmonious agreement as to both its overall success and its very occasional flaws (for example, Chamberlain's brief discussion of Jesus' few Jewish traits, which Cosima herself had denounced as an outrage). Before excusing himself Herr Hansler had invited Herbert to his home to attend his weekly Sunday soiree.

Herbert had changed his plans for returning immediately to Marburg in order to accept Herr Hansler's exceptionally gracious invitation. The house was overwhelming, a veritable palace on Mahlerstrasse, not far from the Opera House. Herbert was not yet in a position to be able to identify the rare art treasures and furnishings displayed in the Hansler domicile. Some years later he would move through the massive rooms and know the joy of being able to place each item in its proper context.

And it was there, on that evening, that Herbert first made the acquaintance of Fräulein Hansler. She was a very serious young woman, full of a reserved dignity. She is definitely *minore,* Herbert had thought, and played *moderato;* no, better: *grave.* Herbert had a great affinity for music written in a minor key. The Fräulein had none of the little frills of flirtation one might expect, eligible young woman that she was—twenty-six, five years older than Herbert himself. She was dressed in a high-necked and rather prim white lace blouse and a simple black velvet evening skirt. The sober modesty of these clothes was set off by the brilliant colors and daring décolletage strewn all about them. There was a somewhat strained immobility to her pale face and her rather rigid posture, which marred what would otherwise have been a rare prettiness of form. But he did take special note of her hands. She had the most elegant and poignantly beautiful hands he had ever seen. White and unblemished, as if carved from a block of perfect marble. She used them very rarely as she spoke, but when she did on occasion raise them up before her breast to make a point, he felt his heart lift up and unfold. They spoke, of course, of music. She told him of her progress through the Liszt opus, and he told her of his Wagnerian studies.

Upon returning to Marburg, Herbert had written the Fräulein a note of gratitude for the evening's entertainment, expecting never to hear from her again. His surprise equaled his delight when he received a response, which was, admittedly, as undemonstrative and unflowery as the young woman's own conversation; and yet! Soon the letters were crossing quite regularly between Vienna and Marburg.

It was at a meeting of the university Wagner Club, late that spring, with the linden all in bloom and a just read—and reread —letter from Elsbeth folded in his breast pocket, that Herbert heard the name of Ernst Brouwer spoken.

"Brouwer," said Herbert, smiling. For despite all that had happened he still could think almost fondly of the young man. "A strange fellow that. No doubt brilliant, but a genuine eccentric."

The student who had been speaking turned and stared at Herbert. "But you're speaking of him as if you didn't know!"

"Know?"

That Ernst Brouwer had died. Shot himself through the head in the icy dawn of Christmas Day. In a remote section of the Marburg woods.

Herbert was at Bayreuth for the opening of the next festival on July 22, 1914. It was less than a month after the assassination of Archduke Francis Ferdinand at Sarajevo. On July 29, while *Götterdämmerung* was making its way to its tragic denouement, the Austrian Army was being mobilized against Serbia. Two days later a new production of *Der fliegende Holländer* played to an emptying *Festspielhaus* as foreign visitors made haste to return home; and a bugler and military escort marched through the streets of Bayreuth announcing Germany's ultimatum to Russia. The last performance of that summer, and of a decade of summers to come, was *Parsifal*, which took place on August 1. That evening, Germany declared war.

Herbert had not even felt it too badly, having to rush away before the conclusion of the festival. He had returned to Marburg and volunteered his service to the Fatherland, the only activity which could possibly overshadow a performance of *Parsifal*.

Oh those glowing days of August 1914, when the historical moment was at last upon us, and all as one seized the rare and precious possibility of heroism. It is a great pleasure to the superior individual just once in his sane and measured life—do you understand, my blessed daughter?—to be able to lose himself altogether in the general sentiment.

I carried the librettos of Wagner's Ring *cycle and* Parsifal *in my army duffelbag. I would pull the books out when I could, gently fingering them. I was unable to manage the act of reading. But the physical feel of them was sufficient to conjure up—there in the mud and the lice and the filth of the trenches, the unremitting stench of death and fear—those visions of a world, remote and idyllic as Valhalla itself, that I myself had once witnessed.*

The story stopped here, abruptly. The next night he went back to reading to her from the magical book of the mythical time.

Each time she took a new book in her hands, Eva turned first, a little sick with the hope and fear of it, to the index at the back, her finger swiftly flying to the M's. Her heart would skip a beat as it fell on the "Mueller." Only it was always another: Heinrich Mueller, a Gestapo functionary, or Dr. Joseph Mueller, a Catholic leader of the Opposition. Never had she found a reference to Dr. Herbert Mueller, of the Westfälische-Wilhelms Universität of Münster. Whatever her father's role had been, it had not been of sufficient stature to merit mention in the history books. The card catalogue at the university listed no books by the professor. (She knew he had published articles in obscure scholarly journals of musicology.)

It had been Martin Weltbaum who had told her of the new Museum of the Holocaust, Yad Vashem, in Jerusalem. (Martin knew quite a lot about Israel, although he had never, on principle, visited. Not surprisingly, he had rather complicated sentiments concerning the existence of the Zionist state. Among his very few friends at Columbia was a professor who was a prominent spokesperson for the Palestinian cause.) Martin too was rather curious to discover who and what Dr. Herbert Mueller had been.

They had written to Yad Vashem with a query concerning the activities between the years 1933 and 1945 of Dr. Herbert Mueller, professor of musicology. In particular they would appreciate any information that could be given concerning a book written by the same Dr. Herbert Mueller sometime between the years 1937 and 1940. Several weeks later they received a letter postmarked Jerusalem. Eva had sat all day, the letter before her, not finding the strength to open it until Martin returned.

The letter was from a Dr. David Friedlander of Yad Vashem. He had been able to find mention of a Dr. Herbert Mueller in connection with the Reich Chamber of Culture, which had been set up by Dr. Joseph Goebbels in 1933 in order to centralize control over the entire range of cultural activities within the Reich. Goebbels himself was the president of the chamber, which had its headquarters in Berlin, and it seems that in practice the organization was little more than a subordinate body of the Ministry of Propaganda. The chamber was divided into six suborganizations: Archives, Press, Radio, Theater, Music, and Creative Arts. These chambers acted through the various professional organizations as sources of patronage, and withdrew financial support and recognition from any artist who incurred the regime's disfavor. There was a Dr. Herbert Mueller who had been made assistant to the president of the Reich Music Chamber in 1937.

Dr. Friedlander had also been able to find that a book by Dr. Herbert Mueller had been published by the Lehman publishing house of Munich in 1937. The title: *The* Ring *Cycle of Wagner and the Critical Moment in the History of the Fatherland.*

"So." Martin had smiled at her. "Assistant to the president of the Reich Music Chamber, subgroup of the Reich Chamber of Culture. I don't mind admitting to you, Eva Mueller von Münster, that I'm the tiniest bit disappointed. I bet the old boy never even beat up a Jew. Maybe burned a few books at most. I personally like my Nazis more of the straightforward thug type. Give me an Ernst Röhm over a Joseph Goebbels any day. Still, I suppose one shouldn't underestimate the power of culture. Maybe Papa even managed to get in a few kicks at enemies of the state like Bruno Walter and Otto Klemperer. What's the matter, Eva, cat got your tongue? Still, I wouldn't mind seeing that book of his that got him all the way from a second-rate provincial university to the Reich Chamber of Culture headquarters in Berlin. He must have said something right. Wagner: say, wasn't he the one who wrote the background music for *Kristallnacht?*" And he had laughed his joyless strangled laugh.

Eva herself was remembering. When she was in *Gymnasium,* she had chosen to study music for her elective, and they had spent several weeks with *Der fliegende Holländer.* It was, in fact, the only opera they had studied in any depth. It had been the class joke. Nobody, not even the teacher, could stomach Wagner, although the teacher felt it was important for them to have some familiarity with him. But even he had smiled over the groaning and the mocking. They could not relate to the arch heroics and passionate excesses.

Eva had never liked opera, but she particularly disliked the works of this composer. She already knew, from her reading, of Hitler's Wagnerian adulation, hatched in the dismal setting of his Viennese adolescence; and she knew too of Wahnfried's reciprocal enthusiasm. Hitler made his first pilgrimage to Bayreuth in 1923, emotionally swearing to the family, beside the Meister's grave: "Out of *Parsifal* I will make a religion." And the Wagner family had, from the first, given themselves wholeheartedly to this religion.

And Eva had remembered Papa's voice in the dark, hushed and distant, different from his daytime voice, talking of Bayreuth and the young Jew, Brouwer.

It was Eva's last year in *Gymnasium*. Her period of obsessive reading about the Third Reich was, for the most part, over. She was in the process of adjusting to the knowledge she had, the knowledge she lacked. But the sense of shame was never far from her consciousness. She often told herself that she could not be alone in this. This thought too had occurred to her very early on in her reading, as she read of the so-called *Gleichschaltung*, or coordination, the "spontaneous" and "voluntary" falling into the party line after 1933. "Wherever the Brown Front moved forward, it ran into no determined resistance. It thrust ahead into empty space," Gisevius had written. There was even a slang word invented, "beefsteaks," for those converted Communists who were "red" on the inside, "brown" on the outside. There was such a rush to join the party that the Nazis were able to extract heavy dues from the latecomers for the privilege. So there must be, she often reminded herself, many, many German children, perhaps some even among her classmates, who carried such a secret within them.

The difference, however, was that the undistinguished masses had, for the most part, left behind no traces of their temporary enthusiasm, had let off only the dissipating vapors of beliefs and shouted slogans. Eva's father was an intellectual. He had left behind evidence of a more tangible sort. Somewhere there was a book.

His hushed voice had throbbed strangely, so that it broke Eva's heart to hear it, when he had spoken of that moment when he had come to accept, at last, his love for the race of Parsifals.

While her classmates poked fun at the high-falutin themes, Eva sat in a haunted silence, her eyes downcast and her cheeks burning. Oh, when would their interminable study of this thing be over? So conspicuous was her discomfort that the teacher even began to tease her about being a closet Wagner fan who resented the class's cavalier treatment of the Meister.

Two years later, when Eva was already an assistant professor, she heard once again from Dr. Friedlander, whose letter had been forwarded from her old New York address. The director said he remembered her request of several years before concerning the book of Dr. Herbert Mueller, and he was very pleased to be able to tell her that the museum had recently acquired a copy of it.

The plane landed at Ben Gurion International Airport with a burst of song. There was some kind of Israeli youth group on board, returning from a trip to the States, and they sang a Hebrew song as the wheels touched down.

Eva had feared just such displays of excess. It was not long after the Davidian triumphs of the Israeli armed forces in what had come to be known as the Six-Day War. Jerusalem had been reunited, Moshe Dayan was a national hero, and the heady emotionalism of this people was running very high. Eva felt herself closing up, like the pupil of an eye drenched with light.

She was already feeling disoriented. She had gotten no sleep. The youths had been up all night, parading up and down the aisles talking, laughing. The airport was a madhouse. A dark-skinned man immediately swooped down on her and relieved her of her suitcase, carrying it out as she protested (were there no official customs to go through?), pushing her into a cab, and holding out his hand for payment before she knew what was happening.

The sun was relentless and the air smelled like diesel fuel.

The hotel was an Arab one, the Pilgrim's Palace, just outside the Damascus Gate leading into the old walled part of Jerusalem. There happened to be a rather large number of West Germans staying there. The room, praise Allah, was clean. Eva pulled down the blinds, crawled into bed, and fell immediately into a dreamless sleep.

She walked the gentle hill of the Path of the Righteous Gentiles leading up to the museum. It was planted with young trees, each one bearing a placard and a name: a non-Jew known to have saved Jews during the Nazi era. The sun was already merciless, though it was still morning, and Eva, squinting, felt herself growing light-headed with the heat of it beating down on her bare head, making the surroundings shimmer and tremble before her.

Dr. Friedlander was expecting her. A small frail man, slightly stooped. Old-fashioned wire spectacles. He looked somehow the German professor, not unlike her own father, in fact. Only, of course, he did not wear a suit. It seemed no men in Israel wore suits. His shirt-sleeves were rolled up so that the blue numbers of the concentration camp were visible. They shook hands.

They spoke at first in English, but very quickly fell into German. Dr. Friedlander spoke with the brittleness of the Berliner, though the harshness had been smoothed by the rigors of a German higher education.

He ushered her into his office, a little bigger than a broom closet, cluttered with papers and books. Apologetically he offered her the only seat, a linoleum-covered kitchen chair.

"Well, you have traveled a long way for this, so I will not waste a moment of your time. Here it is. You may read it at peace in my office. I have work to do elsewhere."

Eva held the book in her hands for several moments, taking measure of its purely physical properties. It was not a very large work: three hundred and fifty pages. Her own book, *Reason's Due*, whose inception she already carried within her, would be about the same size when completed. The volume was well bound. The cover was pale blue, the lettering on the cover black. She opened it. There was a dedication: *For my daughter, Eva.*

But she had not traveled thousands of miles, to this heat-maddened universe, stinking of diesel fuel and rancid emotionalism, to sit here in a collapsed huddle of trembling and tears. All right: he had dedicated the book to his infant daughter, the flaxen-haired, blue-eyed child he called *"meine kleine Fee,"* my little fairy. Yes, she had been his adored object. He had been the most loving of fathers.

Schluss damit! She began to read.

Every once in a while Dr. Friedlander would tiptoe into the room to check on her, quietly placing on the small area of the desk which he had cleared a cup of coffee or orange juice, once a chicken-salad sandwich, all of which she ingested unconsciously.

She had, since receiving her first letter from Dr. Friedlander and learning of the nature of her father's book, read extensively about Wagnerism in connection with anti-Semitism. She had read the composer's *Das Judentum in der Musik*, a fairly early work fueled by his operatic rivalry with the Jewish Giacomo Meyerbeer, which argued that the artistic vacuum which had been created in the wake of the decline of German creativity since the death of Beethoven was being filled by the Jew rushing in with his self-interested entrepreneurial designs. She had also skimmed the works of Houston Stewart Chamberlain, his *Foundations of the Nineteenth Century,* as well as his books on Kant and Goethe, so that she was in a position to see how heavily indebted to this ranting, if erudite, thinker her own father was.

In fact, her father was, for the most part, a mere epigone. The single book of his career was derivative and unbrilliant, a compendium of mediocre monomania. That was the scholarly critical verdict that was forming as she read. There were only a few interesting passages of musical analysis, showing genuine expertise, woven into the overall plan of illuminating the *Ring* cycle's central Teutonic vision.

The book's major modest contention was that the entire history of Western civilization was represented in Wagner's *Ring* cycle, the greatest work of genius ever to have sprung from mortal mind. The representation was accomplished musically and dramatically. Every scene, from the first splashing about of the Rhinemaidens in *Das Rheingold* to the final incineration of Valhalla in *Götterdämmerung*, was analyzed, first in terms of the identification and development of the musical motifs and then, and at much greater length, in terms of the interactions of the characters, all of whom were analyzed in terms of the two fundamental human categories of Aryan and non-Aryan.

For example, the first chapter contained a rather interesting, at least in Eva's non-professional estimation, technical discussion of the E-flat major triad with which Wagner begins *Das Rheingold*, the seven chords with which he represents the primeval elements of the mythical beginnings of time, there in the watery bottom of the Rhine. Dr. Mueller skillfully discussed the nature of the triad, comparing Wagner's use here with, among others, Bach's use of it—again, in E-flat major—in the prelude to his fourth cello suite. He then went on to show how, in Wagner's inspired manipulation of this surpassingly simple element, we are eventually presented with the forging of the mighty structure of the cosmos, as the dwelling place of the gods, the *Götterburg*, musically arises from these chords. In this way, the ontologically elemental is spliced with the musically elemental. "In the beginning is not the Word," wrote Herbert Mueller, "but rather the chord."

The perfection and wholeness of the mythical beginning is fully realized as the Rhinemaidens swim in their self-contained serenity. The absolute order that prevails is not incompatible with absolute freedom, as can be seen by the way in which the motif of the Rhine plays freely over the steady chords in the bass. So it was in the original state which once prevailed, when the needs of the individual were in perfect harmony with those of nature and society, so that the individual could at once act as determined by his own desires and yet not disturb the objective order of things.

Into this ideal world comes the outsider, Alberich the Nibelung, a physical and spiritual grotesque, having crawled out from his rightful place in the bowels of the earth, craving entry into the upper regions. Here, however, he cannot gain a foothold but slips and falls as he curses the "slippery slime." There is a harshness in the music; the flowing rhythm is interrupted in the motif of the Nibelung's bondage. Freedom and disorder are thus, from the very beginning, thrown into opposition, both musically and dramatically. Freedom is possible only when absolute order prevails.

Now ensues the archetypal interaction between the two essential types, Aryan and non-Aryan. Alberich longs, at least at first, for the love of the Rhinemaidens, and in his presumptuous arrogance, his at once pitiful and risible unawareness of his own ineradicable undesirability, he even makes advances toward them. Spurned and mocked, he learns, through the guileless maidens, of the Rhinegold, which they guard and which bestows on its possessor absolute power. The maidens, knowing that whoever would possess the gold must renounce love forevermore, chatter on in their ingenuousness, believing the gold safe: for who would ever pay so precious a price for mere gold? In their Aryan innocence, they do not understand the great differences that exist between the pure of heart and the impure. Alberich, subhuman but cunning, schooled in the ways of darkness and deceit, acknowledges at last the fact that he will never be loved. He is then free to succumb to his raw greed for money and power and steals the gold. And it is from this crime, brought about by the fatal interaction between the two irreconcilably opposed types, that all the tragic events leading to the final *Götterdämmerung* follow with a necessity almost mathematical, a necessity brilliantly mirrored in the musical development.

In this one interchange between Rhinemaidens and Nibelung, we see, as we see again and again throughout the *Ring* cycle, the characteristic weaknesses of the two races, Aryan and Jewish, that have led to the impossible impasse for which drastic steps of remedy are necessary. The Jewish obsession with gold and power, and the Aryans' childlike innocence, by means of which they have fallen prey to the deceit and malice of their blood enemies.

What was of course most distressing was the recognizability of her father's voice. The pages she read, one after the other, unaware of everything around her, in that insufferable Jerusalem heat, surrounded by the clutter of Holocaust documents in Dr. Friedlander's office: those pages sounded like her father. It was his voice she heard, heard it as she had not heard it for years. He had not undergone, as she had half hoped, some sort of trancelike absence, during which an external personality, a *Doppelgänger*, had stepped in and taken possession of him. And, even more difficult to take in, the very qualities for which she had once so adored and revered him were apparent in his work. Yes, it was true. His idealism and high-mindedness, his scholarship and culture: they were here, like poetry in the poison.

Again and again Herbert Mueller wrote of redemption and of freedom. Those were the phrases that he used with obsessive frequency as he sought to illustrate, through the musical drama of Wagner, the eternal struggle which has determined the entire course of Western history until this moment, when we stand poised before the great events which will finally bring a resolution, whether for good, should we succeed, or for everlasting bad, if we do not.

Dr. Friedlander must have tiptoed in at some point and put on the little desk lamp.

Eva was reading now about the last scene of the *Ring* cycle, in the last of the four operas, *Götterdämmerung*. Wotan's daughter, Brünnhilde, perhaps the noblest creature of them all, realizes how the Nibelung, Hagen, son of Alberich, has betrayed the love between herself and the heroic Siegfried. Once again a member of the race of Nibelungs, by practicing the black art in which they are skilled, has betrayed and vanquished the pure. Siegfried's body is laid on the funeral pyre. Brünnhilde removes the golden ring, made from the stolen Rhinegold, from the dead Siegfried's finger and throws her torch onto the pyre, which flares up brightly. And then the noble Valkyrie rides with a single leap into the fire. A Rhinemaiden manages to snatch the ring from her finger, thus restoring the world to the order which had once prevailed. Valhalla is seen in flames. The rule of the gods has descended, while the rule of man ascends to take its place.

Herbert Mueller raced through the action and musical analysis of this final scene, finally out of patience to appear the dispassionate pedagogue. He dutifully pointed out the salient features: the stately Valhalla motif, which collapses in mid-strain, followed by the motif of expiation; the Siegfried motif interrupted by a thunderous orchestral crash; again the theme of expiation. The professor hurriedly enumerated them, in his haste to arrive at his own thunderous crash: "the critical moment in the history of Western civilization," his final statement of a theme which, like all the other themes of the book, had been convulsively reiterated: viz., the incompleteness of the "Bayreuth Idea."

Perhaps this had been the very aspect of the book which had caught the fanatical eye in the hollowed face of the Minister of Propaganda. The professor from Münster had arrived at the conclusion that artistic regeneration was not to replace political revolution after all, as Wagner himself had preached. Rather, the two means of social change are not really contrary. Politics is an extension of art. Just as in the aesthetic realm there is the objective difference between good and bad art, so too in the political realm. And the normative principles are essentially the same; viz., the creation of order out of chaos. The freedom of the artist—which is absolute—consists in his conforming to the absolute necessity immanent within the work; so, too, good politics consists in bringing about that state which conforms to the fundamental social realities, the differentiation of race, in bringing order out of chaos and so making political freedom possible. The opposition between artistic versus political revolution was a false dichotomy.

Such a sentiment would no doubt have met with approval among the forgers of the National Socialist revolution. Hitler and Goebbels in particular would always regard themselves as artists *manqués*. The former's artistic aspirations, his bitterness at having been rejected twice from the Viennese Academy of Fine Arts, are well known. And his Propaganda Minister too had serious artistic pretensions. He had received his doctorate in literature, and regarded himself as a master of film, in the production of which he heavily involved himself, at the risk of boring his audiences into non-attendance with yet further instructions as to their duties to the Fatherland. But for Goebbels politics itself was an art: "Perhaps the highest and most comprehensive there is," he had written. "And we who shape modern German policy feel ourselves in this to be artists who have been given the responsible task of forming, out of the raw material of the mass, the firm concrete structure of the people. It is not only the task of art and the artist to bring together, but beyond this it is their task to form, to give shape, to remove the diseased and create freedom for the healthy." A man like Herbert Mueller might be just the sort to understand what it was to remove the diseased and create freedom for the healthy.

She opened the door of Dr. Friedlander's office. Almost immediately the door across the hall was opened and Dr. Friedlander emerged. The night was already far advanced. The poor man, in his kindness, must have been listening for a long time for some movement from Eva.

She held the book out to him.

"Thank you very much. I am sorry to have kept you so long."

The professor briefly bowed his head in acknowledgment. "You came a long way for your information."

She had not intended to say it: "He was my father, you know."

Again Dr. Friedlander lowered his head in acknowledgment. "Then he is dead?"

"Dead?"

"You used the past tense."

"No. He still lives."

They shook hands with one another. Dr. Friedlander briefly put his left hand, blue-veined and dry as parchment, over Eva's, and patted it in a fatherly manner.

Had Herbert Mueller had some work to do to overcome his initial repugnance for the unsubtly brutal way in which his high-minded theories were applied by the black thugs of the SS and SA? Had he been required to put himself through repeated exercises in self-deception? Or rather had he encountered few difficulties in coming to accept the events which were the logical consequences of those theories of race he had embraced?

Eva didn't know. She had learned what she could, and asked him no questions. She had sought the facts of her inheritance from books, only books, impersonal and public. To face her father directly and demand the knowledge which was by some right her own was impossible for her. Whatever the expression on his face that would have greeted her questions, she would not have been able to look on it, neither his remorse nor his lack of it.

Eventually a kind of escharotic hardness had grown up over the hurtful place, resulting perhaps as much from the great stretch of the Atlantic Ocean she had placed between herself and her father as from the passage of time.

And then of course there had been her study of philosophy, by means of which she had managed to wrap herself in the sterile gauze of genuine high-mindedness. She had found her salvation in the work of that excommunicated Jew from Amsterdam, who, in the grandeur of his modesty—oh, how unlike the Bayreuthian beast of egoism who had claimed her father's reverence!—had quietly gone about the business of revealing the logical structure of truth, and with it the secret of making our peace with the tragic possibilities of this life.

She had come to see her father as one of fate's unfortunates, a victim of the inexorable logic that binds one's action to the determining causes, historical and personal. Had Herbert Mueller not had the great misfortune—a misfortune shared by the more easily identifiable victims of that period—to be present at that place at that time, he would simply have been what she had thought him to be in the first blessedly ignorant years of her life: a man of culture and learning . . . and the most loving of all parents. To be evil is to suffer perhaps the worst kind of misfortune that can possibly befall one. Eva did come, eventually, to acknowledge the truth behind her childhood image: her father did indeed wear the black-and-white pajamas of bondage and stare out, dazed and vacant, from between barbed wire.

It was her father's stroke that disturbed the protective layer of scab and gauze that had settled down over her history. It was more than two years after her sojourn in Jerusalem. Her mother had telephoned, giving her the news briefly and without emotion. The brain damage had been quite severe. He had been left paralyzed and without the ability to speak. However, he did seem to have some consciousness of his surroundings, and had blinked in response to the doctor's questions. It would take several more weeks to see just how much of the loss was permanent.

Eva had returned home immediately.

His face! The room in the central hospital of Münster had reeled about her; she had reached out blindly to grab something and steady herself. He was propped up on some pillows, so that he was half sitting up as she entered, staring right at the door as if expecting her, with that look of pure malevolence into which his face had frozen.

She had stayed in Münster for two weeks, visiting her father every day, sitting beside his bed for the two hours in the morning and two hours in the evening of visiting time. Her mother accompanied her on the great majority of those visits, murmuring her greeting to Herr Professor, settling herself in the chair near the door, occasionally making remarks to Eva, and then formally taking her leave. Eva had stayed on, by herself, her chair pulled up beside his bed, not speaking, not reading, her eyes not moving from the hideous snarl on the so familiar face. And he too had kept his gaze on his daughter.

On the last afternoon of her stay, she got up and stood beside the bed, looking down at her father for several minutes. For the first time she addressed him.

"*Der* Ring *Cycle von Wagner und der kritische Augenblick in der Geschichte des Vaterlandes.* You see, I have read your book, Papa. They have it in Jerusalem, together with other documents produced by your kind. I traveled to Jerusalem in order to read your book, Papa. I know who you are."

The face had remained immobile. Not a flicker of movement, a flutter of an eyelid.

She turned and left, and never saw the living face again.

V

You're gonna wake up
One morning in the cold
You're gonna wake up
And, baby, you'll be old
You've got a chance now
Don't push it all away
You're gonna need love
You're gonna need it on that day.

He had played the song for her again tonight. For surely it was
hers.

She had seen him today. Since midsummer they had made their way through "Of Human Bondage," and had arrived together at last at the final chapter of the *Ethics*, "Of Human Freedom." He had spoken today, excited and happy, about the courses he planned to take this fall, and she had learned that not one of them was hers. She had struggled to maintain her objectivity, to discuss his coming semester in terms of his educational needs alone and to ignore as best she could the tearing within her.

Would he then be gone from her life at summer's end, another student to make his way through the narrow trenches of her teaching? She had loved him even before, when he had sat with the others in her classroom. Even then she had loved. She had been given, miraculously, the gift of him, all through the slowly ripening days of summer. Now it would end, this time surely. There was nothing to be done. Countless students had drifted in and out, flowing like the river of Heraclitus.

What could she do? Speak what she carried within her? She had pictured the scene innumerable times. The word spoken, followed by the high-pitched tinkling sound of his boyhood notions shattering. She had heard him stammer his helplessness in the face of her inappropriate passion, the farce of her delusion. How could she ask him to be adequate to it? She had seen his face, pulled so fine and taut that each movement from beneath vibrated above, registering the shock of his disbelief and horror, the boy's lips mouthing, "Sorry, ma'am, my mistake," as he turned and fled.

Most painful of all was to picture him moved to understanding and pity, the blue eyes welling up once again for what he saw within her. For he had the gift of empathy, the gift of sight recovered.

Don't you remember love?
You must have known it in the past
Don't you remember love?
Why do you put it last?

What wisdom in those lyrics! Wisdom: It is the knowledge that breathes. Perhaps these were the elusive words of her own final chapter, fleeing her every approach as dust motes in the air. What would the horrid Ira Cranshaw have to say to *them*, she wondered.

I love this music; he had spoken softly, looking out at her from half-closed lids and smiling seductively. It goes right to my . . . core. How often she had replayed his remark as she listened to his songs, measuring each curve of melody and entering deep into the pounding rhythm. Belly pressed to the ground, she pushed through the low hidden gate in the moss-covered wall, to wander, dazed with the scent of his desires.

> *Don't you remember love?*
> *You forgot the one thing we know that's true*
> *Let me give it to you.*

Oh, my darling boy, if I could believe that, believe that you would want to give it to me. You are still a cipher. What would *I* not give to know the contents of your soul. What do I know of you?

The sliding up and down of your smooth muscles as you climb the slippery rocks, and the unbroken gliding arc of you hitting the water.

The mottled redness you took on in the moment of your exposure, and the wetness in your eyes at seeing mine.

That you call your mother "Mom," have loved many girls, and like the human condition.

But she knew more. Each time, the sight of him sinking in so deep, the non-transparent aspect of him stopping her gaze, solid and thick with details. The variety of his expressions alone could fill a small treatise. The inertial force of his smiles which could not rest until they were full, and the unstemmable flow of his laughter. The shifting of his weight from one slim leg to another, and the shifting too of his gaze, so that she caught and took in for herself what he was seeing.

The sight of him, again and again, entering her whole and full, with a reality that still shocked, that still hurt her with its hardness, and gave pleasure too from that same hardness.

... And at that moment tastes a pleasure that is sweet beyond compare. Nor will she willingly give it up. All the rules of conduct, all the graces of life, of which aforetimes she was proud, she now disdains, welcoming a slave's estate, and any couch where she may be suffered to lie down close beside her darling.

> *You've got one last chance now*
> *Don't push it all away*

Was it a possibility? It was an axiom of the system to which she had given herself that there were none: no clusters of contingencies, of flickering possibilities, among which to stagger and choose. This is the freedom. Everything hangs by a thread. But the thread is woven of the strongest stuff: of logic, pure and simple.

She leaned back on her couch, her bare feet tucked beneath her, and bit into the peach she was holding, letting its sweet juice run down her chin, wiping it slowly with her arm. She was feeling sleek, savoring with pride the thin cushion of softness which had spread itself over her ribs. She could scarcely believe how good the food of this late summer tasted, the startling intensity of its flavors. And wine! She had never before been particularly sensitive to wine's qualities. But now, like someone tone-deaf suddenly waking one morning to the full voice of music, she found herself tasting deep within the liquid that glided through her, smooth as a Gregorian chant.

She ran her hands over her stomach, contentedly registering its slight roundness. Her breasts too seemed to hang with a new heaviness. She had stared at them this morning in her bedroom mirror, and thought them lovely. She closed her eyes, feeling the starved cells of her plumpening in sweetness and juice, the spreading softening within her. She had moved there, into the body of her.

You're gonna need love
You're gonna need it on that day.

Could it be? Did he too glimpse the possibility hovering in the ghostly anteroom of being? Would he be prepared to pluck it and breathe the wet warmth of life into it? How much did he see?

And as if in a vision she saw it, for it had been only a vision all along; saw the sudden shattering of that crystalline lattice, lit by the frozen flame. Concepts locked into concepts, propositions fused to propositions; she saw the whole immensity of it become in an instant a scattering swirl of broken shards, hard and thin and sharp enough to draw blood. But each a sliver of possibility, splitting the light and releasing the colors.

She had had a strange impulse this morning. And, stranger still, she had acted on it. She had called her mother in Münster.

It was an old lady's voice that answered the phone. A voice brittle as dry leaves blown on the pavement.

Elsbeth Mueller had dutifully questioned her daughter about her work, her health. And then she had complained of the weather. All summer long it had rained in Münster. There had not been a single day without a downpour. The flowers were all drowned.

"And your arthritis, Mother? It must be very bad."

"My arthritis is unspeakable. My hands . . . ech! Like two gnarled old trees."

Eva could see, still, the hands she had stared at as a child. So perfect, as if carved from marble. They had flown across the piano keys as no other hands could. Beautiful music had lain within them.

Her mother wished her a healthful and productive remainder of her summer vacation and a satisfactory school year; and she wished her mother respite from rain.

She hung up the phone with a sad fullness of feeling. She had been moved to pity for this woman who had lived so long with the bitter taste of choked-back ambition. It was the warmest emotion she would ever manage toward a mother who could not love. But pity too can be an achievement of sorts . . .

It was a beautiful day in late summer. The rain the night before had broken the heavy heat and left the world smelling good.

Eva was in her office, blinds drawn, reading a book which she had somewhat impulsively, sight unseen, agreed to review for a philosophical journal. It was extremely hard going. Not to put too fine a point on it, the book was a mess. The author—a great man by the measure of his ambition—claimed authorship of an alternative conceptual scheme that would, among other things, replace the whole edifice of modern science while resolving almost every outstanding issue in the history of ideas. And what a book had burst the bonds of this eidolon, a mass of confusion, non sequiturs, and misinterpretations of others' words.

Yet it was clear that an entire life had been sunk into this production. There was a dedication to a wife, "who stood beside and bore the burden." Of what? The birthing ordeal of this pitifully deformed enterprise? God forbid! For then there was not just one life buried here but two, at the very least. And the children? Had there been children constantly admonished to leave Daddy alone, Daddy must be allowed to work in peace on his revolutionary ideas. Weekend outings and summer vacations sacrificed to the claims of a dubious creativity?

Eva groped her way, trying to make out the form of the fantasy. (The size was self-evident.) It was, as is so much making claims on our attention, at once frightful and funny. It may not be permissible to laugh; that is another matter. But that large gap between the subjective view of the self and the actual state of its affairs is—at least when glimpsed in others—alive with good comedy, even if it is also the dark incubator of much that is sad in our lives.

Why do people do it? There already are enough books on the sagging shelves, works of surpassing significance and beauty; far more than any one person could read in a lifetime.

Eva had believed rather dogmatically in the creative urge as the spark of divinity within us. The creative process is the most nearly perfect, the almost godlike, expression of human freedom. And she had believed as well in the sanctity of the objects thus yielded. Especially books. She loved books, with a passion almost physical, loved even the smell and feel of them. Sometimes, in the university library or bookstore, she would simply take one into her hands and gently and lovingly finger it. Plato's suspicious distaste for the written word had been to her a prejudice most extreme and ill founded. For Plato had committed his views to writing with the most profound of misgivings, having much more confidence in the value of speech:

]237[

[Written words] seem to talk to you as though they were intelligent, but if you ask them anything about what they say, from a desire to be instructed, they go on telling you just the same thing forever. And once a thing is put into writing, the composition, whatever it may be, drifts all over the place, getting into the hands not only of those who understand it, but equally of those who have no business with it; it doesn't know how to address the right people, and not address the wrong.

With this last sentiment, it is true, Eva found herself in some sympathy. She too had had cause to cringe and shudder at the crude misreadings of the non-serious reader, as he skims along on the airy, high-handed presumption of the privileged vantage point of the critic. Eva had never given birth to a living child, but she imagined that the urgent solicitude to keep one's young out of unclean and unkind hands must be consanguineous with the author's hope of having his work left unfingered by "those who have no business with it." (Just exactly so, no doubt, would Eva herself be regarded by the author of the book prompting her present musings on the futility of it all.)

So far she had been able to follow Plato. But when he downgraded the intrinsic value of the misjudged and mistreated objects, she felt a ripple of outrage. For works of art, and most especially books, were to her so much more than the mere mortals by means of which they were begotten; and that is precisely why one would wish to protect them from the unsubtle and unsympathetic minds who would peruse and abuse them.

But why? she now asked herself. Why is a book *ipso facto* a precious commodity, and why is one who is engaged in its production able, by that fact alone, to transcend his meager mortality? Such a query was to her like the act of the biblical Abraham, in taking a hammer to the idols of his father.

There before her sat her own catalectic issue. The summer months had brought it no nearer to completion. It remained as it had been: some three-hundred-odd typed pages, each one of them endlessly worked over, heavily inlaid with penciled remarks and queries. *Reason's Due.* Every day, for over a decade now, she had piously laid her time upon the altar of her project. Staring at the empty page and willing herself to wait; taking the sentences apart, transposing their order, and then putting them back together again in precisely the original way; spinning distinctions so subtle that she herself now had trouble recovering them. At night she dutifully studied the works of others, in search of the elusive insight that would allow her to continue. And if she did not perform these tasks for a goodly amount of time every single day, she felt, quite simply, that her life was a waste. The glories of a day like this would beckon in vain. Blinds closed against the siren song of sunlight, she bent her mind to her work.

And why? So that her book too could find its way to a little niche in the stacks of a university library, those vast Golgothas of our buried literary conceits. Perchance, if she was very lucky, it would be reviewed by a handful of scholarly journals, glanced at by a few of her professional colleagues, who would lay her output, like so much modeling clay, over the mold of the views they already possessed, discarding anything that did not fit in. And really, why *should* they read her book when there already existed more masterpieces than they could ever hope to absorb?

Because, of course, in doubting the sanctity of the written word she was not thinking of those books which were the vessels, no matter how cracked, of the genuine elixir of genius. No, she was thinking of these droppings of solidified thought left behind by the advancing legions of the ungreat, among whom she unhesitatingly numbered herself; for she had never suffered the illusion of being a primary thinker. She was considering those of us who write, not because there is something that must be said, but rather because we must say something. For why do we do this, make sacrifices so great in the service of results so questionable? Well, what else shall we do, then? We are all of us creatures of *conatus,* endeavoring to persist in our own being, one way or another shrieking out our special significance in the face of all the evidence to the contrary. Spending one's life at scribbling isn't clearly inferior to the other possibilities presenting themselves. Only it does leave behind such an awful clutter. Eva suddenly found herself without any desire to add to the heap.

Her manuscript sat in her lap, as she riffled through its pages, reading here and there, recalling the circumstances of the production of the particular proposition before her. She toyed with various possibilities, picturing cutting her *oeuvre* up into paper dolls, or perhaps flinging it out of the window onto the sunstreaked quad below; or better yet, toting it over to the high footbridge suspended over the northern gorge of the campus and heaving it into the wild waters beneath. There would be something rather apt in that, pitching her pages into one of the abysses scaffolding her university.

But in the end she rejected the grand gesture as inconsonant with her personal style. She put the manuscript into the bottom drawer of her desk and quietly closed the drawer. Then she grabbed her bathing suit from the back of another drawer and left her office, the door gently falling to behind her.

She had kept the bathing suit in her office, hoping that Michael might someday suggest they go swimming again. There were times when she even played with the possibility of suggesting it herself.

She was headed for their swimming place of that shared afternoon. The summer was coming to an end. There was the slightest suggestion of an autumnal crispness in the air. Not many swimming days were left.

But wasn't that Sasha Moskowitz sitting on the grass near the waterfall? Yes! There she was, sitting among the remains of her lunch, her reading glasses fallen down over her nose as she hunched heavy over her book. Eva felt an unaccountable gladness at encountering her despised colleague on this day and called out a greeting.

"Hello, Sasha!"

Sasha looked up, frowning, her expression quickly giving way to slight surprise.

"Oh, it's you, Eva." She peered at her over her glasses, her brow furrowed. "Good God, woman, what's happened to you?" she boomed, so that several people turned around. "You look absolutely radiant! What's his name? And don't tell me Benedictus Spinoza either. Intimacy with him never made anyone flush like that!"

She laughed and Eva did too. "Can I join you?"

"Please. I was just beginning to think about getting back to work, but I'm a sucker for a good mystery. And you definitely strike me as a woman with a mystery. I was joking about the lover, but your laughter . . . hmmm. You really do look lovely. I mean it. At least fifteen years younger than when I saw you last."

"Make that twenty and I'll buy you another ice cream." Eva smiled, glancing at the gooey remains of a chocolate Popsicle coalescing to a paper plate.

"Ah, so he's younger, is he?" Sasha winked at her salaciously and again laughed. "Well, more power to you, Eva Mueller. There's a wonderful Yiddish saying: *Vehn der putz shtayt, der saychel ligt in dr'erd.* Is that close enough to the German for you to get it?"

"No. I'm afraid I can't make any sense out of it. *Der Putz?* In German it means a sort of trimming, an ornamentation."

Sasha laughed. "Well, in Yiddish it means something a little different, though related. *Der putz*, as I heard it put with enviable finesse by Isaac Bashevis Singer to Dick Cavett, is Mr. Penis."

They laughed. Eva was sitting on the grass, hugging her knees. "I still don't get it."

"It means that when the penis stands up, then the brains lie down in the ground."

"Ah." Eva smiled. "I see."

Sasha grinned. "You do, don't you?"

"And you, Sasha: how is your love life?"

"Love life? Love life? Oh no. I'm past all that sort of thing. No more *putz-shtayt*ing for me. I'm so past, I don't even miss it. I'm so perfectly content, poking around in my dusty old books, scribbling away my theories, that it's absolutely frightening. Looking at you radiating there, though, I'm thinking maybe I ought to work up a little discontent. If only for the sake of my complexion."

"You, Sasha?" Eva said, genuinely amazed. "Spending all your time in dusty old books?"

"Well, I *am* an academic, you know."

"But all your heated talk."

"My talk has always been the hottest thing about me." Sasha grinned. "But what talk exactly are you referring to? What smoldering sparks of verbiage have I irresponsibly let fly in your vicinity?"

"Oh, all those young bodies in the classroom; how most of the energy generated there was sexual . . ."

Sasha's grin became even wider. "Did I say all that? That must have been my research talking. Actually, that's generally what's doing my talking. Let's see. That must have been when I was working on that monograph 'Inverted Love: Older Women, Younger Men.' "

"Oh, really? How interesting. What form did your research take?"

"Reading novels, of course." Sasha laughed that throaty laugh which had struck Eva as so vulgar the night of her party. "What'd you think?"

Eva smilingly shrugged. "And are there many such novels dealing with this . . . inverted relationship?"

"More than you'd think. Some real classics. My study concentrated on Thomas Hardy's *Two on a Tower*—luscious phallic imagery *there*—Henry James's *The Princess Casamassima*, and of course Colette's *Chéri.*"

"Why 'of course' *Chéri*?"

"Oh, it's the classic treatment of this sort of thing." She gestured breezily, the wide sleeves of her Mexican summer blouse billowing out. "Very thin, less than a hundred and fifty pages. But it's got the best description of an orgasm I've ever encountered. A damned sight better than D. H. Lawrence's attempts at literary invagination. *Very* metaphysical—you'd like it."

She closed her eyes.

"It's their last fuck, you have to understand. Almost certainly the last of Léa's life. She's lived her whole life off her beauty and for the sake of love, and now she's arrived at the horror age of fifty. He's twenty-four years younger, and, though neither of them knows it yet, he'll be leaving her for good in the morning. For a younger woman, of course, who, in an odd twist, happens to be his wife."

Sasha recited, in surprisingly lilting French: " '*Cependant elle voyait avec une sorte de terreur approcher l'instant de sa propre défaite, elle endurait Chéri comme un supplice . . .*' Something, something . . . '*Enfin elle le saisit au bras, cria faiblement, et sombra dans cet abîme d'où l'amour remonte pâle, taciturne et plein du regret de la mort.*' "

There was a moment of silence, as both women tasted the words.

Finally Eva asked, "But why the regret of death? Is death what she finds in her abandonment?"

"Perhaps. Sex sinks us into our creatureliness, and so also our mortality. Or perhaps Colette simply means that there's nothing like a really good fuck to convince a soul that life is worth living."

Both women smiled. And then Eva asked softly, "And does the young man always leave, in the end?"

"Always," Sasha said firmly. "And a vignette that recurs with disheartening frequency is the woman catching sight of herself in a mirror, aghast to see the deflated old creature staring back at her: '*un grand trou . . . le monstre: une vieille femme.*' "

Again there was a full silence. And then Sasha said, "Actually, in my one experience with this sort of thing—oh yes, there was one, sometimes my research takes a more applied turn—I was the one who got bored. It only lasted about a week and a half. No, I mean it, don't laugh. Two weeks at the most. I felt I was wasted on the kid, as if I had laid out an exquisite meal, hours and hours in the preparation, course after course, each one paired with the perfect wine."

"Aged and full-bodied?"

"Exactly. And he just poured ketchup all over it and gulped it down. I mean a Big Mac washed down by a large Coke would have done just as nicely."

They both laughed.

"Hey," Sasha boomed. "I invited you to sit down so that I could extract the secret behind your glow. And here I am spilling my guts while you sit there in maidenly modesty, preserving your mystery intact."

"And so it will have to remain, for now," Eva answered, smiling. Impulsively she reached her hand across her lap and seized Sasha's, which was surprisingly fine-boned and delicate. "But I've really enjoyed talking to you. I want us to be friends."

"Well sure." Sasha laughed, somewhat taken aback. "I'm generally around."

"In the dusty books?"

"In the dusty books."

She had had to rush back to catch the long rays of the sun passing through her prism. She came late to the sight and walked into a room already in the process of transformation. Unhurriedly she undressed and let the glow fall flush on her face and hair, legs and breasts. She sank down on the uncarpeted floor, slowly rolling over so that the softly pelting colors fell evenly. She lay naked on her back, staring into the blaze and feeling the spectrum going molten within her.

He must love me, he must. There can be no life without him. Everything . . . everything hangs by that thread.

So quickly, so quickly, burning sharp for its moment and then over, tracelessly leaving the world. She dressed and rushed out again, bathing suit still in hand, headed once more for the spot of their shared swim.

He would be there. It was altogether impossible that the force of her desire not issue in his bodily presence. Now she did not even need to speak with him. It was not necessary that he even see her. She had need—but my God, what a need—only for the sight of him in the world.

The evening's shadow was approaching, but two children, a boy and a girl, still lay, quiet and subdued, heavy in their sun daze, fused on the boulder rising from the wild water.

Oh, my children, you are beautiful today. Your bodies have lain outside, soaking up the thick and foaming light. You have become full and moistened on luminosity. I would touch you myself if I could, the sun-softened substance of you.

You are young and beautiful and worthy of your reward.

Look at how you move, pretty child, the rounded beauty of you swaying back and forth, the unshamed beauty of you showing itself. You toss your hair in the fallen light, and your thighs like a mare's straddle the boy. Looking up into the softly spreading arc of those limbs, and beyond, the hair falling sweet-smelling from above, falling falling into the deep celebration, all the yearning of him rising up. He is risen out, has traveled the path of his sight into you.

Only beauty can do that, draw out the essence in a self-forgetful stream of liquid pleasure. To dip into that wetness and trace one's word with it . . . that would be, perhaps, to etch the truth. But only one word—in wetness softly breathed against another's ear.

"Damn!"

It was perhaps the fiftieth time in the last half hour that Eva had dialed Michael's number only to be greeted by the maddening repetition of the uninterrupted ringing.

"Damn, damn, and again damn!"

Where could he be at this time of night? Usually, she knew —and the knowledge, so painfully incomplete, of his comings and goings had become first among her occupations—he went straight home after his program, arriving back by twelve-thirty at the latest. But now, when she *had* to talk to him, he wasn't there.

All day she had tried, had run here and there across the campus. At first, only to catch sight of him in the world, but by now more, more.

She dialed, put down the receiver, and dialed again.

"Hello."

"Sasha, it's me. Eva Mueller."

"Eva. Goodness. How are you?"

"I'm fine. I didn't wake you, did I?"

"No, no. Another ten minutes and you might have. I'm in bed, reading a crashingly boring novel."

"Sasha, would you like to go out?" Eva asked somewhat breathlessly.

"Go out? Now?"

"Just for a drink? To the Red Herring, perhaps?"

"I'm sorry, Eva. I'm a great admirer of spontaneity, but also a slavish addict to sleep. I find I need it every night, in unconscionably large amounts. I really am going to be dead to the world in another ten minutes. Why don't we make it another time, at a more conventional hour perhaps?" Sasha laughed good-naturedly.

"Oh yes, of course, I'm sorry." Eva's voice sounded so contrite, it was almost like a young child's.

"Eva . . . are you okay? Look, if there's something the matter and you need to talk . . ."

"No, no." Eva cut her off. "It's nothing like that. I simply wanted to go out for a drink with you. Just fun. A mere caprice. I shouldn't have troubled you."

"*Au contraire, ma chérie.* Fun is a very high calling and caprice is the fairy child of freedom." Sasha laughed.

"You are very kind, Sasha."

"As I said this afternoon, I'm a sucker for a good mystery. How about lunch tomorrow?"

"Yes, thank you. I would like that. You really are very kind. And I'm so sorry."

"No, it's fine. I really wasn't asleep yet."

"No, I don't mean that. I mean I'm sorry about the way I've

regarded you. I've judged you unfairly. I . . . didn't like you very much."

Sasha laughed. "Oh, but you hid it so well."

"What you mean is that I didn't."

"Right." Her voice still held her laughter. "Actually, I always knew exactly what it was about me that offended you. And for some perverse reason I always found myself going out of my way to exaggerate those aspects when I was around you. Even louder and pushier, like some broad-stroked caricature of the vulgar Jew."

"Oh, Sasha . . . that you should say that."

"How do you mean?"

"My father," Eva said very softly. "During the war, in Germany. He was not one of the righteous Gentiles. Do you understand me?"

"Yes," Sasha said quietly. "In fact, I had heard something like that."

"What do you mean?"

"Well, you know how the students circulate these myths about their favorite teachers. I suppose with your accent, and air of remote mystery, it was kind of a natural one for them to fabricate. I simply discounted it, of course. I mean you should hear some of the things they say about me."

Eva passingly wondered how the truth of Sasha could possibly be exaggerated.

"But this story about me . . . happens to be true." Her voice had grown even softer.

"Yes. I understand."

"Do you still want to meet me for lunch tomorrow?"

Again Sasha was laughing. "I never thought I'd say this, not because I've never thought it, mind you, I just never thought I'd say it, but, Eva Mueller, you can be extremely absurd. What have your father's sins or lunacies or whatever the hell they were have to do with you and me meeting for lunch on a bright day in late August? I mean, it's enough to shlep around your own chains, without adding on the weight of your forebears."

"Thank you, Sasha. Thank you for that."

"Tomorrow, then? My office, say one o'clock."

"Tomorrow. Yes. Thank you."

It was close to two now. Eva tried calling Michael again, and once again was unrewarded. She went into her bathroom, switching on the light and standing pensively before the mirror. Sasha had been right this afternoon. Eva did look about fifteen years younger. She looked so pretty now, with so much light in her eyes and color in her cheeks, almost feverish with excitement. Would she ever look so young and pretty again?

She could wait no longer. How much longer *had* she? She would seize this unrepeating moment, seize it and squeeze it and drain it of its rare liqueur.

She ran upstairs to her bedroom, opening her closet to the full splash of her new wardrobe, blazing in warm summer colors against the blacks and grays she had shed. She grabbed a white linen jacket to throw over her shoulders against the coolness which had already invaded the air. She would not sit alone through the long sleepless hours, looking young and lovely, wasting it all on an unseeing night.

It took her about fifteen minutes, going almost at a run, to make her way from her place on the Heights to the house in Collegetown where he lived. How her heart was racing, and her legs pulsing strong as a mare's. She would wait for him, sit on his porch and wait for him to return.

But when she got there she saw with a leap of joy that he was back. The beloved, little red motorbike was parked out on the street and a light spilled its warmth through the windows. How many times had she stood outside and stared at that glow. It had made her happy on those nights, having been all that she had asked for.

She rang the bell and waited, the blood pounding in her ears. She rang again. She began to knock, thinking the bell perhaps broken.

But surely he was home. And then a horrible thought assaulted her with the irreversible feel of revelation. He *was* inside. He was inside and not answering her summons. And for what reason other than that he had a girl with him?

The picture drew itself in the garish hurting images thrown up before her. No doubt they had peeked out the window—they would, wouldn't they? Was it the fat-assed, dim-witted de Witt? The girl who had sat spreading like a mold in Eva's classroom and who could now peer out through the dull slits of her eyes and snicker at Eva Mueller? For of course they would laugh. Why not? What a farcical sight she presented! Trotting over in the panting heat of her late-summer passion, dripping like an over-ripe mango. Or perhaps they did not laugh but rather trembled, that this long arm of parental authority should have reached out to them in the darkness of the night to rap on the door behind which they were engaged in their assuredly unholy hanky-panky. She herself could almost laugh, only there was such a crushing ache.

She gave one more knock, one emphatically angry thump, to convey to them her full knowledge of the situation, and turned and walked away, consciously holding her head high in case the two brats were watching.

It took her another twenty minutes, her gait much slower now, to walk down the steep hill that led into the downtown area. It was almost three in the morning, but there were a surprising number of people still in the Red Herring.

She sat down at the bar and ordered a drink. A Scotch, simply because the name came to her. It had been years since she had taken a drop of hard liquor. It tasted terrible, but she drank it down fast and ordered another. The second one tasted slightly better, and the one after that better still.

After a while Eva became aware that there was some sort of commotion going on toward the thick blackness at the end of the room. There was a crowd. She caught the word "fight." Eva got up, very slowly and deliberately, and went to take a look.

The crowd around the fighters—she still hadn't gotten a glimpse of who they were—was swaying back and forth, moving with the action at the center. It was not to be taken seriously. It was fun. She couldn't see what was really going on, there were excited voices, laughing. She laughed as well. It was so pleasant to be crushed in with this mass, swaying as they swayed. It was wonderful to laugh without knowing at what. A girl next to her laughed back in her face. What a pretty girl! How friendly and good these people were!

Suddenly, she was falling backward. Someone caught her, was helping her back onto her feet, was speaking into her face, laughing: Well, what have we here?

It was a boy. Not hers, of course, but another. Like her own, he was also very nice to look at, with a strong, swelling chest tapering into slim, boy-narrow hips. No taller than hers, but dark where the other was blond. Perhaps not quite so nice, she thought with a faint flicker of rueful loyalty. But still, this one had the virtue of being at hand. His strong arms had caught her, like a hero in a fairy tale. At last. If they hadn't caught her, she would have fallen, and that would have been truly terrible. She would have made a spectacle of herself. Was she perhaps a little bit drunk?

But how wonderful of this boy to have caught her like that in his strong beautiful arms, bursting like unopen buds from out of his tight black shirt. And how unspeakably wonderful of him now to keep his arm around her waist, as they walked leaning heavily together to one of the tables in the back of the dark room.

His name was Robby, or Bobby, or something like that. She told him her name was Sasha. Then are you Russian? he asked. Yes, yes, Russian, from Moscow. Yes, he said knowingly, I could tell right away. I'm an expert at accents. She was sitting right next to him, his arm still around her, and he was still laughing and telling her some kind of nonsense. Only it was very nice. He was a student, he said, and asked her if she was also. Was it then so very dark in here?

A *graduate* student, she told him with much dignity, and then dissolved into laughter. In what? he laughed back. You tell me, she said. Since you already knew I was from Moscow. Oh, I'd say maybe, um, maybe art or something like that. You look artistic,

Sasha. Exactly! she said. Amazing. What mental powers. And what muscular arms; she ran the tips of her fingers over the biceps and triceps while he rippled them for her. He was clearly pleased by this, preening like a male peacock in the heat of spring, and telling her proudly about his exploits in the art of pumping iron. Nevertheless it felt so good to have his hand moving up and down her back, under her jacket, making little circles on her blouse. Unbelievably good. She leaned back into his hand. And now his other hand was working on her knee.

He was whispering in her ear; she had no idea what about, but it tickled so much she couldn't stop laughing. You're pretty silly for a graduate student, he said. I like that.

And then they were leaving together—the Red Herring, it seemed, was finally closing—his arm back down around her hips, pulling her gently up from the chair, leading her slowly toward the door.

Oh, but I can't go home yet, she said. Not yet, she pleaded. I know, let's go to the Brink of Destruction! You know that place? He laughed. Man, you really are a live one. You wanna go danc-ing . . . *now?* You're not tired? No! she shouted. I'm never tired! I'm insatiable! Yeah? He smiled. That sounds pretty wild. I like that. Tell you what, Sasha babe, you come back to my place, I'll take you to the brink. I'll take you over the fucking brink.

He was a beautiful boy, his young hot body poured into his jeans, and the swelling buds of his arms, the ones that had kept her from sprawling out on the floor and making a fool of herself. It was good to be leaving with him, though it would be better still if he didn't say anything more. She glanced around and saw some girls, young and sassy, their little sashaying rear ends so obvious in their skin-tight pants, leaving the place in the company of only one another. Hah! Too bad for them! She would go home with this boy and love him, tonight, when she was still young and pretty.

Strangely, she noticed the motorbike on the side of the street before she noticed him, walking toward her.

"Eva."

He looked so serious, standing there before her on the sidewalk, she had to laugh at him.

"Eva, I'm taking you home now. Okay?" He was laughing back now, which was much nicer than his looking so solemn, his arm around her now instead of Robby-Bobby's, which was also much nicer. Robby-Bobby was suddenly quite gone.

"Can we ride home on my bike, do you think? Can you manage to hang on to me?"

Of course, how ridiculous. Of course she could.

"You're sure, now?" he said, laughing back at her, as she put her arms around him, her head against his back. Oh, how good he smelled! "Now hang on tight! We can't have you splattered on the pavement."

Oh yes! To hang on tight, all through the night. This was more glorious than anything. Sanctimonious Benedictus, initials B.S.: did *you* ever fly through the night like this, with your arms wrapped tight around a boy smelling soapy sweet and the wild wild wind beating out the songs that he loves?

Don't you remember love?
You forgot the one thing we know that's true.
Let me give it to you.

Too soon they were back at her place and he was helping her off the bike, opening the door for her with the key she hadn't been able to get into the lock. The ride had sobered her just enough so that she found herself curious to know how Michael had come to be there.

"Oh, Sasha called me. She said that you had called her earlier, and that you hadn't sounded yourself, and she was sort of concerned. She kept trying to call you back. I figured I'd try the Red Herring because Sasha said you had said something about going down there. I thought you didn't like the place."

He looked at her quizzically, and then when she didn't answer (she had tried to say something, but the words weren't forming themselves), he continued, smiling softly, "I'm sorry if I was like a drag, but I know that character you were with and somehow I just thought I could get you home better. Are you angry with me?"

She shook her head no, and then, with great effort, mumbled, "It was very kind of you. And of Sasha. You are both unbelievably kind."

Michael laughed. "No, not unbelievable. You're the one who's unbelievable." He shook his head, smiling. "Eva, Eva."

"Eva? Since when am I Eva?" she managed to ask.

"Since I retrieved you at four o'clock in the morning from slightly weird circumstances. It's the price you'll have to pay, Eva. God, I like saying that. Eva."

They were sitting beside one another on her couch, and she tried to smile. Her face had gone quite numb, but her head was spinning a little less violently. Perhaps she had drunk somewhat too much? Her head had found its way to Michael's shoulder, and she doubted that she would be capable of raising it ever again.

They must have sat like that for quite some time. She had no idea.

But then she thought she heard something. Slightly revived, she straightened.

"Oh, but listen! He's back!"

It was the long, thin voice of the flutist, returned after an absence of several weeks, pushing its way through the heavy drapery at her window.

"He's back," she whispered again, rising with it, moving to throw open her window to the voice. Michael, too, had gotten up and was standing beside her.

"It's wild, isn't it? It's one of the reasons I really love this town," he said.

"What is it he's playing? Do you know?"

"No, I don't really know that kind of music. I've never really gotten into classical stuff."

"It's Chopin. A nocturne."

Michael shrugged. "I don't know. That music all sounds pretty much the same to me. Hey! Are you cold? You're shivering!"

"No, no. Not really. Tiredness, I think. And the music perhaps. Beauty often makes me tremble."

"Such goings-on." He smiled. "Come, let's go sit back down before you collapse from the beauty of Hunk Beserkowitz."

"What? Hunk what?"

"That's just what we call him, some of us. I mean Hank Berkowitz, of course."

"I still don't know what you're talking about."

"What? You're kidding! You didn't know that the guy who plays his flute in the middle of the night is Hank Berkowitz?"

Eva shook her head.

"That is really amazing. Amazing! So you don't know the story of that crazy music?"

Again Eva shook her head.

"Hunk is this big muscle-heavy guy, I think he's on the wrestling team, and he's over at one of the frat houses, I forget which one. One of those really wild animal houses. And like the thing is, he only plays the flute when he gets completely smashed. They have these parties over there and they all get disgustingly drunk and then Hunk goes out on the lawn and starts blowing away on his instrument." He was laughing.

"That beautiful music . . ." she whispered.

"Right." He laughed. "Out of a mouth thick with booze and slobber and God knows what else. Fantastic, isn't it?"

"Fantastic? Why fantastic? It's somehow awful. It makes my skin crawl. Such a betrayal."

"A betrayal? Why? Of what?"

"Of beauty. Mystery."

"I think this makes the mystery more. I really do. And the beauty is the same, isn't it?"

She turned and looked at him. "You are right."

They didn't look at one another now, but sat side by side on the couch and stared out toward the open window, listening to the delicate notes of the drunken boy.

"Are you sure you're not cold? You're trembling so violently. I mean, you're sure it's just the beauty?"

]257[

"But you too. You're shaking also."

"It must be contagious." His voice was very soft, and Eva turned to him.

He looked at her, his eyes serious on her face, and then he shook his head and whispered, "No. It's impossible."

"Impossible." She smiled. "Why impossible? Logically impossible?"

The authority of his kiss surprised her, before she gave way to its sweetness.

"Eva," he whispered, "beautiful Eva," his lips on her mouth her hair her eyes. "Tell me I'm not dreaming."

She saw what it was he was holding out to her: the joy of the moment. Nothing deeper, nothing more sustained than that. It had seemed too much when she had first felt the possibility of intimacy brushing up against her; now it was far too little. She had opened herself wide at the touch, too wide to be helped by what he could offer.

I am not his salvation. He is not prepared to be mine.

How tender his hands are, how knowing and gentle. His open mouth tastes sweet as a small child's.

Papa's hands were tender when he undressed me at night. He would lift the dress so carefully, as if it were spun of glass, and lay it on the chair beside my bed, his hands gently placing it, as if it might shatter into pieces, an irretrievable loss he would spend his whole life grieving.

His eyes were steady on her face, as he knelt before her on the floor, her clothes beside him.

"I am so afraid," she whispered.

"Don't be afraid."

His voice came with difficulty. His face was so different now, flushed, the desire in it so strong. The morning was whitening, the song of the gifted drunk played out.

She had kept vivid the image of him in his swim trunks. But still his undressed body before her brought a painful spasm of her vision. The narrowing of him into the pale band where the sun had not fallen, startling against the golden brown length of him. He followed her eyes, smiled, and looked back at her, his hands on her waist, his thumbs pressing her belly, as he knelt before her.

Her gaze went out of her, out to the sight of him, joined by the strengthening light coming in at the window. She slid down to the floor where he was. Her hands followed the path of her eyes, trying too to take in the full sight of him kneeling there before her. She bent her open mouth to him, and then looked up to see the pleasure in his face.

"And if we drown in it?" she asked him.

"We won't drown. We're both strong swimmers." She heard him catch his breath and moan. His voice is grown-up, she had said to herself at summer's start. In his voice he is a man.

She believed him, believed the courage of him, even though she knew he didn't know, of course, he couldn't know. And yet there was a kind of knowledge in him, she could feel it coming from him, and she believed him.

He took her hand, gently pressing, kissing each finger with his beautiful man-child lips. His lips opened to her fingers, taking them into his mouth, nectar-sweet, his teeth small and even. His hands were passing over her, parting her, the dissolving strength of them seeping in. And all of her senses struggled to take in the sight of him.

She was descending again, letting herself be drawn back under, into the range of its pull, the relentless current of it, through all the years never weakening. So that she had had to fight against it always, there down down under. And it was a pleasure to let herself go like this, to move without the force of her will, to let her will give way and to be swept along and under, finally. She knew the way to go, knew the direction with every fiber of herself. Had she not been pulling against it, throwing the weight of her whole being against it, for as long as she could remember? The place beyond memory.

Papa's arm around me, reading to me from the magical book of the mythical time.

The little lamp bathes us, softly washing light, only us, the rest of the room in dark, and only we sit in the warmth of this light, side by side, the book between us. I love him so.

Crying from Mama's words, and her hands flying out, burning traces on my face. Her words are the hiss of a snake, and I try not to let them in, soaked with poison. And Papa comes home and I hear her hiss, she is speaking to him of me, trying to make him hate me, and I hear him running up the stairs, and he knows, he understands they are the words of the snake. In his arms, like the branches of my tree. Only hold me!

There is Papa's other face oh my God how ugly, uglier than the snake, than her twisted mouth dripping poison.

Papa's dying face: I know it. It is not new, only the awful unchangingness of it. When he speaks about the ones he hates, who have taken it all from him, and his voice hard and bitter, bad words, the words of a bad man.

I scratched my finger on my tree, put it to my mouth, tasting blood.

Papa's words taste like blood in my mouth and I pray for him to stop, for the words to stop, and the evil taste of it to stop and to stop.

And he stops. And he looks at me, and always his eyes are soft on me, and his face kind and wise. The face of a good man. My papa is a good man. *Mein Schutz, meine Esche.*

He had lifted her from the floor and laid her gently back on the couch. He was on her, raised on his arms above her looking down, and she looked up at his open face and felt the tremor pass through her.

Even he will not be young forever. Now is the moment of his youth. The present is where we live, lit up, the glow of the now, slipping away to the dark, where it stays, in the darkness, all the words that still whisper. He says it is good, it is the zap of poignancy. Only he hasn't yet heard the whispering or the hiss. My child. I would save you if I could.

He was curled up on her now, sitting on her lap, her breast in his mouth, tasting, licking, a hungry baby whom she wished only to feed. Such a greedy boy, to suck like that, and his fingers hungry for the feel of her.

He laid her out again on the couch, his open palm brushing her wet cheek, his eyes on her so closely, as if they themselves would enter her as he did.

Again her hold was loosening as she felt him slide within her, the young strength of him slowly and knowingly moving in her, a fire that doesn't scorch, love is, only warms and melts in its kindness, oh the gift of it! and in the melting to come here, so near, bring me . . .

No!

Had she screamed it aloud? Her eyes were seeking his, grasping on for dear life to his gaze. Hold on, hold on, do not slip back down into that forsaken place.

Only, she had gone too far. The look of concentrated pleasure on his face, his body poured into hers, fusing fire, the moving of him hard, and the . . .

The children. There, as she had always known they would be. Waiting in their silence. Small and shriveled, unformed bodies forever broken, bowed down by the crush of their sadness.

They stared out at her with their hooded haunted eyes, their dark and shadowed eyes, hollowed cheeks, carved with the pain and the fire, the fire that scorches, hate is, cheeks wet with the sorrow, but they did not cry out loud.

There were the babies, ash-gray and shrunken; and cradling them in arms stick-thin, bone-thin, skeletons with skin, other children, all silent but with staring, starving eyes.

They began to march, silently, orderly, all in one direction. Others quickly took their places.

She was meant to be among them. But she searched the lines, the neat rows and columns, each new batch, and she wasn't there. Other children with sky-blue eyes and flaxen hair, but not she, not that child who wore dresses so precious he must lay them down with gentle hands for fear of breaking them.

Papa, have you seen the children? I see them now, and I will see them all, each last one, I will look into their faces, into the unspeakable sadness of them, and I will hold them in my mind forever, mourn them, Papa, mourn them as you would my broken dresses, only I will mourn the broken children, Papa . . . my papa.